HER BAD ALPHA

Her Bad Alpha

Carmalena Winters

Dedicated to my best friend, Michelle Horst and to my daughters Amber and Celina Winters. Without these three women, I do not know where I would be today. Another addition is my grandson Colton, whom I would not have the determination to leave behind a legacy. Also, to Cristal Saxson who always said I was a fantastic writer.

Contents

1

Chapter One: *Death*

It was on this fateful day that she was on the edge of the woods about to take her clothes off and shift into her wolf when someone stopped her. It was Gamma Blake Jeffries. He said, "You need to come back to the pack house with me; it is important!" She hopes that Alpha Colton and Luna Marian Blackwood are doing well. As they reach the pack house, she notices that there are a bunch of the pack members gathered outside the entrance of the pack house. She could see the future alpha, Fallon trying to calm them down. However, that all changed when they caught a whiff of her scent. They knew who she was and who her parents were. They are good people, so they dropped their heads as she came closer to the group.

She wonders why everyone's head was lowered. Gamma Blake ushers her into the house. As she steps through the front door, she can feel that something is wrong, but she does not know what it is just yet. The foyer of the house is massive. The stairs leading up to the four floors of the house split to the left and the right sides. There are rows of rooms, in both directions on all three floors, except the top floor. That is where Alpha Colton and Luna Marian and their son Fallon sleep and live. There is a hallway off to the right side of the stairs where Alpha Colton's office is, and the hugest kitchen known to man. It has steel appliances and modern gadgets. It also has two long tables with benches for seating for the pack members to eat at that live in the pack house. On the left side of the stairs is an enormous family room. It has three long couches, three recliners, and a huge entertainment center complete with a sixty-inch television.

Fallon came into the house right behind them and said, "My father wants to see you two in his office." Gamma Blake led her down the hall to Alpha Colton's office. He then knocked on the door with his signature knock. It is two knocks, a scratch, and another three knocks. He then opened the door when he heard, "Come in. "He had pushed her into the room before he entered the room. Alpha Colton is sitting behind his desk and looks up when they enter the room. He gets up and comes around the big walnut desk. He then takes her hands in his and tells her the most tragic thing that she has ever heard. That her parents were in a car accident coming home from visiting her half-brother in college. A drunk driver head-on hit them. Her father was Alpha Colton's beta, his second in command. Her mother was Luna Marian's best friend.

"They died instantly in the car crash; their bodies are being transferred to the hospital. "Said Alpha Colton.

She looks at him and bursts into tears. He then pulled her into a hug and told her that she didn't have to worry about the arrangements that the pack would take care of them for her and since she was still technically a minor, she could move into the pack house with them, there weren't many rooms taken because most of the pack had met their mates and moved out of the pack house into houses of their own.

Her name is Amber Scott. She is sixteen years old and is about to turn seventeen in a week. She has long blonde wavy hair and piercing silver eyes. She stands about five foot eight inches tall and weighs about one hundred pounds and twenty pounds. Amber is part of the Dark Moon pack, one of the biggest and strongest packs in the United States. The Dark Moon pack controls a big section of green and fertile land near the east coast. She was excited about her birthday because that is where and when she might meet her fated mate. (A fated mate is the other half of your soul, the one picked out for you by the Moon Goddess herself.) With the death of her parents, she does not think she should celebrate her birthday. She voices that thought to the alpha and he says that exactly the right thing to do is to celebrate her birthday with a party like they wanted to do for her birthday originally. She asked the alpha if she could go for a run now because her wolf needed to get out. He allowed it on the condition that someone went with her. Gamma Blake volunteered to go with her.

They go back to the edge of the woods, and Amber goes behind a tree to strip out of her clothes and to shift. Her wolf is a medium size golden-haired wolf, with four white paws and a white star on her forehead. Gamma Blake had already shifted into his wolf. He was bigger than Amber's wolf but not by much. He was also dark where she was golden. His wolf's name is Maddox. Also, Amber's wolf's name is Kia. They took off into the woods, running as fast as they could dodging trees and jumping over fallen logs. They ran as far as the western border and stopped to rest. They had been running for a good two hours straight or more. So, they rested for about an hour and a half, then they started running back home to the pack house.

It took six hours for the bodies of her parents to return to the hospital on pack lands. They were put in the morgue until arrangements could be made for their funeral and cremation. Alpha Colton is in his office making the arrangements for the funeral and cremation when Luna Marian comes in and tells him that she is a little worried about Amber and how she is taking the death of her parents. Alpha Colton voices his concerns about Amber and the situation as well.

Fallon Blackwood, the future alpha, is eighteen years old but has not found his fated mate yet. He decides he will go for a run and let his wolf out for a little while. His wolf's name is Max, and he is bigger than the average wolf. He is black with a white blaze from his forehead to his nose. In werewolf form, Fallon stands six feet and six inches tall. He is well-built and his muscles are well-defined. Many of the single daughters of the pack members all have a crush on him. But Fallon wants to wait for his fated mate, so until he finds her, he has made a vow to still be celibate. Though many of the girls have tried to tempt him into mating with them, he stands strong in his belief that he has a fated mate somewhere out there in the world.

Amber's best friend, Clara Martin who was away visiting her grandparents for the weekend, has just returned home and received the news from her father, about the death of Camron and Olivia Scott. Clara burst into tears. Her father pulls her into a hug and tells her things will be all right. Shortly after that, Clara calmed down and dried her tears, and asked her dad, "Where is Amber now?" She's at the pack house." He spoke. Clara went into her room to put her luggage on her bed, so when she gets back from the pack lodge, she can put her stuff away. She then went back downstairs and told her dad that she was heading to the pack house to see Amber for a while. She went out the front door and turned right to follow the path that leads to the pack house. The walk took about five minutes to get there.

Clara rings the doorbell and waits until someone answers the door. It is one of the omegas that works in the pack house that answered the door. Her name is Jasmine, and she is a petite person with brown hair and doe-like brown eyes. She is also slender and stands five feet tall compared to most other people in the pack. She lets Clara in. Clara asked what room Amber Scott in. Jasmine told her that she was on the second floor on the right-hand side, in the third room. Clara hurried up the stairs to see her friend. When she gets to Amber's room, she knocks on the door and patiently waits for her to answer the door. Amber opens the door with a tear-stained face, red puffy eyes, and a red nose from all the crying she has been doing since the death of her parents.

Clara at once pulled Amber into a bear hug. They both burst into tears as they hugged each other tightly. Clara told Amber that she was sorry for the loss of her parents. She hopes that she can come to depend on Clara's parents like they were hers too. Amber said, "That's the sweetest thing anyone has ever said to me!" She then went back into her room to get ready for dinner, since she had not eaten anything at all yet today. That is when her stomach makes itself known with a loud grumbling noise. The noise was so loud that it startled both girls so much that they jumped in the air and cried out in fright.

Once they realized that it was just Amber's stomach growling, they calmed down and made their way back downstairs to the kitchen for dinner. As they neared the kitchen. However, the girls could hear what was said because of their heightened hearing. As the girls walked into the kitchen, the voices stopped. Everyone that was seated at the tables turned towards the entrance to the kitchen and they all stood up to approach Amber to give her their condolences and sympathies. They also want to give her hugs, so she knows that she is not alone. Amber burst into tears again, but this time they are happy tears because thanks to her fellow pack members, the Alpha and Luna, and Clara, she no longer feels she is alone in the world.

Clara and Amber both took seats at one of the tables to eat. They sat down to eight huge pieces of succulent pot roast, garlic mashed potatoes, green beans with bacon, and for dessert caramel apple pies. Of course, there were generous portions of all the food except the pot roasts and pies. Everyone that was seated at the tables was waiting for one more person to join their group. They were waiting for Fallon to come down and eat dinner with his parents and friends. His beta is Jacob Johnson. Jacob is a gifted wolf. He knows when something is wrong or when something is going to happen. He was the one that informed the Alpha and Luna, about the accident that took the lives of Amber's mom and dad; before the authorities came and told them the news.

Jacob's wolf is of large height for a wolf. However, he is not as big as Fallon's wolf. Although, he is bigger than most of the other wolves in the pack, except for the Alpha, Luna, and Fallon's wolves. His wolf's name is Axel, and he is a dark chocolate-brown wolf with green eyes. He is the only one that has jeweled green eyes like a wolf. In his werewolf form, Jacob stands five feet ten inches tall with chestnut brown hair and sparkling emerald, green eyes. Jacob is the only one who has green eyes as a wolf and a werewolf. Jacob is sitting beside Amber on her left, and Clara sits on her right side at one of the tables.

The three people that are seated across from them are Michelle, Michael, and Ezekiel. They are fraternal triplets, which are exceedingly rare and unheard of in the werewolf community. Michelle's the quiet one. They say you must always watch out for the quiet ones. Michelle's wolf is gray with four white paws. She is of average size for a female wolf. Her wolf's name is Scarlet. In werewolf form, she stands five foot-five inches tall. She has golden blonde hair and bejeweled amber eyes. Michael is the protector of the three. That explains why he is on patrol duty at night. Michael's wolf is large for a wolf; he is as big as Fallon's and Jacob's wolves. His wolf is also gray, but he has brown patches here and there across his body. His wolf's name is Kyle. In werewolf form, he stands six foot five inches tall. He has platinum blonde hair and dazzling blue eyes.

Ezekiel is the funny one to be around. He is always making people happy and makes them laugh at his jokes and silly stories. His wolf's name is Shadow. His wolf is of average size for a wolf. He is tan in color with gray and brown patches covering his body. In werewolf form, he stands five feet eleven inches tall. He has sandy blonde hair and piercing silver eyes. The Alpha and Luna are seated at the head of the front table, Fallon is seated on his father's right side and his mom is sitting on his father's left side. Amber and Clara were sitting towards the middle of the table with Felicity sitting beside Amber on her left side and Clara on her right side.

Amber and Clara were talking about going for a run after dinner. However, the Alpha heard what they were talking about and told them no because rogues had crossed the border on the south side and were being captured by the warriors now. Amber was worried because they have not had any problems with rogues in a long time. When dinner was over, Michael left the house to start his scheduled time on patrol on the northern border. There were about five other people who were on patrol on this side of the border as well. Overall, about twenty-five to thirty people are patrolling the borders. Some adults are trained in their werewolf form and in their wolves to fight the rogues. Most of the adults in the pack are trained as well. It is Gamma Blake who is training them, and they continue their training every day.

Even Amber and Clara are training with the other pack members. They have been in training since they started to shift at the age of twelve. There are quite a few younger members of the pack out on the training field. Today is one of the days that they are training in their wolf forms. Clara has already shifted into her wolf. Her wolf's name is Jaylin, and she is a light tan with four white paws. In werewolf form, she stands five foot six inches tall and weighs about one hundred and ten pounds. She has light blonde hair that is dyed purple and glowing Amethyst eyes. She inherited her father's eyes and her hair from her mom. There was a female wolf of average size for a female wolf. She has black and tad patches from her nose to her tail. She was Gamma Blake's mate, and her name is Abigail or Abby for short. Her wolf's name is Nori. Everyone who was able-bodied was on the training field getting ready to take on the rogues that got away from being captured because they might return.

Chapter Two: *Her Fated Mate!*

The days passed quickly. It is the day of the funeral and cremation of Amber's parents. There are two platforms built out of wood, which is where the bodies of Camron and Olivia Scott are. Alpha Colton, Luna Marian, Fallon, and Amber all wore black and walked to the center of the clearing where the funeral was. Clara and her parents were already there. They were all dressed in black as well. Most of the pack members arrived and were either dressed in black or dark-colored clothes. Alpha Colton must have let the other packs in the area know about the funeral and cremation because the Alphas and Luna of several packs along with their betas showed up that day to pay their respects. They said they would come back for the party next weekend to celebrate Amber's birthday. As the sun began to set, that is when the funeral started. The platforms were set on fire. Alpha Colton gave a speech about how Camron "his beta" was his best friend and he will be missed. Everyone began singing Amazing Grace. Some people were off-key a little bit. Some people did not know that song, so they just hummed to the melody.

The fires continued to burn until the next day when heavy rain came down and put the fires out. Unfortunately, the heavy rain also washed away the ashes into the ground. As the rain continued to come down in a torrent, so did Amber's tears. She has cried so much in the last few days that her eyes are red and swollen. Even her nose is red from all the times she has blown her nose. The last couple of days have been the hardest days she has had to go through. She has the whole pack to fall back on for support, she has not been able to get the thought of her parents never coming back. They are gone forever. That kind of grief takes a while to heal. Amber is just beginning her journey in the many stages of grief.

As the days passed, many of the pack went to the pack house to visit Amber to see how she had been doing since the funeral. She tells them that she is a mess but each day she gets better with the enormous amount of pain she is going through. In two days, it will be her birthday weekend. She does not want to celebrate her birthday, but Alpha Colton suggested that she celebrate her birthday anyway because that is what her parents would have wanted. For the last week, the pack has been preparing to celebrate Amber's birthday party. They have been stringing lights in the bushes and the few trees that are around the center clearing area. They have been setting up tables and chairs around the area. They have gotten a whole hog roast started in a big smoker oven. They also have several different grills going with steaks, hamburgers, hotdogs, chicken, vegetable kabobs, grilled corn on the cob, and potatoes. The buns for the hamburgers and hotdogs are set up on another table with condiments like ketchup, mustard, and mayonnaise, and other toppings like cheese, lettuce, and tomatoes.

As the food was being prepared, the packs from around the surrounding area started to show up for the party. Every member of each pack brought a present for Amber on her birthday. There were at least four packs that came to the party. There is the South Paw pack from the south, the Bright Star pack from the east, the Black Mountain pack from the west, and the Blue Twilight pack from the northern side. There were at least sixty people in all, and they were all dressed up in their party clothes. They also brought dishes like baked macaroni and cheese, potato salad, salad, veggie platter, cheese platter, varied kinds of snack crackers, and many types of drinks.

The Alpha of the Blue Twilight pack has not yet found his fated mate. His name is Onyx Wolfhound. He stands six foot two inches tall and weighs about two hundred and ten pounds. He is about twenty-two years old. He has a very muscular body. He also has short-cropped black hair and deep ocean-blue eyes. He has been alpha since his parents were massacred in a rogue attack when he was eighteen. Since then, he has hunted down the rogue and killed any of them that have crossed over his lands. He is known in the area as a terrible person to be around because he tortures rogues that cross his lands. However, it has been a long time since the rogues crossed to the north.

Amber comes out of the pack house dressed up in a steely gray dress that reaches just below her knees. The dress brings out the silver in her eyes. She is also wearing a pair of silver sandals to match her dress. Clara was dressed up for the party as well, only her dress is a deep purple that highlights her hair and her amethyst eyes. They walked out to the clearing where everyone was collected and were astonished by the sheer number of people who came to her birthday party. She hoped there was enough food for everyone. She began to mix and mingle throughout the party. Clara was at her side the whole time. She begins to smell the most mouth-watering scent she has ever come across. It smells like vanilla and chocolate. She goes to search for the scent, and it leads her to none other than Onyx Wolfhound, Alpha of the Blue Twilight pack. They both say "Mate" at the same time. The next thing he knows she is passing out, but he grabs her quickly, so she does not fall to the ground and hurt herself. He picks her up bridal style and starts for the pack hospital. While he was walking to the pack hospital, Onyx's mind links with Alpha Colton and tells him what is going on. Alpha Colton at once runs to the pack hospital with Luna Marian. The pack doctor, Dr. Claire Blane, who is a werewolf as well, met them at the hospital. The Doctor motioned for Onyx to lay Amber down on a gurney in the room, so she could check Amber out and see what was going on with her. As the doctor takes her vitals, Onyx asks "Will she be okay, doc?" The doctor replies "Well her vitals are good; I believe she has just fainted due to shock."

About half an hour later, Amber wakes up to see the concerned faces of Alpha Colton, Luna Marian, and Alpha Onyx. Amber looks over to the left side of the room and sees Onyx seated in a chair beside her bed holding her hand a little too tightly. Alpha Colton and Luna Marian were talking to Onyx about what his plans are concerning Amber. Now that they know that she is his fated mate. He tells them that he plans to cherish her like his fated mate that she is. He tells them that he has changed he is no longer the killer that he used to be. He promises that Amber will be safe with him. Amber asked Onyx "Do you mean that?" That was when they all realized that she was awake. Onyx got up from the chair and gave Amber a bear hug and kisses on her forehead. Alpha Colton and Luna Marian said they were going to go so they could get to know one another for a while before they had to leave for the Blue Twilight pack.

As Amber comes out of the hospital, she is holding Onyx's hand. When they appeared from the hospital, they faced a substantial number of people who were concerned that Onyx might hurt Amber. They are not aware of the fact that she is his fated mate. They all started asking questions about what was going on and whether Amber was his fated mate or not. Onyx held up his hands for the crowd to quiet down so he could answer their questions. The first thing he did was answer the fated mate question. He told them that yes, she was his mate. The other half of his soul. Then he told them that she had simply fainted due to the surprise that we are mates. He said, "I am a changed man. I no longer have the opportunity needed to hunt down rogues anymore. I have promised the Alpha that Amber will be safe with me and my pack. "Amber raised her hand when the crowd started asking for more inquiries for them to settle down so she could speak. She raised her voice just a little bit to be received behind the crowd. She said, "We plan to spend the day here to celebrate my birthday with everyone and then leave in the morning for the Blue Twilight pack."

Alpha Colton calls Amber to cut the five-tiered cake that stood on one of the various tables and was adorned with flowers and butterflies. The butterflies are created of fondant of an assortment of colors. The flowers are of distinct types and assorted colors. The cake was noticeably big to make sure everyone at the party could have a piece of it. It started with the base of the cake being as big as the table and then it branched out to distinct size tiers of cakes. The tiers were all distinct kinds of cakes from chocolate to vanilla and they were all assorted colors, some cream-filled some jelly filled. Amber had never seen a cake so beautiful and tasty in her life. Onyx came over with Amber to watch as she cut the first piece of this massive, beautiful cake. The catering company that made the cake finished cutting up the rest of the huge cake. There was enough of the cake for everyone to have a second part.

When the cake was demolished and all the rest of the food was gone, Alpha Colton said that it was time for Amber to open her gifts. She goes to the chair that looks like a throne. Beside the chair are a couple of tables piled high with her gifts from everyone. Alpha Colton starts handing her the first gift. The first gift turns out to be a young adult novel by a famous writer. The second gift was a box of hair clips and hair bands. The third gift was a remarkable young adult, book collection. The next gift turns out to be a sixty-inch plasma screen TV. The gifts kept coming because there were so many. When everything was opened and tallied there was approximately twenty-five thousand dollars' worth of merchandise piled high on the tables.

Amber and Clara go to her old house to start packing up the stuff that was left behind when her parents died. When Amber moved to the pack house, she only took some of her clothes. The pack had packed up most of the stuff for her except for her belongings. They started with her mom and dad's room. They were packing away Amber's mama's things when Clara found something that was addressed to Amber. It was a birthday gift from her parents. Amber opened the letter that was with the gift. The letter said that on her birthday she would not only find her fated mate but also come into her powers because she is part witch and a werewolf. She is what they call a hybrid. Her mother continues to explain that she is a half-witch as well. That her papa was her fated mate. But before she met her father, she was in love with another wolf named Thanos Frost who did not take the news very well that she had found her fated mate. He eventually turned rogue. When her mother initially met her fated mate, she said that she passed out and then sometime later she said she started getting her powers. The gift that she left with the letter will enhance her powers she said. It was a gift from her grandmother to her, now it belongs to her. The gift turned out to be a Lunar Gem necklace.

Amber was a little bit in awe. She could not believe that she was a part witch. She hands the letter to Clara to read. Clara reads the letter and faints because she was so shocked by the news that Amber was half-witch and half-werewolf. They both did not believe that Amber's mom was a half-witch and half-werewolf as well. Amber starts missing her parents more than normal and starts crying and sobbing. Fallon comes into the house, and he said that he was there to make sure she was fine. He felt her sadness and distress through the pack link. He tried to comfort her, and she screamed as if his touch burned her.

Onyx came running in to see Amber's tear-stained face and Fallon, talking about something. He was angry because he thought someone was trying to hurt his mate. He said angrily "What did you do?" "What happened?" That was when Fallon realized that Amber had found her mate, and he was not happy with the situation now. Onyx went to attack Fallon, but Amber stopped him by getting between the two men and telling her mate that nothing occurred, and he only touched her with one finger. However, when that finger brushed her skin, Amber felt like she was being electrocuted and that is why she screamed. Onyx felt like he was two years old and then apologized for his rudeness to Fallon and they shook hands creating a new friendship.

Chapter Three: *The Move*

Onyx and Amber have everything packed up into the large U-Haul truck and are about to leave for the blue twilight pack grounds to the north. Clara is coming along for a while to help her settle in as well. It takes four hours to reach the blue twilight pack grounds. By the time they arrived, Amber was so stiff, she could barely get out of the car. The other members of the pack that did not attend the event came from their homes after Onyx used the mind link to tell them to come to the pack house. He told them that he had found his Luna. Before they get to the pack house Onyx is jumped upon by a female werewolf who is dressed like a tramp. Amber gets so angry that she partially shifts and grips the girl by the throat and throws her from Onyx. She growled at her saying that he was hers. The tramp looked at Onyx and asked, "Is this true?" Onyx said, "Yes, Lexi it is." Lexi, it turns out was a short female who stood four foot nine, with an hourglass figure with large breasts that flopped at the slightest movement. She has long wavy black hair and baby-blue eyes and a bitchy attitude. She said, "I cannot believe this! You were going to take me as your chosen mate when you got home!"

"Well, I am sorry about the turn of events but the only reason I was going to choose you as a mate was because I had not found my fated mate yet, but now I have. She is my mate, my Luna." Onyx said. Amber looked at Lexi with a smile on her face when he said that she was his mate and Luna. She was proud to be his mate and Luna. She does not like this chick, who thinks she is entitled just because the alpha was going to choose her as his mate. She is not entitled to anything or anybody else. Onyx then tells Lexi that she can leave. Lexi starts throwing a huff that turned into a major tantrum when Onyx and Amber ignore her and goes ahead into the three-story pack house. Lexi screams "You Will Choose Me!" and sprints away. Lexi shifts and continues to run away from the pack until she runs into the rogue king and his band of rogues. The Rogue King is Thanos Frost, and he stands seven feet tall. He has red greasy, unkempt hair and amber eyes. He has a muscular body with a lot of scary scars crossing it. She tells them that she left her pack because her alpha chose another over her, and it is the truth in a way. Onyx chose Amber over Lexi because she is his mate. She is his other half. Onyx and Amber walked into the pack house. Although it is not as big as the one in the Dark Moon territory, it is significant enough for Onyx and Amber. The Pack House houses the Alpha and now the Luna of the Blue Twilight pack and his beta who is unmated as of right now. Onyx's beta's name is Archer Phoenix. He has mid-length pure white hair and ice-blue eyes, and he stands six-foot-five inches tall with a slightly muscular build. He is the first to notice that Onyx brought some people home with him and for him, he can tell one is his fated mate, but she is not of age yet.

Archer meets Onyx and the other two women he brought home with him when he sees Lexi jump on his alpha and by the look on the one woman's face, she is not supposed to be doing that. Next thing he knows the woman grabs Lexi by the throat and lifts her from Onyx and snarls at her that he is her mate and to back the heck off. He was a little surprised by Luna's actions. He was not surprised by how Lexi acted after being told that Onyx had a mate. As he followed Onyx and Amber into the house, he could not help but stare at her friend Clara, who he learned was his mate but is not of age yet. When they entered the house, it was simply an exceptionally large three-story mansion. On the main level of the mansion, was a decent-sized kitchen with granite countertops and stainless-steel appliances, and mahogany cabinetry. On the other side of the main level is a decent-sized family room with a fireplace and sofas, recliners, and a decent entertainment center with a DVD player, an

XBOX, some DVDs, and a seventy-five-inch TV. Onyx's office is down the hall from the kitchen. His office is about a ten-by-ten size room with a mahogany desk and mahogany office chairs for people to sit down, and a Serta Smart Layers Jennings Big & Tall office chair for Onyx. The second floor is where Clara will stay in one of the many rooms available. The third floor is where Onyx, Amber, and Archer sleep.

One of the omegas that take care of the place, came from the laundry room down the hall from the kitchen carrying a basket full of sheets and things. She was shocked to see the Alpha with someone other than Lexi. She had dropped the basket and apologized for the interruption. Alpha Onyx told her that it was ok he had just gotten home, and that Lexi had left, and he told her who the ladies that stood there with him were. She was happy that Lexi had left and that she had a proper Luna. One that was as beautiful and as kind as their Alpha was. She was happy with the change of events. Lexi was not a stable-minded person when Onyx was not around. She was a veritable witch when he was not around. Everyone hated her but could not do anything because they thought she was going to be their next Luna. What a shock they got when Onyx and Amber got home with the news that their Alpha had found his fated mate. Amber took that moment to familiarize herself with omega. She introduced herself as Amber Scott from the Dark Moon pack and said that she was proud to be her future Luna. The little omega smiled back at Amber and said her name was Sofia and that she was happy that she was Onyx's mate instead of Lexi. She admitted that nobody liked the woman because when the Alpha was away, she was nasty to everyone around her and treated them like they were the dirt beneath her feet.

Onyx asked Sofia if this was a valid statement, and she said it was. Onyx got so angry with Lexi that he wanted to annihilate her for all the pain she caused his pack. Nobody should have treated his pack the way she did. That was when Amber put her loving firsthand Onyx and told him that Lexi is not worth getting so angry over the things she did or did not achieve because she is just a tramp who will never amount to anything, and he calmed down quickly. He then mind-linked to the wolves on patrol to be on the lookout for Lexi that she might come back and if she does, capture her and put her in the cells in the dungeon. He heard a unanimous round of "Yes, Alpha!" through the link. He knew that they would obey his orders. Archer was on patrol that week, so he put in his call with the rest of the people on patrol. After he helped Onyx and Amber with the luggage, he helped Clara with her luggage. He told Onyx that he would see him in the morning because he had patrol duty that evening and out the door, he went. Meanwhile Onyx and Amber were getting to know each other. They were discussing their families and friends. She found out that Archer is not only his Beta but his best friend as well. He found out that Clara had been her best friend since they were three years old. Although she had other friends in her old pack, they were not there for her like Clara was after her parents died. They talked about what to do with all the stuff she got for her birthday and decided to divide it up among the pack members except for the TV, which is going in their bedroom.

They talked for hours until Sofia mind-linked Onyx to tell him that dinner was on the table. So, they went to get Clara and headed downstairs to the magnificent feast the omega prepared for them. They had smoked Turkey, roasted ham, a large pork roast, mashed potatoes, gravy, green beans, Maple baked beans, homemade biscuits, and for dessert a triple-layer chocolate cake. As they were almost done eating, Archer was coming off patrol duty. As he got closer to the pack house, he could smell all the food, especially the cake. His mouth started watering for something sweet. Sofia and the other omegas knew that chocolate was Archer's favorite food. They also knew that chocolate cake was Onyx's weakness. Onyx, Amber, and Clara were about to cut the cake when Archer came into the kitchen and sat down next to Clara and said he would like a piece of cake as well.

Archer got his chunk of the decadent chocolate cake and then helped himself to a plate of food and warmed it up in the microwave that was sitting on one of the countertops. After his food was heated, he went back to sit beside Clara again and started eating. They started talking in between bites of food to get to know each other further. When the food was gone, they decided it was time to go for a run and let their wolves out for a bit. They then went outside and went to the edge of the forest and went behind some trees to strip out of their clothes and shift into their wolves. After they had shifted, they met back in the clearing with their clothes in their jaws and took off down a trail through the forest, Zeus leading the way and Thiago bringing up the tail end. Zeus led them to a medium-sized lake in the middle of the Blue Twilight pack territory. It was like an oasis in the middle of a desert.

It had tall oak trees and bushes scattered around it. It was the beginning of fall so the leaves on the oak trees were starting to change colors. They stopped near the lake to rest for a while before they headed back to the pack house. After about two hours they got up and made the trek back to the pack house. When they got back to the house all the lights were off except for the entrance light which was left on for them. Before they went into the house, they went behind some bigger bushes and shifted and got dressed, then they went into the house and to their rooms to prepare for bed.

Onyx and Amber share his room which is made of the same kind of dark mahogany furniture as the furniture in his office. There are many different paintings on the walls around the house and in his room. Amber asked if he painted them and his reply was "No, my mother did them. She was the painter in the family." With a sad smile on his face, he continued clearing out a dresser for her stuff and half of the walk-in closet. When he was done, he helped her put away her things, it was getting late when everything was put away. They were so tired from the trip and the day that all they did was climb into the massive bed and slept until about ten am the next morning when Clara knocked on the door so many times and so hard, they thought a herd of elephants were at the door. Onyx got up and put on some sweatpants and a T-shirt and answered the door. When he opened his bedroom door, Clara punched him in the face thinking that they were doing something else besides sleeping on their first night as a mated couple. He asked her what that was for, and she said it was for deflowering her friend. It took him a few minutes to understand what she meant, but once he understood he told her that they were just sleeping late and that they did not have sex yet that would come when Amber was ready for it, and he was not going to force it on her. Clara was happy with his statement and was happy that he was going to take care of Amber and not rush things with her. She apologized for punching him in the face and he accepted the apology.

With all the commotion at the door, it finally woke up Amber and she was not in a good mood after being woken up. She got up and dressed in a pair of blue jean capris, and a blue denim shirt. She went up behind Onyx to see who he was talking to about her and found that it was just Clara. Onyx turned around when he heard footsteps behind him and looked down at the floor in shame because he realized that the commotion between Clara and himself that morning woke up his lovely mate, but she had a grumpy look on her face when she got up. Clara realized that when she punched Onyx in the face, she punched hard enough to give him a black eye. However, being a werewolf, he had hyper-healing powers so the black eye would be gone in a few hours. After they calmed down and talked things out, they decided to go down to the kitchen and get something to eat since Onyx and Amber missed breakfast and it is not yet time for lunch. Sofia and the other omegas are busy preparing lunch for the whole pack including the children. So, when Onyx, Amber, and Clara came into the kitchen they asked for something small to eat to tide them over until lunch was ready. Sofia had already thought of something along those lines and prepared little breakfast quiches that looked like little pot pies. They devoured the quiches so quickly and quietly that Sofia had to be sure that they were satisfied with the food. They were so satisfied with the food that they told her they wanted those little quiches tomorrow morning for breakfast.

After they ate, they decided to go for a run. This time, Onyx led them in a different direction. He led Amber and Clara near the northern border where there was a beautiful waterfall that only Archer and him knew about it. He mind-linked Archer and told him that they would be at the waterfall if he needed them. After about an hour or so Thiago shows up and everyone knows that Archer has arrived. Onyx at once asks Archer if anything is wrong with the pack upon seeing him. Archer said that they have visitors and that they needed Amber to come to the pack house right away.

Chapter Four: *Life with the Pack*

Since Amber and Onyx have not marked and mated each other yet she cannot mind-link with anyone to find out who is at the pack house waiting for her. As Onyx and the others set out for the return trip to the pack house, the visitors were getting nervous about what Amber and Onyx would think about her long-lost aunt and uncle, Luna Ember and Alpha Mateo Scott showing up now instead of when she needed them three weeks ago. Sofia and the other omegas were too busy with the preparation of dinner to entertain the Scotts.

Just as Alpha Mateo got up to pace around the family room Onyx and the others came in the door. Archer walked into the family room and got the Scotts. When they came out of the room, Amber had about passed because Alpha Mateo looked exactly like her father so much to be his twin brother. She must have voiced that thought because he hung his head and said "No, I am his twin brother, Mateo." This is my mate and your aunt Ember, and he motions to the woman beside him. Amber bursts into tears and runs over to hug them. She asks them where they have been all this time. Alpha Mateo tells her that they have been on the west coast and are the leaders of one of the strongest packs there. They came back east because they heard that her parents had died and they also felt the connection with them break unexpectedly, so they mind-linked Alpha Colton to see what was going on, he told Mateo what happened, and they made plans to come east as soon as possible. They were unhappy that they missed the funeral, cremation, and birthday party.

Mateo said that he was happy that she had found her fated mate and had moved to his pack. He just was not happy with who her mate turned out to be. However, if she was happy then he was happy for her. She told him that she was happy with her mate. Onyx and Amber asked her aunt and uncle if they wanted to stay the weekend with them and they said they would but then they had to make the return trip home. After dinner, they sat in the family room and talked with Onyx and Amber about their lives on the west coast. They described their lives as busy beavers making a home, but they are werewolves. That comment made everyone laugh so much that they doubled over in laughter. They also talked about the family members that they left behind.

It was getting late, so they all decided to turn in for the night. As Amber and Onyx got ready for bed, Amber could not help but think about all the information she had learned that day. She was surprised that her parents did not tell her that she had an aunt and uncle, let alone cousins she had never met. She voiced these concerns to Onyx his reply was "There must have been a reason for them not telling you." She thought about it for a few minutes and agreed with him that there must have been a reason he was nearing his orgasm he looked into her eyes and saw nothing but love shining there. When he reached his point, he extended his canines and sank them into her flesh at the juncture of her neck and shoulder. When he removed his teeth, he licked the area where his mark now sat.

When morning came, they were wrapped around each other and kissing each other, and they did not want to get out of bed. However, Onyx received a call from his third in command Dante Cambridge through the mind link saying that Alpha Colton and his mate were at the front door. Onyx told Amber that they had visitors at the front door and that they needed to get up and go downstairs. Amber got up and went to the bathroom and brushed her teeth and hair, then came out and went into the closet to get clothes to get dressed. She grabbed a pair of stonewashed jeans and a sweater along with a matching bra and underwear set. Then Onyx went into the closet to get clothes to get dressed. He grabbed a blue T-shirt and a pair of blue sweatpants. When they were fully dressed, they headed downstairs to see what the couple wanted. As they reached the landing at the bottom of the stairs, they noticed Dante standing at the end of the staircase at the side. He told them that he let them in and directed them to the lounge area. Onyx thanked him, took Ambers' hand, and headed that way. Alpha Colton was sitting on one of the sofas with Luna Marian when they came into the room. Onyx asked them why they were there, and they said that they wanted to make sure that they had marked each other shortly after meeting each other because they were afraid Amber might go into heat for the first time if they waited too long. That is when Amber pulled down the neck of her sweater and showed them her mark. Then they looked at Onyx and saw his mark under the edge of his T-shirt.

Alpha Colton looked at his wife and nodded his head and then mind-linked Amber to see if what her mom told him about Amber's powers was true. He was surprised when she replied to him that they were fully mated. She should not be able to do this he thought, nonetheless, she was talking to him with her mind. He realized that she had gotten one of her powers already and she is a telepath. She can read and control the minds of others. Of course, this was a shock to her. Once she realized that she could read their minds, her eyes got big and wide just like her mother did when she mated her father, and she got her first ability. She asked him if her mother could control the minds of others too. When he told her that she could, she was shocked to learn that information.

Alpha Colton and Luna Marian were happy that Onyx and Amber were a fully mated pair. They teased them about the fact that now they need to start having pups, and they took the teasing with a smile on their faces, but they said it was too soon to be thinking about that. Alpha Colton asked them if they used protection when they mated. They looked at each other, dropped their heads, and said no. He then laughed at them and said, "Then it is possible!" They looked at each other and said if it happens then the moon goddess has blessed us. Alpha Colton said that is an effective way to look at the blessing of a pup. Luna Marian agreed with her husband that a pup is a blessing. She wished she could have given Fallon a brother or a sister, but she is happy to have Fallon at least.

Around that time Alpha Mateo and Luna Ember came down to see if breakfast was ready and noticed that their niece and nephew had visitors. As they were coming into the lounge area, they saw Alpha Colton and Luna Marian sitting on a sofa and Onyx and Amber standing at the side of them. They greeted the other alpha and Luna and asked if everything was all right. Alpha Colton said that they were there because they wanted to make sure Onyx and Amber had mated soon after the meeting. After all, they were concerned that she might go into heat if they waited too long. Alpha Mateo looked at the pair and noticed a mark on Onyx's neck and then looked at Amber and who pulled the collar down from her sweater for him to see her mark.

Alpha Mateo looked at them both and said, "Congratulations to both of you!" He also had to tease them a little by asking "So that was what the moaning and groaning were about last night?" They both turned so red, it looked like they had a severe sunburn. They both apologized for any missed sleep that they may have experienced because of them getting loud the night before. They said it with a smile on their faces. They were trying not to chuckle at Alpha Mateo, but they knew that he was just teasing them about making so much noise last night.

Alpha Mateo and Luna Ember calmed down and asked the newly mated pair what they had planned for the day. Onyx said he had a pack to deal with after he gave his mate a tour of the territory. Alpha Colton and his mate asked to go along because they wanted to know if he could provide for and protect his mate from rogues. Alpha Mateo and Luna Ember asked to join the group because they also want to make sure that he and his pack can take on the Rogue King and come out winning. Because they knew that he would come for Amber once the news got out about her abilities. She has the same abilities as her mom and grandmother. It is only a matter of where and when he would strike.

They all left the pack house and turned towards the lake where Onyx had taken Amber and Clara the other day when Alpha Mateo and his wife showed up. Next, they moved toward the northern border where there was a lake with a waterfall. They hang around the lake with the waterfall for about two hours. Then the group headed South toward the town that accept the southern half of the territory and where most of the pack worked to make ends meet. As they got to the town, they could see that there was a theatre, a hair salon, a dog grooming salon, a supermarket, a bank, and a police station. Most of the townspeople were werewolves and were oblivious to the fact that a pack of wolves surrounded the town and worked beside them every day.

A few of the werewolves knew that there was a pack of werewolves living around the area of the town and promised not to say anything to anyone else. These few werewolves are mates of some of the wolves in the pack. They were sworn to secrecy about the situation they found themselves in with their mates and their other friends who are mortal. After the group explored the city, the women said that they would like to go shopping later at the boutiques that they just passed, before they headed to the western side of the territory. On the western border of the territory was the biggest training camp on the east coast. Onyx and his warriors train wolves from other packs in hand-to-hand combat techniques and fighting skills in their wolf form. The reason they trained warriors from all over the country was that they are deadly to any rogue that comes near the territory. However, they have not killed the Rogue King and his band of rogues yet.

Chapter Five: *Life with the pack part 2*

Amber and Clara are planning a birthday party for Onyx because his birthday is Christmas Eve. Everyone is preparing for the holidays and his birthday. He always gets extra presents this time of year because his birthday is the day before Christmas. The weather service is calling for a major snowstorm to hit the eastern seaboard around midnight on Christmas Eve, bringing up to ten to fifteen inches of snow to the area. The Blue Twilight pack territory had already been hit with five inches of snow a week ago. Now they are supposed to get another ten to fifteen inches. If they get that much snow, they will be snowed in for a while. They will not be able to go outside for runs if they are hit with that much snow that the weather service is calling for.

The Blue Twilight pack is not worried about the threat of this big snowstorm that is about to dump a lot of snow on them, they are concerned about the party they are about to throw for Onyx on his birthday. The omegas, Amber, and Clara are standing in the kitchen making sure that they have enough food for the party and the whole pack, they had gotten word that the snow that they got last week made the roads impossible to travel on. Some of the roads have not been plowed yet, so some of his friends will not be coming to the party.

As the party began at around eight pm, the snow started falling and it was in large heavy flakes. Amber was looking out one of the windows at the falling snow, it looked like a blizzard outside, it was zero visibility. The pack members had a challenging time finding the pack house in the blinding snow. They mind-linked the Alpha to tell him that they are not able to make it to the party this year because of the blinding snow. It snowed for a day and a half, dumping a total of ten inches on top of the five that they already had, making the total amount of fifteen inches of snow. The party consists of just Onyx, Amber, Clara, and Archer. They decided to go ahead with the party even if it was just them.

They started with the succulent dinner that was made for Alpha's birthday. The omegas made butterfly shrimp, scallops, lobster, mashed potatoes, gravy, mixed vegetables, and a triple-layer fudge cake. Then they moved on to the gifts that everyone got Onyx for his birthday. The pack plans to give their gifts to him when they can dig their way through the snow and reach the pack house. Amber got him an iPad to help him keep track of all the paperwork he had on his desk. Clara got him a Bluetooth scanner and printer. Archer got him a shredder machine.

Onyx did not know what to do with all his gifts other than to say thank you and that he would put them to effective use.

It took several days and many hours of challenging work to get the paths shoveled out with all the warriors working to get to the pack house to make sure everything was fine there before clearing up more paths around the area. The snow was so high that it covered most of the houses that the pack members had built for themselves and the children could not play in it without being buried in the deepest snow. When the warriors got all the paths uncovered and plowed a new year had started. 2001 is going to be a momentous year to look forward to.

By the time the snow melted, Spring had arrived, and the ground was soggy from too much moisture. The pack was learning about Amber's new power that Onyx and she were trying to keep quiet about. The pack members that found out about it promised to keep quiet about her new ability. The new power that Amber has developed over the past few months is telekinesis. It is the power to move things with the mind. Thus far Amber has developed two different gifts or powers, they are telepathy and telekinesis. Onyx tells Zeus that he thinks she will be formidable in a fight. She has learned that she can freeze someone with her telepathy ability and then move them somewhere else with her telekinesis and unfreeze them. She mostly does it to Onyx and Archer because she thinks it is funny to see the look on their faces when she unfreezes them. They do not like it when she freezes and unfreezes them because they cannot get back at her to do the same thing to her.

She has used her gifts on a few of the wolves also. However, she has mostly been using her telekinetic power on inanimate objects to practice with. She can now move things with her hands. Before she had to use her eyes to move things and over time that gave her headaches. Onyx, Clara, and Archer are all debating on what Amber's next gift is going to be. One thinks that it will be pyrokinesis. One believes that it will be to control the weather. The last one seems to think that she will get the power to freeze time.

With those three debating on what power Amber will get next, she has continued to practice moving items around the pack house and in the training field. She has found out that she can only use her telepathic ability in wolf form. She has found that this comes in handy in a battle with other wolves. She freezes the attacking wolf and then she or any other wolf can attack it. She has also found that she is faster than any wolf when she uses her powers say, for instance, she froze a wolf in battle, but she was werewolf she then used telekinesis to throw it into a tree with great force. With enough force, she can kill a wolf that way by throwing them into a tree with her power. So far, she has only broken bones on the wolves who have volunteered to be her guinea pigs to practice her gifts.

When she started breaking bones, she stopped tossing the wolves into the trees. Now she just tosses them around the training area or into another wolf. Her powers are getting stronger the more she uses them. The weather has gotten hotter, and that means that Summer has arrived. Somewhere around the middle of Summer is when Clara turns eighteen. Amber and Archer have been waiting to throw her a party that everyone could come to, unlike what happened at Christmas. They have been planning in secret with Onyx because he has connections with many people and packs. Because after her birthday she will be the Beta female and mate to Archer. However, only Onyx, Amber, and Archer know that Clara is his mate. Clara and Archer have been getting along very over the last six months.

About a week before Clara's birthday party Onyx stepped up the border Patrol because there had been Rogues spotted on the west side of their territory. Alphas around the area have been trying to figure out what was going on. As Amber was getting ready to decorate for Clare's birthday party. Amber was outside in the backyard when she spotted a man in the tree watching her. She tried to play it off like she did not see him. By the time Onyx and Archer got to her. He was gone. Onyx stiffened the air as soon as he got there. And caught the smell of the Rogue

King himself! After that, a message arrived saying "I will be back to come get you soon." Signed "The Rogue King!"

Two days before Clara's birthday party, a rogue was seen extremely close to the western border of their territory. Onyx tells Amber to stay with the guards he assigned to her. Clara was informed to stay with Amber by Onyx. There was a total of ten wolf guardians. One at each entrance to the house. There are at least four different entry points into the house. There are two guardians on each floor. There are three floors. The rogue that was spotted near the western border was really a lure to get Onyx and Archer out of the house and away from Amber. So, the main group of rogues makes their way from the eastern area of the territory. The rogues do not know what is waiting for them at the house. Amber knows that the Rogue King is coming for her right now, but if he thinks she is going to go without a fight he does not know what kind of woman she is.

The rogues make their way to the house, they see the guards at the entrances to the house and plan an attack. They waited for the change of guards to attack. There were so many rogues that the guards were overpowered and torn apart. They crashed through the doors and flooded the house looking for Amber. The first wave of rogues takes out the guards in the house. The second wave is destroyed by Amber and her gifts. With the third wave, there were so many that Amber could not fight them all, and she and Clara were pinned in a corner of the master bedroom on the topmost floor. The rogues were waiting for the rogue king to get Amber. It does not take long for him to show up. When he comes into the room you can smell the stench that is coming from him. It is so foul that it makes you gag. When Amber caught his stench, she passed out. That is how awful the smell was. With Amber passed out, all the Rogues King had to do was pick her up and carry her away. The rogues left the house as quickly as possible. It was almost destroyed, and it would take a while to repair the damage that was caused. The rogues headed to their hiding place in the Northeast region near Canada.

By the time Onyx and Archer got back to the house it was a disaster and Clara was in the lounge area crying her eyes out and saying "He took her! He took her!" Onyx asked "What do you mean he took her I had ten guards in here! Clara yelled at him "They were not enough! The first wave took out your guards. In the second wave, Amber took care of herself! However, in the third wave, there were so many that she could not defeat them all at once, and they cornered us in the master bedroom until the Rogue King came to get her! He stank so badly that we both passed out! When I woke up again, they were gone, and the house was in shambles!"

Onyx's eyes turned black, and a fierce growl came out of his chest. He said with a gruffer tone to his voice "We will get her back!" He looked at Archer and said, "Gather the gammas, deltas, and the rest of the warriors!" "I will contact the alphas around us, we are going to need an army to get my mate back!" The first person he contacted was Alpha Colton. His beast also came to the surface, growled through the phone, and said, "You did this! You left her alone! But I will help you get her back. I will send my warriors and Fallon is one of my best fighters."

The next call he made was to Alpha Mateo to let him know what had happened. Alpha Mateo said he would send several of his warriors if he needed them. Onyx told him to hold on to that thought until he contacted the other alphas around him. He contacted the alphas of the South Paw pack, the Bright Star pack, and the Black Mountain pack for help to go after his beloved mate. They all agreed to send their best fighters. However, he was still going to need Alpha Mateo's support to get Amber back because the force he had gathered was not enough. While Onyx was gathering his army, so was Alpha Mateo. He was calling the alphas around him and asking them to help him get his niece back from the Rogue King on the east coast, and they agreed quickly. They gathered and hopped on a couple of private planes and flew to the east coast to help rescue Amber. They came prepared with camping gear.

When they landed, they bought various travel buses and made their way to the Blue Twilight pack. It took them about three hours to reach the pack grounds. When they got to the pack lands, they disembarked from the buses and headed to the pack house. Alpha Mateo let Onyx know that they had arrived and were ready to go on the journey to get Amber back. The trackers were already on the trail of the rogues that took her. As the mighty group was getting ready to get her back, Amber contacted Onyx through the mind link even though it should not be possible. She told him that she was in the Northeast near Canada. She sent him a picture of the area where she was being held captive.

He roars at the indifference she has received from the rogues and especially the Rogue King. She was confined in a dark basement chained to the wall with silver handcuffs. The Rogue King at least did make sure she was fed regularly even though it is flavored oatmeal. As she was held by the Rogue King and his rogues, Onyx and his army were making their way to the northeast to achieve a few things one: rescue Amber, and two: kill the Rogue King.

Onyx, Archer, Alpha Mateo, Fallon, and the rest of the army have tracked the rogues to an abandoned mansion in the Northeast near the Canadian border. Their trackers have found that just a limited number of the rogues are living in the mansion, and the ones that survived the fight against Amber, are living in the woods around the mansion. They waited for nightfall to take out the rogues in the woods. Onyx's mind linked with Amber and told her that the army had come to rescue her and for her to be calm and wait for them to get to her. She told him that she was shackled in the basement with silver handcuffs. When she told him that it just made him and his beast all the madder. They went on a killing spree, killing everything that was not a friend. When all the rogues outside of the mansion were dead, Onyx pushed into the building and started killing all those rogues too. When all the minor rogues were dead, he went looking for the Rogue King. Onyx found him in the basement holding a silver knife to Amber's throat. He roars "It is between you and me now! Leave her alone!"

Onyx shifts into his wolf. He is massive compared to Amber's wolf. The Rogue King shifts into his wolf. He is a large rust-colored wolf with scars crossing through his fur. Compared to Onyx, he is half the size of Onyx. They circle each other for about ten minutes. Then the Rogue King suddenly attacks Onyx. However, Onyx is younger and smarter. He jumps to the side and swipes his claws down the Rogue king's side making him roar out in pain. He then uses his claws to cut into his hind leg on the same side that he swiped his claws down. When the rogue king went to attack again Onyx was ready for him and used his jaws and snapped the Rogue king's leg. The Rogue king has lost a lot of blood, you would think that he would not have the strength to still fight. However, just as Onyx turned to look at Amber, the Rogue king grabbed him by the throat and was about to snap his neck when the whole room lit up like a Christmas tree. Onyx and the rogue king both turned to look at Amber. She was glowing and her hair had turned red, the silver handcuffs melted off her, and even her eyes had turned red. The next thing Onyx knows is there is a huge ball of fire where the Rogue King was. He looked at Amber and saw that flames were coming from her hands.

After about an hour or so Amber calmed down and the flames died away. Her eyes went back to their natural color. She looked at Onyx, he was in awe of her for the second time. He loved the latest look. He even told her how much he liked it. By the time everyone else found Onyx and Amber, the rogue king was dead. He was nothing but a pile of ash in the middle of the basement floor.

The survivors of Onyx's army found automobiles and buses in the area to drive home in. Fallon was one of the survivors. It took them about four to five hours to get back to the Blue Twilight pack. When they got back, they were encircled by the pack. They were so happy that everyone was back unharmed. They started cheering for everybody that survived the battle with the rogues. Clara came running out of the pack house to welcome the survivors. As soon as she hugs Amber, she gets a whiff of something delicious. It smells of rainfall and fresh-cut grass. She follows the scent until she runs into Archer. When he turned around, he said the one word she had been longing to hear and that is "Mate!" She also said, mate at the same time. They at once fall into each other's arms and lock lips. They kiss for so long that they run out of air and must separate after a few minutes. By this time, their lips are bruised and swollen but each has the biggest grin.

They walked into the pack house and saw that the omegas had decided to decorate for Clara's birthday everyone missed it because of Amber's kidnapping. Omegas were all surprised that Sophia and the other omegas thought to do something like that for them when they got home. By the time they all settled down to eat, the daylight had fallen into the night. They sat down to a delicious meal. There were two-inch steaks, twice-baked potatoes, green beans, buttermilk biscuits, and a large birthday cake. Clara's cake was half the size of Amber's.

The wolves that had gotten to know Clara came to the party and brought her gifts. They brought her gifts of jeans, T-shirts, jackets, dresses, and an iPod. They also brought their gifts for Onyx too. Their gifts for Onyx ranged from a German Shepherd puppy to a ham radio for learning to communicate with the other packs around the area. Since he already has his federal license for the ham radio. This gift he adored second to the puppy.

Onyx named the puppy Arlo. After a while, the puppy started to come to the name when called. Amber loved the puppy as well. It came to Onyx's attention that everyone loved the puppy. However, he was supposed to be Onyx's dog, but he would come to Amber more than Onyx even though he was calling the pup. The puppy was only about three to four months old.

As time went on Amber's powers grew and became stronger every day. Onyx, being the concerned mate that he is, sent a message to the Werewolf Council asking for help for his mate. He knows that the Werewolf Council has witches working for them when they need them. After about a week, the Council sent a reply, they said that they would send their highest level which they have to them to train his mate on how to use her gifts. They said she should arrive in about a week and a half to two weeks. She arrived after two weeks. She introduced herself as Sarafina Evergold. She is the high priestess of her coven. She is a fire witch, like Amber.

Sarafina and Amber got along well with each other considering that Sarafina was much older than Amber. Sarafina taught Amber how to control her fire gifts and harness the power of the mind. As they were training Amber developed another power. This one was that she could control the weather. When she gets upset it snows and when she gets angry, she causes thunderstorms. When she is sad it rains. This unique power surprised Amber and Sarafina because now she can control the elements.

This new power of Amber's really surprised everyone in the pack because one day they were sparing each other on the training field, and she got mad at herself and the next thing they knew there was a dark thunderstorm brewing overhead of everyone. However, it could come in handy in a battle with the enemy. Amber could cause a major fog bank to roll in and cover the battlefield to blind everyone. Amber likes this gift because she can use it while she is in Kia's form, and nobody would know that she was a hybrid or the one causing the fog.

Amber and Onyx found out just how effective her gifts are in a battle with the rogues that survived the battle to rescue her. The rogues thought they would get revenge on Amber and Onyx. However, Amber showed that she is stronger than the average wolf, and her gifts are unique or so they think. She not only inherited some of her mother's powers but also some of her grandmother's as well.

After about a month and a half of training with Sarafina, Amber has become more confident in herself and controlling her emotions and her gifts, especially her pyrokinesis because before when she got upset everything started burning and getting hot now, she can control that element and herself. When she gets super angry and lets her power free it is like an atomic bomb went off around her. You would think with that much heat she would be burnt from the inside out, but she does not have a mark on her.

After training for six months with Sarafina, Amber was able to suppress certain gifts when she needed to. She has grown into her gifts exponentially and she also developed a gift. This one is the ability to move through solid matter. She thought that this ability was cool because she does not have to use a door anymore. After getting control of this new gift, Amber comes home from a run with Archer and Clara to find that she has a visitor. It turns out that her grandmother has come to visit, a grandmother she never knew about. Her grandmother is at the highest level in the coven as you can go, she is also on the werewolf council. Her grandmother's name is Gilda Morningstar.

Chapter Six: *Unexpected Things*

Now that Amber's grandmother has come to visit, Amber is in total amazement because her mother never talked about her mother, and Amber never asked about her growing up, she thought that she was dead. When Amber found out she had a grandmother that was not dead it was quite a shock to the system. They talked way into the long hours of the night. They talked about her grief and her gifts, and her carrying on the family legacy by having pups of her own.

The one thing Onyx and Amber have not talked about yet is having pups of their own. The thought never occurred to them. Even when they mated for the first time the thought of pups was never brought up. Except when Alpha Colton asked them about it after they were fully mated. As they were lying in bed, they were talking about what Amber and Gilda had talked about, having pups of her own. Onyx said he did not think he was ready to be a father yet but if a pup came along right now, he would be happy about it.

As they were lying in bed that night, they were discussing the topic of children of their own. The more they talked about the idea of having a pup of their own they began to like that idea. So that night they made love to each other like it was the first time. They made love to each other with reverence and so much heat and passion that they fogged up the windows. It was the first time they have made love to each other since the kidnapping, they were not sure how to still be calm as they were making love because the full set fire to everything thing is a bit of a turn-off. However, they got through their insecurities.

When they woke up the next morning, they could see a few scorched marks on the blankets, sheets, and the wall behind the bed and the ceiling above them. They were shocked to see the marks, it implied that it got a little too hot in their room last night and they are going to have to do some painting here soon to get rid of the marks. They are surprised that the blankets did not catch on fire.

They got out of bed and got ready for the day. Onyx had alpha duties to conduct, so he went to his office after they had breakfast. Amber and Clara talked about going shopping for some things, especially new bedding for the bed in Amber's and Onyx's room.

Onyx told Amber and Clara to take some of their warriors with them to provide protection. He does not want to lose her again, especially if she might be pregnant with his pup. Amber agrees with his request with no complaint. When Amber and Clara and the four warriors that came with them got to the city, they decided to go to the mall that was situated on the far side of the city. The group first went to the department store on the first floor of the huge mall. Amber decided to get new bedding for her bed. She chose to get a set of deep blue blankets, and a sheet set to match.

They then went to the clothing area to see if they had anything that caught their eye. They found some lingerie to match the bedroom bedding that Amber had just bought. Clara found some lingerie that might spice up her love life with Archer. Not that they needed any help in that department, but she likes to keep him on the edge of his seat. They also went by the paint area and picked out new paint for the master bedroom.   They hoped the color they picked would go with the mahogany furniture in the master bedroom. They then went around to the other different areas of the space and picked up various things from body wash to makeup. They also found some dog toys for Arlo to chew on instead of the furniture and shoes.

Once they had everything, they needed they headed to the checkout counter. Before they had left the pack house Onyx had given Amber his black card which has an unlimited limit. The cashier was a werewolf and very plain looking, even her clothes were plain a white shirt with black pants. The only thing that set her apart from the other employees was her eyes. They were an amethyst color. She asked Amber if she found everything she needed, and Amber replied, "Yes, she did." As they were checking out, the girl noticed the mated mark on Amber's shoulder. The Mark now looks like a tattoo. She asks her about her tattoo. The Mark resembles the symbol of two wolves lying under a full moon. It is Onyx's mark.

Amber told the girl that when she met her boyfriend several months ago, they decided to get these tattoos. Meanwhile, the girls were shopping at the mall, Onyx was planning the most romantic double proposal, he and Archer could think of. They were hoping for it to be a double proposal, but Onyx said they better propose to their girls in private. They decorated their rooms with bouquets of roses and rose petals scattered on the bed and all over the floor. Onyx chooses purple roses because that is Amber's favorite color, what he does not know is that she has recently changed her favorite color to deep blue. She made this decision because she loves Onyx's eyes. She has never seen anything so blue before. Archer chose red because that is Clara's favorite color and just happened to be the most popular color of roses, so he ordered more than Onyx did. Archer hopes that Clara is surprised by all his efforts.

As the girls were coming into the house from the trip, the guys were waiting for them in the lounge. They each told their girl that they wanted to talk to them alone. Each couple went into their respective bedrooms. However, before the girls could enter the rooms the guys covered their eyes and guided them into their decorated rooms. The guys sat them down on the beds and uncovered their eyes. As the girls got their first look around the room and saw all the roses they were surprised and each of them felt like their mate must love them a great deal to do something special like this. As Onyx was getting down on one knee in front of Amber, Archer was doing the same with Clara. Each of them had separately gone out shopping for a ring to complete the proposal. The girls were shocked and in amazement at their men as they spoke.

Onyx and Archer said at the same time "Will you marry me?" While holding up a diamond ring that looks like two hearts surrounding the diamond that was at least three to four carats. Amber and Clara at once said, "Yes, I will marry you!" That night the house was not a quiet place to live as not only were Onyx and Amber making wild animalistic enthusiastic love to each other. Archer and Clara were making just as much noise as they were making wild enthusiastic love to each other. The windows in Onyx's room fogged over from the heat they were producing. The flowers on the dressers began to wilt and the petals fell off.

The petals on the bed began to wither and burn due to the heat that Amber was unknowingly making. As the petals were burning, they were leaving holes in the bedding on the bed thus ruining another set of sheets and comforters. With as much heat as Amber was making in the room, it is surprising that Onyx is not affected. Their wolves were in a blissful state. They were overjoyed that their werewolf halves had mated again. This time, Kia knew that Amber had become pregnant. However, she was not going to tell her it was twins, she would let her find out the old-fashioned way.

After several weeks of being nauseous in the morning and eventually throwing up in the toilet, Amber began to think that she was pregnant. She asks her wolf, Kia, if she is, and she says she is. She told Onyx to get some home pregnancy tests because she might be pregnant. She was not going to tell him right away that she was. Onyx was on cloud nine when Amber told him to get pregnancy tests which means she thinks she might be carrying his pup. He drove into the city that was in his territory, went to the nearest drug store and got several kinds of tests. If the tests were positive, he would make an appointment with the pack doctor the next day to find out how far she was.

When he got home, they used one of each kind of the five diverse types of tests. Onyx had gotten four of each type of pregnancy test. After waiting the required amount of time, they looked at the tests and each one was positive. Onyx let out a loud whoop full of joy causing Archer and Clara to come knocking on the bedroom door wanting to know what that noise was. When he had let out his joyful call, he had grabbed Amber in a bear hug and lifted her in the air and jumped up and down unknowingly making her already upset stomach that much worse. She told him that if he does not put her down right now, she is going to get sick all over him. He dropped her on her feet like a hot potato. She then ran to the bathroom and unloaded her stomach with what little bit was left in it. Onyx was holding back her hair while she was unloading in the toilet.

She looked so pale after she was done. Onyx picked her up off the floor of the bathroom and put her in the huge tub and started the warm water. He then adds her strawberry-scented bubbles to the bath. When he was satisfied with the amount of water in the tub, he begins to wash her body with a soft washcloth and her strawberry-scented soap. He loved her scent, it was a mix of vanilla, cinnamon, and strawberries from her soap and bubble bath liquid. She also had his scent mixed in. He is wondering about who the pup will look like, him or her, and if it will be a boy or a girl. After he was done washing her, he pulled the plug into the tub to drain it and helped her stand up and get out of such a large tub. He then reached for the towel that was lying on the counter and began drying her with it. When he went to dry her under her arms, she giggled because it tickled, which made him look up at her. She told him it tickled, which made him realize what he was doing, and he moved to another area.

Once he made sure she was completely dry, he picked her up and carried her out of the bathroom into the bedroom and sat her on the bed then went to get her some comfortable clothes out of the huge double walk-in closet. He came out with her Victoria's Secret purple lounge pants and matching sweater and her matching bra and thong. He then helped her get dressed and into bed with the new bedding she bought in the city the last time she went shopping before he proposed. They were planning a double wedding already and now they are pregnant. They are going to have to tell Gilda the news as soon as they see the pack doctor tomorrow morning. Onyx had already mind-linked the doctor and told her that they needed an appointment in the morning because Amber is pregnant and needs to be checked out. He then went into the bathroom and took an exceptionally long cold shower.

The next morning was Amber's appointment with the pack doctor. To say she was nervous was an understatement. She did not sleep well the night before, all she did was toss and turn all night, and having terrible morning sickness did not help the situation. However, she mustered her strength and got up to go to the hospital to get checked out and to make sure everything with the pup was fine. As Amber and Onyx walked into the hospital, they had a shock to their system, one other person was also waiting for the same appointment. It turns out to be Clara. They both got pregnant on the night that the guys proposed. She also has terrible morning sickness. She was so weak from throwing up in the bathroom that all she had on under her robe was her bra and underwear. Archer had to carry her in, luckily, they had a wheelchair they could use to get her through the building while they were there. Archer and Clara had already checked in with the nurse and were waiting to be called back into a room. Onyx and Amber walked up to the nurse's station to check in themselves before having a seat.

Archer looked at Onyx, Onyx looked back, and the biggest grin spread across their faces as they started to chuckle about the things that were crossing their minds at that moment. They were mind-linking each other and asked if their girl was pregnant, each other replied yes, she was that was when they began to grin like the Cheshire cat. One nurse came through the door and called Clara. Archer got up and wheeled her through the door down the hallway into a room on the right that the nurse showed him. He made sure that the wheelchair would not move while he was trying to lift Clara out of it. Once he got her out of the chair, he moved over to the exam table that was in the middle of the room and laid her down on it. He took the seat that was beside the table and faced the nurse and helped answer questions about her pregnancy that they knew of.

Out in the waiting room, it was Amber's time to be called. She too was weak from throwing up from the morning sickness, but she was stronger than Clara because of her wolf. Her wolf was stronger than Clara's because her wolf was an Alpha female. Which is extremely rare if not unheard of. She slowly got to her feet and made her way down the hallway to the opposite room to Clara. She went to the exam table and got on it, faced the nurse, and started to answer questions about her pregnancy that she knew about. Onyx sat in the chair beside the table and helped answer questions that only he could answer about his family history.

The nurse finished writing down all the information in Amber's file and said that the doctor would be in to see them in a few minutes and quietly left the room. Meanwhile, across the hallway, Clara's nurse was also just wrapping up in her room and told them that the doctor would be with them soon. The doctor came in to see Amber first, she greeted Onyx and Amber with a smile on her face. She jumped right to the subject of why they were there, Amber's pregnancy. They nodded yes, she was correct. She explains that an alpha pregnancy lasts for up to five or six months depending on how healthy the mothers are. She then told them that she was going to use a machine to check the pup's heartbeat.

What a shock everyone got when they heard two different heartbeats. Kia chose that moment to pipe up in Amber's mind and say "Yes Dear! You are having TWINS!" and then trotted off into the back of her mind with a wolfish grin on her face. The doctor also apparently came out of shock and said the same thing as Kia did. She then had to adjust the timetable for Amber's pregnancy because the Twins were a rare occurrence in the werewolf community and had never happened in this pack until now. She also wanted to get a measurement of the twins as well. She told them that it means that a probe would be inserted into the privates to get an ultrasound of the twins in the womb. The ultrasound shows that the twins are about six to eight weeks old. They look to be healthy as far as their development goes. It was too early to tell what sex the twins were yet. She asked them if they wanted pictures of the ultrasound, and they almost shouted yes. She pressed a few buttons on the machine and then it printed out several different views of the twins and handed them over to Onyx. She then removed the probe and wiped Amber clean from the ooze used for the machine and told them that she wants to see them back in a month.

She got up from the little stool and said that she was going across the hall to see Beta and his mate next. Amber turned to Onyx and said, "Clara's pregnant too?" He told her yes, she was. Meanwhile, in Clara's room, the doctor had just entered and apologized for taking so long with the Alpha and Luna. That was when Onyx's mind linked with Archer and told him they were having twins. At the same time, Amber was doing the same with Clara and telling her about the twins. When the two heard this, they looked at each other and yelled "TWINS?" The doctor looked at them and realized that they already knew that Luna Amber was carrying twins.

She had a big smile on her face. As she got closer to Clara, she could see how pale and weak she was just from a few feet away. She asked Clara if she had been able to keep anything down at all in the past few weeks. Archer and Clara tell her that she has been able to keep saltine crackers down sometimes and potato chips sometimes. She told her that she was going to prescribe something that should help with the morning sickness. She then asked them if they wanted to hear their pup's heartbeat. They put a lot of energy into the words "Yes, please!" The doctor got her little machine and squirted some gel on Clara's belly and used the probe to listen for the heartbeat. However, instead of one heartbeat, there were distinct sounds of at least four heartbeats. It means that Clara is carrying quads which have never happened before in the pack or the werewolf community. This announcement shocked everyone in the room. The doctor said she had never heard of a quadruple pregnancy and could not make the best decision for the future of Clara's pregnancy and the safety of the pups. She told them that she was going to have to call some friends for help with their case.

However, she could make sure that the pups were developing as they should for werewolf pups. A normal pregnancy for a werewolf is about 7-8 months. With quads, it will be difficult to keep them from coming too early. The doctor brought in her ultrasound machine and explained that the probe was inserted into Clara's private, and it would look at the pups on the screen of the machine. She could tell that they were worried about the situation, and she easily calmed them down by showing them the four pups on the screen. They appeared to be a little on the small scale for being six to eight weeks old. She asked them if they wanted pictures of the quads and they both yelled, "Yes!" scaring the poor doctor. She printed out the pictures of the pups even though they scared the daylight out of her.

She gave the pictures to Archer, and he gave them to Clara. The doctor finished in a few more minutes with the machine and then said that she was done and pulled out the probe and wiped Clara clean with a towel. She said to come back in two weeks for a check-up, at least until she makes some calls to get help from some of her colleagues who may know something about a quadrupled werewolf pregnancy and got up from the stool and left the room. They look at the door as Onyx and Amber come in and they yell "We are carrying quads!" Clara starts to cry, and Archer tries to soothe her, but he has no effect. Amber walks over to her and hugs her and tells her she is beside her down the road for the months ahead until they have their pups. That calms Clara down quickly.

Amber released Clara from her hug and stepped back. The nurse knocks on the door and comes in holding some papers in her hand. She explains that she has a presentation for prenatal vitamins and something that might help with morning sickness. She handed the papers to Archer and asked if they had any questions or concerns. Archer and Clara said that they had a lot of concerns but would wait for the next appointment with the doctor to voice them. She goes to leave and notices that Amber is in the room as well, she tells her that the doctor also prescribed prenatal vitamins and the same medication as Clara for the morning sickness they are at the front desk waiting for her. Archer picked Clara up from the table and placed her back into the wheelchair and followed Onyx and Amber out of the room. They stopped to pick up Amber's presentations and then everyone left the hospital, got into their separate cars, and headed to the pharmacy in the city.

Onyx and Archer took the prescriptions into the pharmacy to be filled while the girls waited in the car and mind-linked each other about their situations with so many pups due in a few months. They were both worried about how fragile they felt, especially Clara. The guys came out of the pharmacy, and each one was carrying a bag of stuff. While they were waiting for the medications to be filled, they went shopping. They got crackers, ginger ale, and their mate's medications. The pharmacist recommends that they try to take the morning sickness medication after they have emptied their stomachs in the morning and tried to eat something. Onyx and Archer relay this message to their mates after they got into their cars and handed them the bags and six-pack of ginger ale. All Amber and Clara could do is say ok to this and started to open the vitamins and they both took the specific dose. They were going to wait until they got home to try and eat something and take their other medication, and hopefully, it works especially for Clara who is on bed rest until she can keep food down for more than an hour.

As they arrive at the pack house, the omegas are in the foyer of the house waiting for the announcement of whether they are going to have a pup or two again running around in the house soon or not. As the couple come into the foyer, Sofia asks if everything went well with the doctor. She does not see Archer carrying Clara behind Onyx and Amber. Amber tells her she is carrying twins. Sofia's eyes got so big and round that they resemble a doe's eyes. Poor Sofia got an even bigger shock when Clara told her that she was carrying quads. The shock of it all was too much for Sofia because when she heard Clara mention quads she fainted into a puddle on the floor. She was an older woman in her late forties with graying auburn hair and golden eyes. Like most omegas, she was on the short side of the spectrum. Onyx went over to Sofia to make sure that she was all right and that she did not injure herself when she fainted. He gently shook her awake and asked if she was hurt anywhere. She replied that she was fine, he asked if she needed help getting up off the floor, and she nodded her head yes. He then helped her up from the floor and into a chair in the lounge area. He asked one of the other omegas to get her some water. She quickly brought the water to him, and he handed it to Sofia with instructions to sip it slowly.

Sofia looks at Amber, then at Clara, and cannot imagine so many pups being born to the two of them. The Moon Goddess must have blessed both. Clara asked Archer to take her to their room so she could lie down for a while because she was getting tired already. He picked her up from the couch in the lounge, where he had sat her down when the commotion happened with Sofia and carried her to the room. He made sure that she ate enough crackers to settle her stomach and to take her medication. He then covers her up and leaves the room, promising to check on her in a couple of hours. Meanwhile, downstairs Amber was talking to Onyx about the twins, and they were discussing names for the pups already but had not decided on which name to go with for each sex of pups.

Onyx made sure Amber ate enough to take the medication. By the time lunch came around she did not have an episode of morning sickness and was hungry for food. Clara is also feeling better and wanted to try to eat something for lunch and hopefully, it will stay down. Archer came downstairs to the kitchen to see what Sofia and the other omegas prepared for lunch. They had made beef broth with veggies, crackers to go with it, a hot roast beef sandwich with gravy. Sofia made a tray up for Clara and gave it to Archer to take it up with him.

As Archer was taking the tray to Clara, Amber was sitting down at the table to eat her lunch. She started with the broth, and when that stayed down, she continued eating the rest of her lunch. Clara had the same reaction when she ate her lunch. By the time both were done eating, they had inhaled all their lunch because they were so hungry and could finally keep it down. Clara sent Archer down to the kitchen for more, and Amber asked for more as well. Sofia gave Amber a second helping of the hot roast beef sandwich and gravy and the broth with veggies and crackers. She then made up another tray for Clara and sent it up with Archer. This time the second helping of food filled their stomachs, and they were happy to be so full. Onyx and Archer were only glad that they were able to keep the food down this time.

Clara decided that she would watch a movie on the sixty-inch tv that was mounted on the wall above one of the dressers in their room. She decided on a romantic comedy she had never seen before. Meanwhile, downstairs Amber and Onyx were discussing what they wanted to do. They decided to go for a walk around the pack grounds. They were talking about proclaiming to the pack that they are going to be parents in a few months. They mind-linked, Clara and Archer, and asked if they wanted them to announce that they too were going to be parents in the coming months. Clara said that she liked the idea. However, she did not want them to announce how many pups are being born to both. She wants that to be a surprise for everyone. Amber and Onyx agreed with her wish to keep the number of pups they are carrying a secret for the time being.

They agree not to talk about them aloud in front of other people. They had already told Sofia and the omegas, and they agreed to stay quiet for the sake of their privacy and the safety of the pups. The omegas and Sofia were happy with the knowledge that they would hear little feet running around the house again.

They will help with the many diaper changes and the late-night feedings because, with so many pups on the way, Amber and Clara may run out of milk soon after the pups are born. They are planning to make sure that Amber and Clara eat as much healthy food as possible while they are pregnant and after they deliver their pups so that they produce enough milk for six pups in total.

To do this, they need to contact the doctor and ask her what foods they should stay away from to make sure that Amber and Clara are getting the most nutrients for the pups to grow strong and healthy. She said to try to limit junk food. However, if that is what they are craving then give it to them but in moderation. Amber was already starting to crave weird foods. She is craving peanut butter and chocolate ice cream, avocados, sour cream, and onion chips all these things at the same time. Clara is craving mint chocolate chip and strawberry ice cream, mangoes, and barbecue chips all of them at the same time. Onyx and Archer have no idea what to do. They think these combinations of foods are disgusting. Onyx keeps getting upset because his sour cream and onion chips keep disappearing. However, he knows it is Amber taking them, but he wishes she would save him some, but no she eats the whole party-sized bag. Archer and Onyx were worried that their mates were going to gain a tremendous amount of weight by eating so much junk food. However, what they do not realize is the Amber is not just eating for herself, she is eating to feed two pups in her womb. Clara is eating for herself and four pups. She needs to eat more food than Amber does because of the sheer number of pups growing in her womb.

Sofia and the other omegas started to make more healthy food choices for the families at all the important mealtimes, especially at dinner when the mothers needed the most nutrients to sustain them through the night. However, they still send Archer and Onyx down for something to snack on in the middle of the night. For example, last night around one is Amber sent Onyx down to the kitchen for some of the double chocolate cupcakes that Sofia had made the day before. At the same time, Clara sent Archer for some of the same things. By the time the guys got back upstairs the girls wanted something else. They did not want to bother the house by yelling down the stairs, so the girls stayed quiet. When the guys got halfway up the stairs, they linked with them and told them that they changed their minds and wanted something else, so they turned around and went back to the kitchen and put the cupcakes away, got what the girls wanted, and headed upstairs.

They got upstairs with the stuff that the girls requested and split into different directions. Archer went into his room and Onyx went into his room. Amber and Clara were eagerly awaiting their snack. By now they were about two to three months long in their pregnancies. Clara has a bigger bump than Amber does. However, she is not angry that her best friend has a bigger bump than she does, it means that her friend's pups are growing because she is carrying quads. It also means that the pups are healthy and have a steady heartbeat. They go every two weeks for a check-up because Clara's pregnancy is unheard of in the community. It is rare in the werewolf community and has happened very rarely.

Amber's pregnancy is just as difficult for her as Clara's is for her. As the pups grow bigger, the more checkups they need to make sure there are no problems with the pups in their developmental stages. They both get weekly ultrasounds to get video documents of the developing pups. They were developing fast, healthy, and strong. The pack doctor was in the office when she got a phone call from the Dark Moon pack doctor about Amber, Clara, and their pregnancies and the possibility that they might deliver the pups incredibly early depending upon what they were doing. Amber looks like she has swallowed a beachball. Clara looks like she swallowed two beach balls.

Onyx and Amber are in their room onyx says "I cannot wait to be a father! Of twins for that matter!" Amber replies "I am excited as well… I am just a little scared because of something happening with the pups." Onyx said, "Do not worry too much baby! I will be there every step of the way!" They made plans with Archer and Clara to spend time together, so they go downstairs Clara then asks Amber, "How are you feeling? The pack doctor said with us having more than one baby each we might go into labor early!" Amber says, "I am feeling fine just a little bit scared" Clara replied, "So am I with having quads." Amber says back "What are your fears, Clara?" Clara says, "I am worried that something might go wrong!" Amber said" I have the same fear" Archer and Onyx are listening in on their conversation and say at the same time "I will be there for every step of the way baby!" They go to relax at the lake…

about 20-30 minutes later Clara and Amber start to scream in surprise when their water breaks … and when Onyx and Archer jump up and ask, "What's wrong?!" The girls yell back "THE PUPS ARE COMING!!!" Archer and Onyx look at each other and yell "OH SHIT! WE HAVE TO GET THEM TO THE HOSPITAL!!"

Onyx and Archer rushed into action. They mind-linked one of the omegas at the pack house to grab the bags that Amber and Clara had previously mentioned that they had prepared for when they go into labor with the pups. Amber's bag was found just inside their bedroom door, on a chair. Clara's suitcase was on top of the standby their bedroom door. Onyx told them to meet them at the hospital with the bags because the pups were coming, and they were heading straight there. When both parties got to the hospital, the doctor rushed them into separate rooms. They put Amber in a normal delivery room. However, they feared that Clara might need a C-section to deliver the quads safely.

They prepared an operating room just in case Clara needed a C-section to deliver the quads safely. Amber's contractions started to be one minute long and five minutes apart. By the time they got to the hospital, the contractions were upon each other. Clara's contractions started ten minutes apart and were two minutes long. When Archer got her to the hospital, her contractions were a minute long and two minutes apart. When the doctor checked Amber to see if she was ready to deliver the pups, she was fully dilated, and she kept saying "It hurts, I want something for the pain!" However, it was too late to give her anything for the pain of delivering her pups because the first one was coming at that very moment. The first pup was a boy. He weighed four pounds, four ounces, and was nineteen inches long. The second pup was also a boy. He weighed five pounds, five ounces, and was twenty inches long. However, they were surprised by a third pup, a little girl, who was hiding behind her brothers. She weighed three pounds, four ounces, and was nineteen inches long. All three pups were tiny for werewolves. However, they were healthy, strong, and had a good set of lungs. Each one let out a fierce scream when they were born.

After the pups were cleaned and swaddled, they were then put into their parents' waiting arms. Onyx held the two boys, while Amber held the tiny girl. They looked at each other with awe on their faces that turned into immense joy. Onyx looked at Amber and asked, "What are we going to name them?" Amber thought for a few minutes and produced the names Griffin, Koda, and Aislin.

In a room down the hall, Clara was preparing to have her quads. She was hooked up to a lot of leads and wires. By the the time they got her into bed her contractions were on top of each other. She delivered her first pup twenty minutes after Amber had her last pup. Clara's first pup was a girl, who weighed four pounds and four ounces, and was nineteen inches long. The second pup to arrive was a boy, he weighed five pounds and five ounces and was twenty inches long. Her third pup was a girl. She weighed five pounds, four ounces, and was nineteen inches long. Her last pup to arrive weighed was a boy, he weighed six pounds, seven ounces, and was twenty-one inches long. Clara and Archer are shocked that they have two of each. They have the look of amazement on their faces. Clara points out that the pups came before they could decide on names. Of course, they did not know that they had two of each. Clara and Archer started thinking of names. They chose the name Leilani for the oldest girl. They chose the name River for the oldest boy. They chose the name Dahlia for the second girl, and they chose the name Paxton for the second boy.

They mind-linked Onyx and Amber to see how they were fairing with the twins when Onyx told them that they truly brought into the world triplets. When Archer and Clara were notified that Onyx and Amber had triplets, they were stunned with shock. Then they looked at each other and said, "TRIPLETS! No wonder she was bigger than normal for carrying twins." Onyx answered them and commented that "Yes, she was larger than normal for carrying twins." Archer said, "It is a good thing we got the nurseries set up before they came." Onyx agreed. The pups were too small to tell which one looked like which parent just yet. However, Onyx's and Amber's boys did favor Onyx in their hair coloring and complexion. Whereas Aislin resembled her mother with her hair coloring and complexion. Clara's and Archer's girls took after their father with their coloring, and their boys took after Clara with their coloring.

Aislin had to stay in the NICU for about two to three months until she was up to six or seven pounds or more before the doctor would release   her to go home. When Onyx and Amber were told that they could take Aislin home four months after she was born, they were overjoyed. They had added a crib for her in the nursery with the boys, Griffin, and Koda. She was still smaller than her brothers because while she was in the NICU they were growing bigger every day. They had already decorated the nursery in pastel colors because they did not know what the sex of the pups was.

Chapter Seven: *Living With Multiples.*

Life with the pups was not what Onyx and Amber expected. They knew that there would be a lot of dirty diapers and more than their share of dirty clothes, but they did not anticipate the shear load of what the triplets produced in a single day or in a single hour. They were doing more laundry for the triplets than they were doing for themselves. They were also not getting as much sleep as they thought they would, because when they got two of the three down to sleep the other would wake up and start crying and wake the other two and start the process all over again.

Clara and Archer had decided to move out into a place of their own before the pups came so that they would have room for the quads when they got older. Their house is not as big as the pack house. However, it is big enough for the six of them. They have a big bedroom dedicated just for the nursery for the quads, and it is decorated in pastel colors like Onyx and Amber's house. They also were not prepared for the sheer number of dirty diapers they went through or the sheer number of dirty clothes. They were not expecting the pups to have so many blowouts, where they exploded in their drawers and the poop goes halfway up their back and down their legs, requiring them to need a bath several times a day. The same situation was happening with Onyx and Amber's triplets.

All the pups were being breastfed, which meant that Amber and Clara had to eat a lot of food to produce enough milk for the pups to consume. Sometimes they were fed with a bottle, but it was still breastmilk they were being fed in the bottle. Usually when they get a bottle, their father feeds them. It has been two months since the pups came home, and they have doubled in size and weight. Aislin has tripled in her size and weight since she has been home with her family. She is growing so fast that you would not believe she had such a rough start in life.

Onyx and Archer are always trying to find ways to help their mates with the many feedings that the pups demanded every day. They ate more than normal. Instead of them eating every two to three hours, they were eating at least every hour. Onyx and Archer would help Amber and Clara by bottle feeding the pups while they were taking a nap, which was as often as they could, because they were up at odd hours of the night feeding the pups. The pups ate so much that Amber and Clara thought that they would run out of milk before the pups were six months old. The pups grew so fast, that by the time they were eight months old they were the size of a werewolf, three to four-month-old.

As much as the pups are eating, you would think that they would be bigger than they are at this time. Aislin was growing much faster than her brothers and Clara's and Archer's pups. Onyx and Amber believe she will be the next alpha of the pack since she is bigger than her brothers. Also, she is a lot more dominating than her brothers when she is around Clara and Archers pups. Onyx told Amber that one of his great- grand- mothers was the first female alpha of the Blue Twilight pack and he be- lieves that Aislin will follow in her footsteps and be a great alpha so when she is old enough, he wants to start her alpha training. Amber agrees with him on her being the next alpha, also she made the agree- ment with him that when she is about fifteen to sixteen years of age to start her alpha training, so she has a few years to train with her father before the time she starts attempting to find her mate and take over at nineteen as alpha. They share their thoughts with Clara and Archer, they agree with them, but Archer thinks she should start her alpha training at fourteen not fifteen.

This makes Amber start to think about it and agrees with Archer and therefore tells Onyx. To which he says, "I think you both have a point there seeing as that's when I started my training" Amber replies "there we go it is settled she will start her training at fourteen, so she has enough time to learn as much as possible before finding her mate. Also, she has enough time to understand the rules of the pack before taking over as alpha when she is nineteen." Onyx said, "That is a great idea, it works for me. I love the idea that Aislin will be the next alpha of the pack."

Clara and Archer agreed that it was a clever idea for Aislin to start her alpha training at fourteen. They also discussed the idea of one of their sons being her beta. They also discussed the position of Aislin's gamma and decided to let her pick him herself. When she is older and has taken the alpha position then she can fill the other slots of her command, (as in delta and so forth). She may appoint her brothers to some of those positions. The choice is entirely up to Aislin. As of this time, the pups are nine months old.

As the pups got bigger, their appetite increased. Amber and Clara have to use a pump to increase their production of milk because the pups are just too big to be held and are now being bottle fed. The pups are a year old and have grown a lot. Aislin has gotten so much bigger than her brothers, even though she eats just as much as they do. Clara's and Archer's pups have also grown much bigger in the last few months. Although her girls are smaller than her boys, they are smaller than Onyx's and Amber's pups. Onyx and Amber believe that their pups are bigger because of their alpha ancestry.

Time Jump

Years go by and the pups have grown up, Aislin has become the leader of the gang, River has essentially become the second leader of the gang when Aislin is not around due to her training with her father since she will grow up to be the next Alpha of the pack. Also, River is always looking at Aislin when they are studying, and Aislin does the same thing.

Aislin's POV, she is currently training with her father.

Well, when training is over, I am going to take about an hour nap then study the history of the pack with River, oh wait that means being alone with River… this is going to be fun. "AISLIN! PAY ATTENTION!" says Onyx, Aislin responds "Sorry dad! But did you really have to knock me on my ass?!" Onyx chuckles. "Well, if you were not daydreaming about River, you would have noticed my attack!" Aislin's jaw drops open "DAD! SHUT UP BEFORE THE WHOLE PACK HEARS YOU!!!" This reaction makes Onyx laugh even more. At that moment, Amber comes to the training field to tell them that dinner will be ready in about half an hour,

In which they all turn to go to the pack house to get ready for dinner. As they sat down to dinner, there was a commotion at the back of the house. Onyx gets up from the table to see what all the ruckus is about. He came to find Sebastian, the gamma holding his son who had just shifted into his wolf. He looked so worn out from the transition that he could not stand on his own feet. His name was Caleb, and his wolf was large compared to the rest of the pack. However, he was not as big as Griffin, Koda, and Aislin, who would be the next alpha of the pack like Onyx and Amber thought she would. Aislin's wolf is bigger than her brother's wolves because she is to be the next alpha. The alpha is usually bigger than the rest of the wolves in the pack. Although some are bigger than others, the alpha is usually the biggest because they have more power than others.

Onyx looked over at Amber and Aislin and said, "One of you two want to help me get him upstairs and into bed so he can relax and the other bring him up a plate of food because he will not be able to sit upright to eat at the table." Amber and Aislin looked at each other and Aislin said" Mom you get the plate of food, I will help Dad get Caleb upstairs" Amber looked at her daughter and nodded showing she understood. So, she and her father went ahead to guide her friend up to his room and sat him on his bed. He almost fell towards his pillows, but Aislin grabbed him quickly and said to him. "You need to eat, Caleb" he responded with "But I'm tired Aislin" she replied, "I understand that, but you just lost strength due to your first shift, it happens until you get used to shifting, but you still need to eat because you missed lunch due to you being worried about failing a test again."

Caleb looked at his next alpha in shock, "How did you know about that?" Aislin looked at him dumbfounded, "River told me last night" Onyx looked between both and said, "What are you two talking about?" Aislin and Caleb looked at each other and looked back at their alpha Aislin muttered "SHIT!" while Caleb sighed and looked at his alpha and explained "I failed a test at school because me and the gang minus Aislin and River were training and I forgot to study because well… I was spending time with Leilani."

Onyx looked at Caleb with a perplexed look on his face and then looked at his father and said, "If you do not ground him for the test and not eating, I will!" Sebastian, his Gamma replied "Hell Yes, I will ground him for two months for the test and not eating. Will that work for you Alpha?" Onyx replied "That will work but the only things he can do aside from school and home is that he can shift and spend time with Aislin's gang. He will learn a thing or two from them on discipline." Baxter looked at his son and said "You heard the Alpha that is your punishment for the next two months" Caleb looked between his father, his Alpha, and Aislin. He put his head down and said, "Yes father, I know, I did wrong by not eating and failing my test." Right about then Amber knocked on the door with the plate of food.

Amber placed the plate of food on the bed beside Caleb and told him he better finish it all or he would be in trouble with her. Onyx agreed with her and looked at his gamma and said that if he comes out with anything left on that plate, he is going to get his tail chased by the alpha and luna. Aislin then agreed with her parents with the implementation of punishment. Caleb just looked at the plate of food and started eating like he had not eaten in a week. He scarfed the food down so fast that he hardly chewed it. In the end he cleaned the plate and was better than he was before he shifted. Aislin had watched him eat and sent a message via mind link to her mother that the plate was clean and that he was now resting on the bed.

Amber came to collect empty plates. She asked Caleb if he felt better, He said that he did and that he would make sure he ate more often than he has been. Aislin also said that she would make sure he ate on a regular basis. Amber gave her daughter a look and spoke to her in a private mind link involving what Leilani feelings might be about it and Aislin responded in voice "She will understand because if she were to find out he hasn't been eating she would freak out." Amber nodded her head in acknowledgement and understanding and told her daughter "You should probably tell her what is going on but leave that piece of information out" Aislin replied to her mother's comment "I will see what River thinks about that since it is his sister" Amber agreed with her daughter's wisdom regarding her leadership in her group and told her daughter to handle it as she will.

Aislin left Caleb's room and went to her own room but when she got into her room she was pinned to her door and when she looked up to see who had the guts to sneak into her room she looked into the angry stormy blue eyes of River. She paused as she tensed up to throw out her attacker when she realized it was him who held the lock to her heart without her knowing it. She asked him "Why are you so angry that you snuck in my room?" River investigated her scared but questioning hazel green eyes and said "You stink of Caleb! Why?" she kept his gaze in her eyes and said, "If you would please relax and let go of me I will explain after I get a shower" his eyes widened and he asked, "Can I join?" She denied his request therefore he relented and let her go shower. When she came out and got her pajamas in her towel that's when she felt Rivers arms come around her waist and he whispered into her neck "I'm sorry my love I didn't mean to get mad but when I smelled Caleb on you Rowan was mad, and his anger influenced mine" Aislin let out a sigh and turned around in his arms and looked up at him and replied "It's okay Aqua said he would be mad. How she knew that is beyond me" then the realization came to both, and they said at the same time "They know because they are mates!" a second later came the replies of their wolves "You finally got it, Idiots!"

Aislin and River were both shocked to hear their wolves call them idiots. Then they burst out laughing at the fact that they had in fact been idiots not to recognize that they had been mates all along. This was something that their parents suspected from when they were at an early age. Aislin and River were always together all the time. It started about the time they started walking and has progressed to where they are now. Griffin has been spending time with Leilani and it looks like they may be mates as well. A twist of fate that has happened is that Leilani and Caleb are also mates. So, this means that Caleb and Griffin are mates as well, which is unheard of in the pack, but the moon goddess had other ideas. Koda and Dahlia have also been spending a lot of time together, it turns out that they are mates as well. All these revelations come as a shock to Onyx, Amber, Archer, and Clara.

The fact that they have kept this matter a secret from their parents puts them in a foul mood. It was the Moon goddess that chose their mates for them long before they were born. River is happy that his mate will be the next alpha of their pack. Griffin and Koda were glad that they were not chosen to be the ones to lead the pack next year. Onyx and Amber decided to host a ball in honor of their children finding their mates. When they spread the news that they were hosting a ball the whole pack erupted in cheers. Clara and Archer could not believe that Onyx and Amber had decided to host a ball in honor of their children finding their mates in each other.

Paxton is the only one who has not found his mate yet, but he feels she is near. He thinks that she may be from one of the neighboring packs, but he will wait until the ball happens to see if she comes to meet her. If she does not come and he does not find her at the ball, he will leave the pack to go search for her. Paxton brought this to his mother as she was the easier one to talk to between both of his parents. His mother was disappointed but agreed with his choices and she said to him "I do not want you to go but I understand you need to find your mate; you will be lucky to run your own pack one day. I must say is there anyone I would entrust this pack to aside from Aislin it would be you Paxie." He replied to his mother with a teary smile "I love when you use the nickname that you used to use when I was a child, mother, and I appreciate the trust and faith in me, but we shall see what the moon goddess has in store for me."

With tears streaming down her face, she replied "If you feel you must leave the safety of the pack to search for your mate, then by all means you go with your father's and my blessing." She gave him a hug, before walking away to go in search of her mate. She went in search of her mate to talk to him about her ideas for the ball. She found him in his office with the of the pack gamma discussing something. She looked at her mate with tears in her eyes and cried "Our baby boy might be leaving the pack if he does not find his mate among the she wolves at the ball." He looked at his mate and replied, "That would be a very bad thing for the rest of the family, they will miss him too pieces." Clara then looked at Sebastian, the gamma and exclaimed "At least you won't lose your son because he has yet to find his mate and your daughter is just a child still."

Sebastian looked at Clara and then at Archer, then hung his head and sighed and pinched the bridge of his nose, then calmly lifted his head, and said, "I do know what you are going through. My oldest left the pack to search for his mate before Onyx became alpha of the pack, I do not know whether he has found her or not, he renounced ties to me and to the pack before he left." Clara was too stunned to say anything after he said that. She just sat down on the couch in the office in a flopping motion. She was completely at a loss for words as to how to respond to Sebastian's statement. She did not know that he had an older son.

Meanwhile, Archer was watching the two with a perplexed look on his face. He looked at Sebastian and asked "Is that why Falcon left the pack? I thought he left because you two had a fight or something." Sebastian just shook his head no, meaning that this was not the reason. He then looked at Clara and said "Marcy was devastated when Falcon renounced ties to the pack and us. I pray your son does not do the same thing." Clara looked at Sebastian and asked, "How old was Caleb and Alora when Falcon left the pack?" Sebastian looked over at Clara and replied, "Caleb was only 15 and Alora was 6 when Falcon left at 19" Amber and Onyx looked at each other and said to Sebastian "Maybe Caleb might have contact with Falcon?" Sebastian thought about it for a minute and then said, "He might they were really close before Falcon left" Amber said "I will go to Aislin and see if she might be able to ask him because they are very close rather than you going to ask him and end up arguing" Sebastian nodded and then Amber went in search of Aislin.

Amber found Aislin in the library studying the history of the packs in the surrounding area. Aislin looked up from the thick tome she was reading. Amber looked at her daughter and asked, "can you do something for me Aislin?" Aislin made eye contact with her mother and nodded "sure mom, what's up?" Amber sighed and said, "is there any way you might be able to ask Caleb if he has a way to contacting his brother Falcon?" Aislin gave her mother a quizzical look and replied, "Falcon? As in gamma Sebastian's eldest?" Amber nodded to her daughter, "yes that is correct, honey." Aislin then said, "yea mom let me call him and have him come down here" Amber looked at her daughter and said, "where is he right now?" Aislin looked up from her phone and said, "he's with Leilani at the moment, don't ask me what they are doing because I don't want to know!" Amber laughed and said "okay."

Aislin then called Caleb and asked him to come to the library and he told her he would be there in 20 minutes.

20 minutes later

Caleb walked into the library and found Aislin but did not expect Amber to be there as well "Luna, Aislin, is everything okay?" Aislin grinned and said, "yes everything is okay just mom wanted to know if you might have any contact with your brother Falcon?" Caleb was surprised to hear Falcon's name come from her because nobody really talked about his brother by his name everyone normally calls him "The gammas eldest who left" Caleb has had contact with his brother for a while, but he did not know what Aislin wanted to know.

Amber noticed the hesitation in Caleb and said "Caleb, she's asking you because I asked her to because I know you mainly talk rather easy to them as you and your father don't get along much" Caleb looked at his Luna and replied, "I have contact to him yes, but why did you ask Aislin instead of just coming to me? I told you I will tell you anything to you and the Alpha because you two are the Luna and Alpha of the pack" Amber sighed and looked at Caleb "The reason I did not come to you is because I did not want to upset you, also because your father is very touchy on the subject of your brother" Caleb looked between Amber and Aislin, "So my father is the one who wants to know if I have been in contact with my brother?" Amber replied, "Yes and no, yes your father wants to know, but also Onyx and I wanted to contact your brother to see if he would be willing to come back and speak with your father."

Caleb then said to his Luna "My brother has found his mate and she's very nice the only problem is that she is a rogue and Falcon is scared that if he were to come back and ask to rejoin the pack he would be denied and banished from the pack" Amber then understood just why Falcon has never come back. Amber asked Caleb to call Falcon and let her speak to him, Caleb did so and when Falcon answered on the second ring "Caleb? Is everything okay?" Amber took the phone and said "hello, Falcon this is Luna Amber I asked Caleb to call you for me as I don't have a way to contact you personally, but I wanted to invite you and your mate to the ball we are having at the pack house if you would like to come?" Falcon was silent in shock "Luna? A ball? Umm... sure may I ask who the Alpha is now?" Amber chuckled "the Alpha is Onyx now and I am his mate" Falcon then said "Oh, I remember him, we will be there, just have Caleb text us when it is" Amber replied, "Will do see you and your mate soon."

As Amber and the girls started planning for the ball and the banquet that will follow the men were getting fitted for their tuxedos with matching color pocket handkerchief, bowties, and cummerbunds to match their lady's dress. For instance, Amber's dress is an aqua blue color, Onyx has matching things. Clara's dress is a dark red, and Archer got his items to match. Aislin chose a royal blue color for her dress. They decorated the ballroom, which was hidden at the back of the big house, with multicolored streamers and balloons.

Chapter Eight: *The Return of a Son*

While the Blue Twilight pack was spreading the news about the ball to the packs in the outlying area, Falcon and his mate, Ciara were preparing for the trip back to the Blue Twilight pack lands. They were in the middle of the country, found around the area where Oklahoma City is now. It will take them several hours to get to a bus terminal, and then at least a few days travel to get to the East Coast and to The Blue Twilight pack.

While the girls of the pack were getting fitted and measured for their dresses, the men were installing a crystal ball in the ballroom along with various lighting. The omegas had decorated the ballroom with colorful streamers, lights, and balloons. There were also tables along the walls for people to sit and talk and rest in between songs. The tables were decorated with a tablecloth that was in a rainbow of colors as the room was decorated in many colors. The walls were painted an eggshell white color halfway and wood paneling the rest of the way down the wall.

The packs from the surrounding areas sent their RSVPs to confirm that they were either coming or not to the ball. The news even reached King William and Queen Andromeda of the Lycans, who are the beginning of the species of werewolves. Their son, Prince Henry Blackthorn said he would attend this ball to see what it was about and to pass on the well wishes of the court. When he got to the pack grounds, he caught a whiff of something sweet and tangy.

The something sweet he smelled was a mixture of cherry blossoms and lemons. His wolf went nuts trying to take control, he knew that their mate was near, and he could smell her scent. However, Henry won control and calmed his wolf Ajax, and promised him they would search for their mate. He began to search through everyone at the ball, determined to find his mate. He knew she was here somewhere, he just needed to find her before he lost control of his beast.

Piper who was half fae, half dragon, and half wolf caught the scent of her mate and her beasts, dragon, and wolf, started shouting "MATE!!!!" in her head. His scent was a mixture of chocolate, strawberries, cinnamon whisky, like Fireball whisky. She found him standing by the fountains in the garden. He was tall, around six foot five inches. He also had the wide strong shoulders of a linebacker. He also had dirty blonde hair that fell to his shoulders, giving him a rugged look, his eyes were hazel. His mouth was thin and wide, above a square chin. He had a two-day growth on his beard, but he had plans to trim it into a goatee.

Piper, a princess in her own right in the fae world, was floored by the emotion that rushed through her upon meeting her mate. Her beasts were both going crazy inside her head trying to take over at the same time, but she finally got control and calmed them down. She had the lightest blue eyes anyone has ever seen. Her hair was red so vibrant it looked like it was not hair at all but flames running down her back. She had rosy cheeks and a fair complexion, her lips were as red as her cheeks, needing no added coloring to make them stand out. Her visage made for a striking image to look upon because her features captured the eye and held a person's gaze for a long time.

When Henry turned around and saw Piper for the first time, he lost his ability to breathe correctly. His breathing was very shallow, like he had something heavy sitting on his chest. When Henry turned around to face Piper, she did not know what he looked like, as he turned around, she began to see his face and intuitively knew who he was. He was not only her mate but the heir to the Lycan throne. Henry also knew who Piper was as well after looking at her face for about five or ten minutes.

They began to talk to each other to explore the new bond that was forming between them. They talked about their families, friends, and worlds because they came from diverse cultures. It was the Moon Goddess who chose them as mates before they were even born into the world. As they talked, they gradually got closer to each other until they were so close she could feel and smell his warm sweet breath on her face. He slowly dipped his head closer, his eyes on her red lips, he then laid the barest of kisses on her lips. She thought that she was imagining things when he came back and kissed her harder. He started out slow, but then he grew hungry for more. He almost took her breath away he had kissed her far longer than a normal person would. He had kissed her so hard and so long that her red lips were a deeper red, bruised, and swollen.

By the time he lifted his head and let her get some air she was out of breath and her chest was heaving like she had run ten miles. She was so shocked by his move that she just looked at him with wide eyes and a look of utter astonishment on her face. She then reached up to touch her lips, thinking they might be bleeding from his ravishment. He was watching her with a hungry look in his eyes again. In just the brief time they got to know each other he became addicted to her taste and scent. His beast was still pacing around in his head wanting to take over to claim her right there in the garden. However, once he got a taste of her sweet mouth, he knew that his grip on his beast was limited.

Her beasts were also going crazy in her mind after the kiss he laid on her. As for Asia, her dragon, was concerned she was in heaven after that kiss. Blaise, her wolf, just closed her eyes, rolled over and played dead for a little while. This time she started the kiss by throwing her arms around his neck and full-on French kissed him, which caught him by surprise. He was not expecting her to return and kiss him with abandon like he did her. She virtually pawed at him to mate with her right there in the back of the garden, but he wanted their first mating to be special for them both.

They did not know that someone was watching them. It was Piper's father and mother, Soric Frostflash, King of the Fae and Dragon shifters, and Aria, his mate. Aria was also a werewolf as well as being half fae. They were thinking, who is this man their daughter is kissing? Just now the couple parted Soric was going to go and stop his daughter from making a gigantic mistake if the man she is kissing is not her mate. What they do not know is that he is her fated mate, as well as the next heir to the Lycan throne.

Meanwhile inside the ballroom, Falcon and his mate are just arriving at the event after seeing his family and preparing for the ball. They had some news to tell Onyx and Amber, the current Alpha, and Luna of the Blue Twilight pack. It appears that on their trip back to the pack, Ciara has conceived a pup, she does not think she is extremely far in her pregnancy, but she has been ill the last few mornings. When they found Onyx and Amber they were with Sebastian and Caleb. Caleb saw his brother and his mate and said "Falcon! I am so glad you made it!" Falcon smiled at his brother and replied, "I'm glad we made it as well, aside from the fact that we had to keep stopping due to Ciara feeling sick."

Sebastian and Caleb looked at both and said at the same time, "Sick? What do you mean by that?" Falcon and Ciara looked at each other and then at the group that was forming around them, and Falcon said, "Dad this is not the place or time to be discussing this." Amber looked at Ciara with a knowing look on her face, and came close enough for only Ciara to hear her and said, "How far a long are you?" Ciara just gazed at Amber with such a shocked look that she could not believe her ears heard correctly.

Ciara asked Amber "How did you know that it is about that?" Amber laughed and said "I had triplets, I know when someone is pregnant" Ciara then smiled so widely that she resembled the Cheshire Cat. The thought of having a pup with Falcon put her in a better state of mind. She sent her thoughts to her mate Falcon and when he realized what she said he let out a joyous cry that made everyone in the room turn and stare at him like he grew two heads.

Amber just had a knowing smile on her face when she looked at Onyx. She did not want to tell him here at the ball that she was pregnant also. She wanted to be at home to tell him this news. It was just the other day that Clara and she were talking about having more pups if they could and the very next day Amber started feeling ill in the mornings, so she and Clara went to the store and they both secretly bought tests to take. Amber and Clara took the tests at the same time and they both had the same results; they were pregnant again. When you have multiple pups the first time, the odds of having one the second time are remote.

Amber did tell Aislin the news because she came into the room unexpectedly when they were taking the tests. Onyx gazed at his mate and then it dawned on him what the smile meant on her face, and he dropped to his knees and wept for joy! He thought after their triplets were born that she might not want any more pups. He told her as much when he asked her through their link if she was pregnant again and when she confirmed it, he told her about his thoughts on the news. He was beyond happy, but he was worried how this news would affect their grown pups.

Aislin was ecstatic that her mother and father were going to have more pups, which meant more siblings. She would like to have a sister to spoil. When her mom told her she could tell her brother's news she wasted no time in spreading it to them through their mind link they shared. When Aislin told her brothers, they were so shocked that their eyes went wide open, and their mouths formed large O's. They just stared at their mother like she lost her mind. Clara wanted to keep her secret a little longer. She wanted to tell her mate first that he was going to be a father again. She did not want to tell him here at the ball.

She has a feeling she is going to have multiples again this time around she just does not know how many yet. She also had no idea how to bring up the subject with her pups since they are adults. She does not know how they will react to the fact that they will have more siblings in a few months. However, if the reactions of Griffin and Koda are anything to go by the reactions from her own pups might be just as bad. She had a secret smile on her face just thinking how she would tell her whole family she was going to have more pups in a few months and hoping their reactions were not the opposite of what she hoped their reaction would be.

She plans to tell her family at dinner tomorrow when they are all gathered in one place and cannot run away from her. She hopes for her family to be happy about the pups coming. Although they tried to get pregnant after the quads were born, it never seemed to happen for them, then they decided to try one last time and low and behold she was pregnant, but Amber is also. What is surprising to her, is that Falcon's mate is also pregnant.

There were so many people at the event that not everyone could fit in the ballroom at one time. One of them attending the ball was Fallon. He had come to the ball in search of his mate. It was during the moment he was talking to Amber and Onyx that his wolf started to pace around in his head and quietly growling. He asked his wolf what was bothering him. He said flatly that their mate was nearby. Just as he said this, Fallon looked at the doorway and saw a woman in an elegant red ball gown, with matching jewels dripping from her ears, wrists and adorning her slender neck.

She was scanning the room when their eyes met. Her wolf let out a cry screaming "Mate, mate!!!" He almost lost control of himself and his wolf when his wolf yelled "MATE!!!" He at once started moving across the room to reach her. When he got close to her, he could smell her scent, it was a mixture of raspberries and peppermint. He searched her face for any type of emotion that would hurt them both. When he found nothing but kindness and love, he leaned in and gently kissed her cheek, and when he raised his head, he asked for her name.

She calmly told him that her name was Alexa Cornakova. She was the only daughter of Miles and Lilly Cornakova of the South Paw pack. Her brother Rowan, who was just three years older than her, is becoming the next alpha of their pack. He is learning the ropes of how to be the alpha from his father and grandfather. He already has strong leadership skills but the training for alpha will enhance those skills. Rowan is also at the ball hoping to find his fated mate.

Rowan knows she is somewhere in the building; his wolf can feel she is near. His wolf, Ajax was going crazy in his head because he can feel their mate is near but cannot seem to find her yet. Calogera was coming down the main stairs leading to the front of the pack house when she caught her mate's scent. Her wolf demanded that they follow that scent. It was a mixture of musk, vanilla, and spearmint. She followed it outside to the garden that was situated behind the house. It was an exceptionally large garden with fountains all over the place and so many distinct types of rose bushes scattered here and there. In the far corner of the garden, she saw a couple talking and then they kissed, she turned away from the intimate scene and searched for her mate, he was standing in another far-off corner of the garden.

When he caught her scent, he at once turned around and just watched as she slowly came closer. She was dressed for the ball, in a figure-hugging gown in a pale blue color that matched her eyes. Her hair was so black it looked blue in the moonlight. When she was within speaking distance, he asked for her name. She responded with "I am Calogera Snapdragon of the Woodland elves." She also had a wolf, but she was raised in the fae world. Her wolf's name is Sabine and when she transformed into her wolf, she also had fur so black it looked blue, and pale blue eyes that is uncommon in a wolf.

Rowan was shocked that his mate was half-elf and half-wolf. He did not think that his mate would want him because he had a huge scar running down half of his face. It is rare that werewolves are scared, it takes a silver weapon dipped in wolfsbane to cause the scar. Calogera looked at him, saw the scar and gasped at the site. He bowed his head and went to turn away when she stopped him. She gently ran her fingers down the length of the scar and then kissed the area that covered his left eye. He was lucky he was not blinded in that eye.

When Calogera raised her head and looked at Rowan, she showed him that she was not disgusted with the way he looks. She told him that she thought it gave him a dangerous look and that appealed to her. He kissed her with so much passion that it left her breathless. He almost stripped her out of her dress in the corner of the garden where many people could see them. Instead, he took her to one of the vacant rooms on the second floor of the huge pack house.

This room was decorated in hues of blue; everything from the curtains to the bedding was blue or a different shade of it. Rowan led Calogera to the bed and gently laid her down after he peeled off her form fitting dress. She had barely anything on under her dress. She was wearing a lace strapless bra and matching lace panties. She started to help him take off his clothes, piece by piece. As she uncovered a section of his skin, she gently kissed the bare area.

When Rowan was stripped down to just his boxers, he reached behind her to undo her bra. The last thing that was left to come off them both was their underwear. After Rowan had freed her lovely breasts, he reached up to cup one in his hand and it filled it with truly little space left over. As he was playing with the one breast, he leaned in to take the other in his mouth. This action made her let out a loud moan. When he had brought her pink nipples to hard peaks he started to run his free hand down her body. Rowan felt every curve of her body and it made him harder till he was bulging in his boxers. Calogera noticed this and slid her easily from his neck to the band of his boxers then she proceeded to slip her fingers under the band of his boxers and remove them. Rowan looked into her eyes and asked, "Are you sure you want this right now or did you want to wait till after the ball?" she then replied, "I am ready if you are."

Rowan was surprised by her answer that he proceeded to take off her underwear and expose the scent of her arousal, the air, when they were both completely naked he looked at her and said, "Once I mark you there is no turning back" Calogera made eye contact with him and said, "There was never any turning back when I first saw you I knew from that moment that it was you and I till the end of our time." Rowan kissed her with renewed passion. He slowly began to work his way down her body until he reached the juncture of her thighs.

Rowan gently pried her long, gorgeous legs apart to settle his face there. He took a deep breath in her luscious, intoxicating scent. He licked her from her anus to her clit. This made her moan aloud again, so he repeated the action several times. She gripped his hair with both hands and pulled him up her body until he covered her. Rowan gripped his huge cock in one hand and used the tip to tease her a little bit before slowly inserting it in an inch at a time. Calogera let out a breathy moan, and gripped his hips as he was easing back out to push in harder. Rowan started to pick up his pace and the strength of his push in. The faster he pushed in the harder he got until he was about to explode, but he wanted her to find her release before he let go and marked her as he found his release.

Calogera felt the tension in her come to a peak and on his next push she fell off that cliff into ecstasy. When she fell off that cliff, she let out a loud cry of pleasure that caused him to lose the grip he had on his pleasure and as he was reaching his own peak and going over it, he let his canines extend and bit into the soft tissue of her shoulder. She let out a moan of utter ecstasy and marked him as her mate.

Their wolves Ajax and Sabine were in complete heaven as their werewolf counter parts completed the mating and the bond slid into effect. As Rowan pulled out of her warm tight entrance, the door to the room swung open and an astonished Clara and Archer both yelled at the same time "What the hell are you doing in our bedroom?!" Clara recovered quicker than her mate and realized what had just happened. She quickly covered her eyes and tried to back out of the room to allow the newly mated couple time to get dressed before confronting them about them being in the wrong room. Her mate Archer had no qualms telling them in a menacing voice dripping with anger to get dressed and get out.

Archer turned on his heel and grabbed Clara's elbow to lead her out of the room. Before they could go to sleep that night, they would need to change the sheets and bedding on the bed to get the scent of sex out of them. They could not freshen the air around them because that would just irritate their senses. Rowan and Calogera dressed in hast to follow Archer's command. They did not want to offend the Blue Twilight pack because of their actions that night. When they were dressed, they left the room and left the building in a rush. Rowan linked his father and told him what happened and that they were leaving before they caused any more trouble. Calogera also linked her parents and told them what had happened between her and Rowan, and that she would come home later and collect her things.

Meanwhile at the ball

Onyx and Amber were talking to Miles and Lilly, the alpha and Luna of the South Paw pack, when their expressions dropped and the Miles looked at Onyx and said, "I apologize for my son and his mate it seems he could not control himself when he met her and had to immediately mark his mate, and please give your beta my sincere apologies as well" Onyx was confused and mind linked Archer to see what happened and Archer replied to Onyx through the mind link "Clara and I walked in on them mating in our room" Onyx was shocked, then he doubled over with laughter, Amber looked at him and asked "What happened?" he told her what archer told him through the mind link right as Rowan, Calogera, Archer, and Clara came down the stairs.

Amber was so shocked by the news of what happened in the room that she just stood there with a confused look on her face which soon turned to shock, and her mouth unhinged and stood open for a few minutes before she found her composure and retracted her jaw. Archer and Clara were talking to one of the omegas that took care of the house and told her that their bed needed stripped and freshened before they could go to bed that night. They did not explain why this needed to be done, just that it needed to happen fast because Clara was getting tired after a long day.

Miles and his mate looked at their host and bid them farewell as they were taking their son and his mate home and going to have an exceedingly long talk with them about courteousness and responsibility of an alpha. When they got back to their territory and pack, Miles tore into his son about what he did and how it was an embarrassment to him, his alpha and father. Rowan and Calogera just lowered their heads because they knew he was right. They should have waited to mark and mate each other when they got home. However, the damage has already been done and they did the deed in the wrong place and got caught.

Miles hoped that this kind of news does not spread like wildfire. He does not want his pack to be a laughingstock of the werewolf community. He hopes that Onyx and his pack can keep this quiet, and it will eventually go away. He hopes that his son and now daughter in law have learned their lesson on how to act properly at a formal event hosted by someone else. Lilly was too overwhelmed by the news of what her son and his mate did to say anything that her mate did not. Miles was so upset with his son and his mate for what they did at the ball, his face was starting to turn purple.

Lilly noticed her mate's face and at once called for the pack doctor. She feared he was having a heart attack. The doctor arrived in seconds with his bag of things. This bag held his equipment and various medicines. The doctor quickly took Miles's blood pressure. When the doctor found that it was extremely high, he gave Miles fast-acting medicine to bring it down. The doctor then told Lilly and Miles that he should lie down for a while because he was on the verge of an attack if he did not rest.

Lilly helped Miles climb the stairs to their room so he could do what the doctor ordered. Rowan and Calogera followed behind them to go to Rowan's room. His room was decorated in shades of green because he liked green. It was a large room with a queen-size bed in the middle and dressers scattered around the rest of the room. Two of these dressers were meant for Calogera, and they were empty. Half of his closet was empty as well, meaning, he left the space open for his mate to fill.

Calogera was astonished by all the space he left for her things when she brings them to her new home. As she looked around the room, she noticed it had a complete bathroom off to the right side. She was in love with the large tub, but what caught her attention the most was the updated shower. It was large enough to hold five big men comfortably. The shower also had shelves built in for their bath products. The bathroom even had a linen closet so that they did not have to go out of their room for towels and such. It was fully stocked with towels, comforters, and sheet sets.

Rowan linked his mother and asked where his sister Alexa was, he could not feel her in the house. This meant that either she found her mate at the ball, or she was still there. Lilly replied that Alexa had indeed found her mate as well and was travelling to his pack. Rowan asked who her mate was. His mother said, "Fallon Blackwood of the Dark Moon pack." Rowan was shocked that his sister was the mate of someone specializing in warfare. Fallon had made a name for himself when he went on the warpath with Onyx to free Amber from the rogue king.

Fallon and Alexa were making their way to the Dark Moon pack just as the sun was topping the mountains in the distance behind his pack lands. His father Colton had stepped down as alpha several years ago, after he came back from rescuing Amber. The news that she had been taken took a toll on his father, and it had aged him prematurely. He no longer had the will to lead their pack. His mother Marion agreed that he step down, and let Fallon take over.

Fallon could hardly wait to get Alexa alone and in their room. He had been semi-hard all the way home just thinking about what he was going to do too when he got her in his room. As they got out of the car they were in, Alexa noticed the bulge in his trousers. Her eyes became as big as saucers, and she said, "Are you really that eager to have me all to yourself?" He replied, "Hell Yes!! I have been waiting all night to take you to bed. You smell divine and it is making my mouth water just thinking of how good you are going to taste on my tongue."

As they were going through the main door, Marion was coming down the stairs from the second level of the pack house. She stopped where she was on the stairs, she had some shocking news for her son. His father had taken a turn for the worse and might not make it through the night. She hopes the news that Fallon found his mate will bring him back from the brink of death and give him renewed energy to live to see their grandchildren grow and find their mates.

Fallon stopped just in front of the door after closing it. He had seen movement on the stairs and looked up to see his mother descend them to meet her daughter-in-law. It was the look on her face that made him start to chant the words "NO, NO, NOT DAD!!!" She stopped him after he said it four times and told him he was hanging on, but barely. She told Fallon her idea that the news of him finding his mate might give his father a new lease on life. With a sense of urgency Fallon, Alexa, and Marion went up the stairs to the second level and into Marion and Colton's room, where Colton laid on the bed looking pale as a ghost and thinner than he used to be when Amber lived among them.

Colton did not know that Amber and Onyx had delivered triplets eighteen years ago and that they were now adults and finding their mates. He thought that the rogue king had harmed her somehow. That thought running through his mind for years took away his reason for living. Fallon went to Colton's bedside and told him that he had found his mate. He also told him that Amber was alive and well and a mother of three, and that she was pregnant again. This news woke Colton up and made him smile with joy. He had feared that Onyx and Fallon and the others that went with them to rescue her were not be successful in freeing her from the rogue king.

Fallon also told his father that Clara, Amber's best friend, was also a mother of four and that she had found her mate in Onyx's beta. This news gave Colton renewed energy. He slowly sat up on the bed and faced Alexa and Fallon. He looked at her over from head to toe and declared her fit to be Fallon's mate and the mother of his grandchildren. This statement made everyone in the room laugh.

After about an hour or so, Colton started to get tired again. This was Fallon's cue to take Alexa to his room on the third floor. He had moved into his parents' room when he had taken over as alpha. Colton and Marion had moved to a smaller room just one floor down, they were still in the same house they were just on a different floor so they would not hear if Fallon got busy with Alexa and made her scream at the top of her lungs. Which is exactly what was happening the first time he made love to her. They took things slow to build up the pleasure, but it did not have the effect he wanted but the opposite. Alexa so loud it shattered the glass sitting on the nightstand beside them. Glass went flying everywhere. It was like glass just exploded.

When the glass shattered, it made Fallon jump off the bed. He told Alexa not to move off the bed that he would clean up the broken glass. She felt a little embarrassed that her scream had caused the glass to break. She hoped he did not step on any of the pieces and needed first aid. Although, if that happened, she would tend to his wounds herself. However, he managed to clean up the broken glass without getting cut. It was a clever idea to take the carpeting out of the room that his parents had in there and put down laminated flooring. It tended to be cold in the wintertime, but he had a rug put down in certain areas of the room.

The next day, they got up and made plans to go to her family's home and get her things that she would need for her life with Fallon. Things like the cradle their pups would lie in when they were born just as her and her brother did, and the blankets that were made for her by her grandmother. Her grandmother and grandfather passed away, within months of each other, two years after she turned eighteen.

When she told Fallon this, he said "You were lucky you got to know them! I never knew my grandparents. They died when I was extraordinarily little." She stopped in her tracks on her way to her old front door, and just looked at Fallon like he grew a second head. When he saw her expression, he explained that his grandfather died in battle with a group of rogues that at the time was being led by a young wolf, they dubbed the rogue king. He continued to explain that the same rogue king later captured his friend Amber from her very own home, and that him and her mate with a large group of other went to rescue her. There was a fierce battle, and they succeeded in killing the rogue king and freeing Amber. What Fallon did not know was that Amber was half witch and had used magic to help Onyx defeat the rogue king.

His grandmother passed away from a broken heart because she missed her mate. His father told him that she passed just four months after his grandfather died. That was when Colton took over as alpha, he was still a teenager at the time. He was barely sixteen and had not met his mother yet.

Colton took over as alpha in a turbulent time. Rogues were attacking packs left and right, many people died, but there was hope for the future in the young ones that were born out of the chaos.

Chapter 9: *The Moonlit Reckoning*

In the heart of the ancient forest, where the light of the city never reached, and the stars painted stories in the night sky, Fallon and Alexa stood side by side. They were bound by destiny, though their paths to this moment had been as divergent as the river's course.

Fallon, with eyes like the stormy sea, carried the weight of heritage in his every step. His lineage, traced back through generations of powerful werewolves, bestowed upon him legacy of strength and an acute sense of responsibility to both his kind and the werewolves who dwelled unknowingly beside them. Yet, it was not his heritage alone that defined him; it was the choices he made in the face of the eternal struggle between coexistence and isolation, peace, and conflict.

Alexa, on the other hand, was a maverick spirit whose life had been irrevocably changed by a chance encounter under the full moon's haunting glow. Once a student of the stars, her gaze was now drawn earthward, toward the mysteries that lurked in the shadowed glades. Her transformation into a werewolf had been an unasked-for gift—or curse, depending on the moon's phase. Yet, she embraced her new existence with a fierce determination to forge her own path, guided by a moral compass that owed nothing to legacy and everything to the heart.

Together, Fallon and Alexa stood for the convergence of old and new, tradition and rebellion Their alliance had been forged in the heat of battle and deepened through shared quests that evaluated their limits and expanded their understanding of the world and themselves.

On this night, as the moon ascended to its throne in the sky, casting a silver sheen over the forest, Fallon and Alexa faced a reckoning that had been centuries in the making. A rogue faction within their own kind looked like shatter the fragile truce with werewolves to claim the night as their exclusive domain, heedless of the chaos such a war would unleash.

The clearing where they stood had been chosen with care, a neutral ground steeped in ancient magic that amplified their strength and ensured no unwelcome eavesdroppers could intrude. Around them, the forest held its breath, the usual chorus of nocturnal life silenced by the palpable tension in them.

Fallon spoke first, his voice a deep rumble that seemed to emanate from the very earth. "Tonight, we decide the future of our kind. Will we be tyrants lurking in the shadows or guardians of the balance that has allowed us to survive amidst a changing world?"

Alexa nodded her expression resolutely. "Our strength lies not in dominance but in harmony. To choose war with werewolves is to embrace a path of destruction that will spare neither side. We must stand against those who would lead us into darkness."

Their plan was audacious, a blend of ancient werewolf lore and modern cunning. Fallon's knowledge of the old ways, combined with Alexa's strategic brilliance, formed a strategy that would outflank the rogue faction before they could launch their first assault. Yet, success relied not only on their preparations but on their ability to unite the disparate elements of their own community, to awaken a collective desire for peace that transcended personal grievances and historical biases.

As the night deepened, Fallon and Alexa moved among the shadows, their senses heightened to the presence of friend and foe alike. They communicated in the silent language of gestures and glances, each movement a testament to their finely honed instincts and unwavering trust in one another.

Their first encounter of the night was with a patrol of their allies, a diverse group including the oldest families and those, like Alexa, who had been singularly chosen by the moon. These were werewolves who shared a common vision of a future where their kind could live in secret harmony with the werewolf world, safeguarding the balance of nature from the encroachments of modernity and the darker impulses of their own people.

Under the canopy of ancient oaks, they met a council of war lit by the ethereal glow of the moon. Fallon addressed them with a gravity that belied his years, every word infused with the urgency of their cause. "This night could very well determine the fate of all we hold dear. Our adversaries mistake our desire for peace as weakness, but they do not understand the true power of our resolve. Together, we stand as a testament to what it means to be guardians of the balance, protectors of both our hidden world and the werewolf realm that moves beside ours."

Alexa's voice rose in tandem with Fallon's, her tone imbued with a fiery passion that ignited the hearts of their assembled allies. "Our strength lies not in the ferocity of our bite but in the courage of our convictions. Tonight, we fight not for dominance for the right to exist in harmony with the world around us. Let our actions this night echo through the ages as a declaration that we choose a path of unity over division, light over darkness."

With their forces rallied and their strategy laid bare, Fallon and Alexa led their allies through the veiled paths of the forest, each step bringing them closer to the confrontation that awaited. The rogue faction, emboldened by their own certitude, had gathered in a clearing not unlike the one in which Fallon and Alexa had forged their plan. The air was charged with the potential for violence, a palp tension that sought release in the clash of ideals.

The battle, when it came, was swift and fierce. Fallon and Alexa fought as one, their movements a dance of light and shadow, striking with precision and retreating before their opponents could counter. Their allies, inspired by their leadership, fought with discipline. Also, resolve that belied the ferocious nature inherent to their kind. Together, they turned the tide, not through brute force but through strategic superiority and an unbreakable will to secure a future worth living.

As dawn streaked the sky with hues of pink and gold, the conflict ended. The rogue faction, though formidable, had been outmatched by the unity and purpose of Fallon, Alexa, and their allies. The victory, though not without cost, marked a turning point in the hidden history of the werewolves, a moment when the path of peace and coexistence was chosen over the allure of dominance.

After the result of the battle, as the forest began to stir from its nocturnal silence, Fallon and Alexa stood once more in the clearing where their journey together had reached its crescendo. They were weary but unbroken, their spirits buoyed by the knowledge that they had defended the very essence of what it meant to be werewolves in a world that balanced always on the edge of darkness and light.

"This is but the beginning," Fallon murmured, his gaze meeting Alexa's, finding there a reflection of his own determination and hope for the future. "Our victory tonight does not signify the end of our struggles, but it illuminates the path we must walk together. We have shown that unity and understanding can triumph over division and hatred."

Alexa nodded her eyes alight with a resilient fire. "We must now build upon this foundation, ensuring that the peace we've fought so hard to achieve becomes a lasting legacy. This means reaching out to those who were led astray, offering them a place within our ranks, and teaching them the true meaning of our existence."

In the days that followed, Fallon and Alexa took on the mantle of leaders within their community. They worked tirelessly, not only to mend the fractures within their own ranks but also to safeguard the fragile peace they had secured. They showed councils that included both old and new members, creating a forum where voices could be heard, and disputes settled without recourse to violence.

Their efforts extended beyond the confines of their community. Aware of the necessity of coexisting quietly alongside werewolves, they strengthened the words and enchantments that kept their world hidden from werewolf eyes, all the while watching for threats that could upset the balance they so carefully kept.

As the seasons changed, news of their victory and the new era it heralded spread throughout the werewolf world, continued the whispers of the wind and written in the stars above. Fallon and Alexa became celebrated figures, symbols of hope and change, but they never lost sight of the fact that their true strength lay not in accolades or honor but in the simple acts of courage, compassion, and leadership they showed each day.

Their love for each other, too, deepened in the crucible of shared struggle and triumph. It was a love that transcended the physical, rooted in a profound connection of spirit and purpose. Together, they were a beacon for their kind, a reminder that even in the darkest of times, light could be found and nurtured.

Even as they built this new future, Fallon and Alexa remained vigilant. They knew that the world was ever-changing, and the peace they had won could be threatened by forces both external and internal.

They prepared for the challenges ahead, training new guardians and forging alliances with other creatures of the night who shared their vision for harmony.

And so, under the ever-watchful gaze of the moon, Fallon and Alexa continued their watch over the forests and the beings that called it home. They were guardians, leaders, and lovers, bound by a shared destiny to walk the line between two worlds. Theirs was a legacy of light in the darkness, a testament to the power of unity and the unbreakable strength of the heart.

As the moon rose high in the sky, casting its silver light through the trees, Fallon and Alexa stood together, looking out over the world they had vowed to protect. They did not know what the future held, but they faced it together, with courage and hope, as guardians of the night and keepers of the peace they had fought so bravely to secure. As the seasons turned, the bond between Fallon and Alexa deepened, their shared life filled with both the joys and challenges of their roles as guardians. Amidst a dance of duty and passion, an unexpected but joyous discovery became known: Alexa was pregnant with twins. This revelation brought a new dimension to their existence, intertwining their personal and communal responsibilities with the anticipation of a new life.

The news of Alexa's pregnancy spread through their community like a warm breeze, stirring a wave of excitement and celebration among their kind. The prospect of twins born to such distinguished parents was seen as an auspicious omen, a sign of prosperity and strength for their future. Fallon, ever the protective partner, watched over Alexa with a tenderness that belied his fierce exterior, his love for her and their unborn children shining in his eyes.

Alexa, for her part, embraced the changes within her with a warrior's heart and a leader's mind. Her pregnancy did not dim her spirit or her resolve; if anything, it strengthened her commitment to creating a world where her children could thrive, free from the shadows of old conflicts.

As the months passed, Fallon and Alexa prepared for the arrival of their twins with the same meticulous care and strategic planning they applied to their duties. They fortified the safety measures around their home, weaving ancient magics with new to create a sanctuary that was both a haven of peace and a bastion against any who dared threaten their family.

The entire community rallied around them, offering support in various forms, from patrolling the territories to ensure their safety to providing counsel on the ancient traditions and modern considerations of raising the generation of werewolves. Fallon and Alexa found themselves at the heart of a network of love and loyalty, a vivid reflection of the unity they had fought so hard to achieve.

Alexa and Fallon were getting to know each other, every day that passed. It was not long after they mated that she began to have symptoms of Morning sickness. It was only known to the luna Marian that Alexa might be pregnant. On this day Marian and Alexa were doing the laundry and Marian asked Alexa if she might be pregnant. Alexa replied "I really do not know; I have been getting sick in the morning uncertain smells make me sick. Mama Marian, do you think I am pregnant?"

Marian replied, "Yes honey, I do. I do not know how far along you are, but you are showing the signs of being pregnant." Alexa just bowed her head and gently touched he stomach and muttered "I am going to have Fallon's pup." She had a serene smile on her face when Fallon came to find her on the back patio swing, just swinging away without a care in the world lost in thought. It was the look on her face that had Fallon worried. She was smiling, and since the time he had known her, she never smiled.

He asked her if anything was wrong. She replied "Everything is simply fine. I just have some news for you. You might want to sit down for my news, it is shocking." Fallon went to sit in the chair that was in their room, Alexa said, "You know I have been getting sick in the morning and certain smells make me sick." He nodded his head yes but stayed quiet. She continued, "Your mother has concluded that I might be pregnant. This means we are about to have a pup in a few months."

His mouth dropped open at her news. He was so shocked that he could not close his jaw. He had to reach up and close it with his palm. When he got his jaw working again, he asked "Are you sure?" She replied "No, but I will go to the pack doctor to confirm it." Fallon sent a message to the pack doctor that his mate, Alexa, needed an appointment as soon as possible. The doctor informed Fallon that he could see her in fifteen minutes. They waited around the house until it was time to see the doctor.

Alexa told the nurse that she might be pregnant when she was taking her vitals. Nurse Amy at once told the doctor this information and he ordered tests to confirm the suspicion that Alexa was thinking. The blood and urine tests came back positive. The Doctor, Manuel, smiled at the couple sitting in his office. He happily told them that Alexa was indeed pregnant. All three of them went into another room where a machine would take pictures of the growing pup. The first testing for this was completed, but the doctor wanted a video of the pup. He had her get undressed and into a gown that was provided and had his nurse take her into the imaging room. In the room was a machine to do ultrasounds. For her only being a few weeks into her pregnancy, the nurse had to use the vaginal probe to see the pup and to confirm the pregnancy.

With the images in hand, Fallon and Alexa left the hospital for home. When they got home, Marian and Colton were waiting in the lounge or family room for the news. Alexa and Fallon had nothing but smiles on their faces because they had good news to share. When they told Marian and Colton the news, Marian just screamed with happiness, making everyone in the room wince from the noise.

This would be the first time their son gave them a grandchild. They were ecstatic about the news they were going to be grandparents soon. Marian made sure Alexa took her vitamins and ate correctly. After two months Alexa was starting to show. She had a little bump, but she was concerned that the pup was not growing the way an alpha pup should be. She went to the hospital to see the doctor and told him her worry.

Manuel ran a series of tests to see what the problem with the pup was. It turned out that the pup was growing healthily, but there seemed to be a second pup hidden behind the first pup. However, Manuel could not tell the sex of the second pup because it constantly moved away from the ultrasound probe. Manuel happily told her she was carrying twins. Alexa was too shocked to respond.

When Alexa went home, she told everyone that the pups were growing at the right stages and then she told everyone she had a surprise as well, they all looked at her quizzically, but she informed them she would wait for Fallon to come back from training with his beta and gamma. When Fallon got home, she told him the news, that she was carrying two pups instead of one. He was so shocked by this news that he just collapsed into a chair and took a siesta.

His parents were dumbfounded that they were going to grandparents to twins. They were overjoyed to be grandparents. Marian said that they needed to turn one of the five bedrooms of the top floor into a nursery. Alexa agreed that they needed to start on it tomorrow.

When the time came for the twins to be born, the forest itself seemed to hold its breath, the very air charged with expectancy. The delivery was a blend of ancient ritual and the deep, unspoken bond between Fallon and Alexa. With the moon casting a soft glow through the window, illuminating the space they had created, Alexa brought their twins into the world, their first cries harmonizing with the whispers of the night.

The twins, a boy, and a girl, were named with care, their names a testament to the legacy they would inherit and the path they were yet to forge. The boy, bearing his father's stormy eyes, was named Ronan, meaning "little seal," a symbol of protection and guidance. The girl, with eyes mirroring the depth of Alexa's spirit, was called Elara, meaning "moon," a nod to the force that had shaped their destinies.

Ronan and Elara's arrival marked a new chapter not only for Fallon and Alexa but for the entire community. They stood for hope, a tangible symbol of the future that could be crafted through unity, love, and a deep respect for the natural world. Their presence strengthened the resolve of their parents and all those who looked to them for leadership, underscoring the importance of the legacy they were creating together.

Fallon and Alexa, now parents, faced the joys and challenges of raising their twins with the same courage, love, and wisdom that had guided them through their own journeys. They knew that Ronan and Elara would grow up in a world that was both beautiful and fraught with dangers, but they also knew that together, as a family and a community, they would provide a foundation strong enough to support and nurture these new lives. They envisioned teaching their children the values that had guided them: respect for the balance of nature, the importance of and peace, and the strength that comes from compassion and understanding.

As Ronan and Elara grew, their personalities began to appear, each reflecting aspects of both their parents. Ronan showed an early affinity for the natural world, much like Fallon, his curiosity leading him to explore the forest's secret places and learn the language of the wind and trees. Elara, with a spirit as luminous as the moon after which she was named, showed a keen intuition and empathy that reminded all of Alexa's innate ability to understand and comfort.

Fallon and Alexa balanced their responsibilities as leaders and protectors with their duties as parents, often blending the two. They introduced Ronan and Elara to the intricacies of their world, teaching them about the delicate balance that governed their existence alongside werewolves and other creatures of the night. The twins learned to walk softly on the earth, to listen deeply to the stories it told, and to always act with a purpose that honored the legacy they carried.

The community, too, played a significant role in the twins' upbringing, embodying the proverbial village it takes to raise a child. The twins were taught the history of their people, the struggles and triumph that had shaped their present. They learned the art of shifting, the deep magic that allowed them to embrace their dual nature, under the watchful eyes of their elders. But most importantly, they were raised with love and a profound sense of belonging, knowing that they were part of something greater than themselves.

As Ronan and Elara's understanding of their place in the world deepened, so did the bond between Fallon and Alexa. They watched their children grow, each day a mixture of wonder and challenge, knowing that the future was in capable hands. They had faced adversity, fought for peace, and now, they were witnesses to the next chapter in their family's story, one that Ronan and Elara would write in their own time.

Under the guidance of their parents and supported by a united community, the twins flourished. They became symbols of hope for all, living proof that a future where werewolves could live in harmony with the world around them was not only possible but already beginning to unfold.

In the quiet moments, beneath the watchful glow of the moon, Fallon and Alexa often reflected on the journey that had brought them here. They pondered the legacy they were creating, not just in the achievements of peace and unity, but in the love and guidance they offered their children. Ronan and Elara, born of love and raised in a world of endless possibilities, stood as a testament to the power of hope, the strength of community, and the enduring bond of family. Together, they faced the future, not as individuals, but as part of a continuum that stretched back through generations and forward into the unknown, illuminated by the steady light of the moon and the unwavering love of their parents.

Chapter 10: *Expecting Multiples Pt. 2*

In the quaint town of Silverwood nestled along the rugged East coast, the moon cast its silvery glow over the dense forest that surrounded the small werewolf community. Among the Blue Twilight pack, two extraordinary women, Amber, and Clara, stood at the heart of a love story that transcended boundaries of species and destiny.

Amber, a striking witch-wolf hybrid with fiery red hair and eyes that sparkled like amber, had a rare blend of magic and primal strength. Clara, the spirited female beta of the pack, carried herself with a grace that belied her fierce nature and unwavering loyalty to her packmates.

Their mates, Onyx, and Archer were strong and protective alpha and beta of the Blue Twilight pack, who had found their destined partners in Amber and Clara. Onyx, with his obsidian black fur that shimmered under the moonlight, was a formidable presence, while Archer, with his piercing ice blue eyes that mirrored the depths of the nearby lake, exuded a quiet strength that drew others to him.

Amber sat in the living room of the Blue Twilight pack house, her hand gently resting on her large, round stomach. She was eight months pregnant with triplets, and she could not be more excited to welcome them into the world. She had never imagined herself settling down with a werewolf, let alone having children with one, but Onyx had changed everything for her.

Onyx, the alpha of the pack, was a powerful and commanding werewolf with a heart of gold. He had swept Amber off her feet from the moment they had met, and she could not believe how lucky she was to have him as her mate. He was currently out patrolling the pack territories, ensuring the safety of their pack and their unborn children.

Clara, Amber's best friend and the beta of the pack, sat beside her on the couch, rubbing her own swollen belly. Clara was also pregnant with triplets, sired by Archer, the strong and loyal beta of the pack. Clara and Archer had been together for years, and their bond was unbreakable.

"Can you believe we're both going to be mothers of three at the same time?" Clara said with a laugh, looking at Amber with a grin.

"I know, it's crazy," Amber replied, feeling a surge of happiness at the thought of raising children alongside her best friend. "I never thought I'd be here, carrying Onyx's pups."

Clara nodded in agreement, her eyes sparkling with excitement. "I never expected to fall for a werewolf, let alone have his pups. But Archer has shown me a love like no other, and I can't wait to see what the future holds for us."

Just then, Onyx and Archer entered the room, their faces filled with pride and adoration as they caught sight of their mates. Onyx swept Amber into his arms, pressing a gentle kiss to her lips as he whispered words of love and devotion.

Archer pulled Clara into a tight embrace, resting his head against hers as he whispered sweet promises of a future filled with love and happiness. The bond between the two couples was strong and unshakeable, and they knew they would do anything to protect their growing families.

As the days passed, the two couples prepared for the arrival of their pups, buying cribs, diapers, and all the essentials they would need. The pack rallied around them, offering their support and love as they anxiously awaited the births of the newest members of the Blue Twilight pack.

Finally, the time came for Amber and Clara to give birth, their mates by their sides every step of the way. Amber brought three beautiful, healthy pups into the world, a boy and two girls, while Clara welcomed three strong and handsome pups, all boys.

The pack celebrated the arrival of their newest members, showering them with love and affection. Amber and Clara looked at their mates and pups with tears of joy in their eyes, grateful for the love and happiness they had found in their werewolf mates.

As the pack celebrated under the full moon, a sense of joy and anticipation filled the air, for Amber and Clara were both pregnant with multiple pups, a rare occurrence that spoke of the powerful bond they shared with their mates. The pack rejoiced in the promise of new life and the continuation of their legacy.

Amidst the festivities, Amber and Clara found solace in each other's company, their bond as sisters-in-arms deepening with each passing day. As the moon wove its magic around them, they confided in each other, sharing their hopes and fears for the future, and finding strength in their unbreakable bond.

Amber, with her knowledge of both magic and the ways of the wolves, guided Clara through the challenges of her pregnancy, offering her wisdom and support as the female beta prepared to welcome their pups into the world. Clara, in turn, stood by Amber's side, her unwavering loyalty and fierce protectiveness a shield against any threat that dared to come near her beloved sister.

As the days turned into weeks and the weeks into months, Amber and Clara's bellies swelled with the promise of new life, a testament to the enduring love they shared with Onyx and Archer. Together, they navigated the trials and joys of pregnancy, their bond growing stronger with each passing day.

And on a moonlit night, as the pack gathered around them in a circle of support and love, Amber and Clara brought forth their pups into the world, a miracle of nature and magic that filled their hearts with wonder and gratitude. As they cradled their newborns in their arms, surrounded by the love of their mates and packmates, Amber and Clara knew that their family was complete, bound together by a love that would endure for all eternity.

The arrival of the newborns brought a renewed sense of joy and unity to the pack. The tiny pups, a mix of witch-wolf and purebred werewolf blood, brought a spark of magic and vitality to Silverwood. Amber and Clara watched over their offspring with a mix of wonder and determination, knowing that their children would be raised in a community filled with love and acceptance.

As the pups grew, it became clear that they inherited traits from both their mothers and fathers. Some displayed a natural affinity for magic like Amber, while others showed the strength and agility of their werewolf lineage. Each pup was cherished and nurtured, their unique personalities shining through as they explored the world around them under the watchful eyes of their parents and the pack.

Amber and Clara, with their bond as strong as ever, found solace in the shared experience of motherhood. They supported each other through the sleepless nights and the challenges of raising multiple children, drawing strength from their unbreakable connection and the love that bound their family together.

Meanwhile, Onyx and Archer stood by their mates, proud and protective fathers who ensured the safety and well-being of their growing family. They imparted their wisdom and guidance to the young pups, teaching them the ways of the pack and instilling in them the values of loyalty, courage, and unity.

As the children of Amber and Clara grew, they formed strong bonds with each other, forging friendships that would last a lifetime. They roamed the forests of Silverwood together, exploring the mysteries of nature and honing their skills under the guidance of their parents and the elders of the pack.

And amidst the laughter and playfulness of the young pups, a sense of harmony and peace settled over Silverwood. The love that bound Amber and Clara, Onyx and Archer, and their children together created a tapestry of unity and strength that would withstand any challenge that came their way.

As the moon rose high in the sky, casting its silvery light over the werewolf community of Silverwood, Amber and Clara stood side by side, their hands clasped together in a silent vow to protect and cherish their family for all eternity. In that moment, under the watchful gaze of the moon, they knew that their love was a force of nature, as enduring and unyielding as the bond that connected them to each other and to their pack.

As the seasons changed and time passed in Silverwood, the bond between Amber and Clara, Onyx and Archer, and their children only grew stronger. The young pups grew into confident and capable members of the pack, each one finding their place within the tight-knit community that had become their home.

Amber, with her unique blend of magic and wolf instincts, became a mentor to the young ones, guiding them in harnessing their powers and embracing their dual heritage. Clara, the steadfast female beta, led by example, instilling in the pups the values of loyalty, courage, and compassion that defined the pack.

Onyx and Archer, as proud fathers, and leaders of the pack, watched with pride as their children thrived under the care and guidance of their mates. Together, they ensured that the next generation of werewolves in Silverwood would be prepared to face whatever challenges lay ahead, united by a bond that transcended bloodlines and boundaries.

As the children of Amber and Clara reached adolescence, they faced new trials and tribulations, evaluating their strength and resilience. But with the unwavering support of their family and packmates, they overcame every obstacle, emerging stronger and more determined than ever to uphold the legacy of their ancestors.

Amidst the ebb and flow of life in Silverwood, Amber and Clara found moments of quiet reflection and joy, savoring the precious moments they shared with their family. They knew that their love was a beacon of light in the darkness, a source of strength and hope that would guide them through any challenge that came their way.

And as the moon shone down upon the werewolf community of Silverwood, casting a silvery glow over the forest that surrounded them, Amber and Clara stood together, their hearts filled with gratitude for the love and unity that bound them to their mates, their children, and their pack. In that moment, they knew that their bond was unbreakable, a testament to the enduring power of love in all its forms.

Under the watchful gaze of the moon, Silverwood thrived with life and love. The bond between Amber and Clara, Onyx, and Archer, remained unshakable, a beacon of hope and unity during a world filled with uncertainties.

As the children of the pack grew into young adults, they each embarked on their own journeys, guided by the wisdom and teachings of their parents and the pack elders. Some chose to explore the world beyond Silverwood, eager to discover new lands and forge new alliances, while others remained within the comforting embrace of their home, dedicated to protecting and preserving the traditions of their ancestors.

Amidst the ever-changing dynamics of the pack, Amber and Clara found themselves at the heart of it all, their roles as mothers and leaders intertwined with the responsibilities they carried with grace and strength. Together, they navigated the challenges of parenthood and leadership, their bond as sisters-in-arms serving as a source of unwavering support and understanding.

As the seasons turned and the moon waxed and waned, Silverwood stayed a place of peace and harmony, a sanctuary where werewolves of all backgrounds came together as one. The legacy of Amber and Clara, Onyx, and Archer, lived on in the hearts of their descendants, a testament to the enduring power of love and unity in the face of adversity.

And so, as the moon rose high in the sky, casting its silvery light over the werewolf community of Silverwood, Amber and Clara stood side by side, their hands clasped together in a silent vow to protect and cherish their family and pack for generations to come. In that moment, under the eternal glow of the moon, they knew that their love was a force of nature, unyielding and everlasting, a bond that would endure through the ages, shaping the destinies of all who called Silverwood home.

As they settled into their new lives as mothers, Amber and Clara knew that their love for their mates and pups would only grow stronger with each passing day. Love and family bonded them, and nothing could ever tear them apart.

Chapter 11: *Moonlit Confessions*

Under the glow of the full moon, the hidden world of the werewolves came alive in a way that daylight could never reveal. It was a time when true nature was empowered, secrets unearthed, and destinies intertwined.

The night throbbed with anticipation as the pack assembled in the ancient clearing, their eyes gleaming in the moonlight. This sacred spot, encircled by guardian trees older than memory, had borne witness to the rites and celebrations of their kind for generations.

Elena, a fierce and spirited young werewolf, lingered at the clearing's edge, her heart syncing with the primal drumbeats that reverberated through the wilderness. This evening held a significance beyond the communal ritual—it marked Elena's moment to shine, to ascend within the pack's hierarchy. Yet, her thoughts were not dominated by the forthcoming trials, but by Alex and Alexa, the Alpha twins, who governed the pack's heart and soul.

Alexa's grace and wisdom balanced Alex's fierce leadership, making them an indomitable duo. Elena's heart, however, beat a wild rhythm for Alex, whose strength and complexity had ensnared her since their first encounter.

Alex, the embodiment of dominance and raw power, was more than a leader; he was a force of nature. Yet beyond his imposing facade, Elena had glimpsed a warmth and depth that few others saw. Tonight, she faced him and the trials, eager to prove her worth—not just as a guardian, but as a partner and equal in Alex's life.

As the trials started, Elena's senses honed to razor edge. She navigated each challenge with a blend of grace and ferocity, embodying the spirit of the werewolf. Her performance was a testament to her unyielding spirit and determination.

Yet it was only after the trials, amidst the pack's jubilant celebrations, that destiny truly took its course. Elena found herself secluded with Alex, away from the pack's prying eyes. Bathed in moonlight, the night took on a dreamlike quality.

"I saw you tonight," Alex said, his voice a deep rumble that resonated within Elena. "You were remarkable. You've always been more than you realize."

Surprised by his words, Elena's defenses crumbled. "Alex, I..." she began, her voice a mere whisper. "Let me speak," he interjected, closing the distance between them. "I've watched you evolve, embrace challenges, and grow stronger. Yet, it is not solely your resilience that captivates me—it is your heart, your spirit. You're meant to stand by my side, as my equal, my partner."

In that moment, under the moon's watchful gaze, the world around them faded. Elena looked up into Alex's eyes, finding truth and sincerity. Her doubts evaporated, replaced by a sense of clarity and purpose. "I, too, have waited for this moment," she said, her voice now steady with resolve. "I have harbored feelings for you, thinking them unreciprocated. But tonight, under the moon's light, I see our truth."

Their union was written and sent with love and care, a bond formed not by words, but by the unspoken language of their hearts. It was a promise sealed under the eternal moon—a love that had once dwelt in shadows, now brilliantly illuminated. Their kiss, a melding of soul and spirit, marked a turning point. The world resumed its rhythm around them, yet for Elena and Alex, everything had shifted. There was a new vibration to their bond, luminescence that echoed the moon's approval.

"I never dared imagine this," Elena, her forehead against Alex's. "I thought my feelings would linger in obscurity, recognized by neither you nor the moon." Alex's hands cradled her face, his eyes reflecting the night's infinite depth. "My fears mirrored yours," he confessed. "Fear of disrupting the pack's balance, of the ramifications for us. But I've come to realize that strength lies in embracing vulnerability, in acknowledging the power of our connection."

Their exchange was a revelation, simple yet profound, capturing the essence of their beings not just as werewolves, but as creatures capable of profound emotional bonds. The intimacy of their moment gradually faded, replaced by the sounds of celebration. The pack's laughter and music, floating through the trees, beckoned them back to the communal heart. Yet, as they joined hands and walked together, Elena and Alex knew they were embarking on a new era, not only for themselves but for the entire pack.

Together, they would face the challenges that lay ahead. Pack dynamics to navigate, external threats counter—all would be met with a united front, their partnership a testament to their commitment to each other and to their kin. As they approached the celebratory gathering, illuminated by firelight and the lingering moonlight, Elena felt a profound sense of peace. Besides Alex, every obstacle seemed surmountable, every victory sweeter.

The transition from night to dawn approached, yet the events of the evening—their confession of love and partnership under the moon's vigilant gaze—would remain indelible in their hearts. This new chapter in their lives, replete with promise and the assurance of shared battles and joys, signified more than personal fulfillment. It heralded a new era for the pack, one where love and leadership intertwine to forge a stronger, unified front. As the first rays of dawn painted the sky with streaks of pink and gold, Elena and Alex stood on the threshold of their future. The pack awaited, ready to embrace its Alpha and his chosen equal.

The essence of their journey was love. A force unparalleled. Beneath the vast, shifting skies, they moved forward, not merely as leaders but as living proof of love's transformative power—a love affirmed and sealed beneath the gaze of a benevolent moon, underpinned by the strength and unity of twin hearts beating as one.

Their path ahead was one of shared promises and challenges, but illuminated by the steadfast glow of their bond, Elena and Alex stepped into the dawn of a new beginning. As the sun crested the horizon, bathing the world in its golden hue, Elena and Alex joined their pack, now not just as members, but as symbols of unity and strength. The pack gathered around, sensing the change, welcoming their leaders whose bond had been forged under the moon's approving gaze. Their union promised a new direction, one anchored in trust, respect, and an unyielding love that promised to guide them through the times ahead.

The celebration took on a new fervor with the rising sun. Drums beat a lively rhythm, mirroring the heartbeat of the pack, as they danced and rejoiced in the light of a new day. The air was filled with the smell of roasting meats and fresh earth, a testament to the pack's resilience and connection to the land.

Alex and Elena, at the heart of the celebration, were more than just the focus of attention; they were the embodiment of the pack's hopes and dreams. They danced with a grace and passion that left no doubt of their deep connection, their movements telling a story of two souls intertwined by fate and choice. As the celebration wound down, the couple stood together, overlooking their kin. Alex took Elena's hand, turning to the pack with a clear-eyed gaze. "Today marks a new chapter for us all," he began, his voice carrying over the quieting crowd. "A chapter where we not only survive but thrive, guided by the principles of loyalty, courage, and love."

Elena's eyes sparkled with emotion as she continued, "Together, we will face whatever the world throws at us. With Alex by my side, and all of you with us, I have never been more confident in our pack's future. We are stronger together, united by the bonds that tie us." The pack responded with a unified howl, a sound that resonated with power and unity, echoing through the forest and into the sky.

As leaders, Alex and Elena were acutely aware of the challenges that loomed on the horizon. Territory disputes, werewolf encroachments, and the ever-present threat of rogue werewolves would evaluate them in ways they could only imagine. Yet, standing together, they faced the future unflinching, knowing that their bond was not just their strength but the pack's as well.

In the days that followed, they worked tirelessly, not only to protect their borders but also to strengthen the ties within the pack. Training sessions, council meetings, and shared hunts became part of their routine, each activity reinforcing the unity and power of their collective spirit. As the seasons changed, so did the pack under Alex and Elena's guidance. They became a beacon among werewolf communities, proof that love and leadership could coexist, that strength did not need to exist in solitude.

Their love story, born under the watchful eye of the moon and sealed in the light of dawn, became a legend. A reminder that even in a world fraught with danger and uncertainty, love could be the most potent force of all, capable of overcoming any obstacle, any challenge. And so, under the endless cycle of moonrise and sunset, their story continued. A story not just of power and leadership but of hope, of the enduring belief that together, they could face the darkness and emerge into the light, stronger and more united than ever As the leaves turned from green to vibrant hues of red and gold, marking the of time in their hidden world, Alex and Elena stood as steadfast leaders, their love an unwavering beacon for their pack. The challenges they faced were many, each a test of their resolve, their unity, and their commitment to each other and to the welfare of their kin.

On a night when the moon hung low and full, casting a silver glow that sanctified the forest, the pack gathered once more. This time, it was to celebrate the Harvest, a time of thanks for the abundance the earth provided and for the strength of their community. Under the Harvest Moon, traditions long held were honored, pledges renewed, and bonds strengthened. Alex and Elena, encircled by their family—blood and bond alike—reaffirmed their commitment not just to each other but to the ideals that held their pack together: loyalty, respect, and the shared duty of protection.

It was a moment of reflection, as much as celebration. Looking into the fire that danced and crackled with life, Elena saw not just the flames but the faces of their pack, illuminated by light and shadow. There was strength there, and hope, and she felt a profound gratitude for the journey that had brought them here, to this moment. With the first light of dawn breaking over the horizon, Alex of the future of the challenges still ahead but also of the opportunities those challenges presented. "We stand on the threshold of a new era," he said, his voice resonant with conviction. "Together, we will navigate the uncertainties of this world, protecting our home, our family, and the values we hold dear."

Elena, moved by his words, added, "In each of you, I see the future of our pack—a future bright with promise. As we stand here today, let us renew our pact, not just as members of pack but as guardians of the world in which we live. Let our legacy be one of courage, compassion, and unyielding love." The pack responded, their voices mingling in a chorus that rose to the heavens, a powerful affirmation of their shared will and purpose.

In the weeks and months that followed, Elena and Alex led by example, turning challenges into opportunities for growth. When tensions arose with neighboring packs, they sought diplomacy over conflict, strengthening alliances through mutual respect and cooperation. When the threat of werewolf encroachment loomed, they worked to safeguard their territory, not through aggression but by using the land wisely, ensuring their presence remained hidden. Each decision and each action were guided by the principles they had vowed to uphold, and under their leadership, the pack flourishes. The bond between Alex and Elena, too, grew stronger with each passing day, their love a constant source of strength and inspiration.

As seasons changed, their story became a legend, not just within their pack but beyond, a tale of two souls who crossed paths under destiny's grand design and forged a love that transcended challenges, a love that unified not just two hearts but an entire community. Their legacy, however, was not just one of love but of leadership that inspired a generation, proving that true strength lay in unity, compassion, and the courage to face the unknown together. Theirs was a tale for the ages, a reminder to all that in the deepest of, the rawest challenges, love and unity can not only survive but indeed thrive and become a beacon for others to follow.

As the wheel of the year turned once more, bringing with it the whisper of winter and the promise of renewal, Alex and Elena stood side by side, watching as their world transformed under a blanket of snow. It was a time for quiet reflection, for appreciation of the journey thus far and the path that lay ahead.

The cold months were a time of gathering close, of sharing stories by the firelight, and of planning for the year to come. It was during these intimate gatherings that the truth of their leadership shone brightest, in the thoughtful way they listened, the wisdom with which they spoke, and the openness of their hearts.

The trials they faced were not few, but each was met with a resilience that served to only strengthen the bond within the pack. When illness touched their community, they came together, each their strength until health was restored. When the harsh weather threatened their provisions, they pooled their resources, ensuring none would go without. In every challenge, the unity of the pack was their greatest asset, a living testament to the power of the collective over the individual.

Alex and, through their actions and their unwavering commitment to each other and their family, symbols of hope and endurance. Their love, evaluated and tempered by adversity, appeared all the stronger, a guiding light through the darkest nights. One night, under the burgeoning light of the year's first full moon, Alex and Elena stood before their pack, reflecting on the past and envisioning the future. "Our journey together has been one of both challenge and immense joy," Alex voiced, his gaze sweeping over the faces gathered before him.

"And through it all, one truth has remained constant—the strength draws from each other, the strength we offer back to our pack," Elena added, her hand finding Alex's. "Our promise to you, on this night, is to continue to lead with both heart and might, to protect this family and the love that binds us all." The pack, moved by their words, howled in unison, a sound that carried far into the night, a declaration of their shared strength and undying loyalty.

The path forward was lined with both known and unforeseen challenges, but guided by Alex and Elena's steady hands, the pack navigated each with grace and fortitude. With every passing season, they grew not just in number but in spirit, their legacy a beacon across the shrouded landscapes of the werewolf world.

Their story, a tapestry woven from threads of love, bravery, and the unyielding bond of family, continued to unfold under the watchful gaze of the moon. Through every hardship and joy, the love that Alex and Elena shared—the love that had blossomed under a moonlit sky and been solidified through trials and triumph—remained the heart of their story, a reminder of the transformative power of love and unity in the face of all adversity. In the endless cycle of day and night, through changing seasons and the passage of years, their legacy endured. A legacy not just of power, but of love's indomitable spirit, echoing through the ages, a testament to the enduring truth that together, nothing is insurmountable.

As keepers of their kind's history and guardians of the future, Alex and Elena's roles evolved far beyond the daily leadership of their pack. They became lore keepers, ensuring that the tales of their ancestors, their own story, and the lessons learned would be passed down through generations. In the heart of the forest, under the wide canopy, they proved a place of learning, where young werewolves were trained on the importance of harmony with nature, the strength in community, and the sacred bond of the pack. This sanctuary became a beacon of wisdom, drawing not only their own young but those from distant packs, eager to learn from the Alpha couple who had become a legend in their time. Here, among ancient trees and the ever-watchful moon, stories were shared, traditions honored, and a new generation was imbued with the values that had seen their pack through times of plenty and want.

With each challenge faced and overcome, the fabric of their community grew ever stronger, woven from countless acts of courage, kindness, and unity. Yet, it was not just within their own borders that their influence was felt. Alex and Elena's vision of a world where werewolves lived in peace and mutual respect with werewolves and other supernatural beings began to take root beyond the hidden sanctuaries of their kin.

Through careful maneuvering and the fostering of alliances, they worked to bridge the gaps of understanding and mistrust that had long isolated their kind from the rest of the world. Their efforts, slow and painstaking, sowed the seeds of change, hinting at a where coexistence was not just a dream but a possibility.

As the years passed, Alex and Elena saw their pack flourish. Cubs born their leadership grew into strong, wise wolves, embodying the ideals and strength of their elders. The couple, now seasoned leaders, watched with pride and a touch of wonder at the legacy they were building, a testament to the power of love and the unbreakable bonds of family and pack.

Their own love, as profound and unyielding as the earth, continued to be the cornerstone of their life together. It was a love that had weathered countless storms, a beacon that guided them through the darkest nights and into the light of dawn. They knew, as did their pack, that if they stood together, there was no challenge too great, no hurdle too high. And so, Alex and Elena's story, etched in the annals of their kind and whispered in the winds that roamed the wild lands, became a legend. It was a tale of two hearts united under a moonlit sky, of strength found in unity, and of a love that transcended the ordinary, becoming a beacon for all.

Their legacy, carved not just in the minds and hearts but in the very soul of their pack, continued to inspire, to guide, and to serve as a reminder of what could be achieved when hearts are united in a common cause. In the endless dance of the cosmos, where stars are born and fade, their story—a testament to the enduring power of love and unity—stayed a constant light. Alex and Elena, through lives lived with courage, love, and unwavering dedication to their family and ideals, became not just leaders but legends, symbols of what it means to lead with both strength and heart. As the world around them evolved, so did the tales of their exploits, each retelling adding a layer of myth to the fabric of their legacy, yet their essence remained rooted in truth.

Within the heart of the forest, where ancient trees stood as silent guardians of time, Alex and Elena often walked together under the canopy, their steps light upon the earth that had seen the unfolding of their love. This sacred grove, untouched by time, held the essence of their journey—a testament to resilience, the power of unity, and the indomitable spirit of love.

In these quiet moments, away from the responsibilities of leadership, they found solace in each other's presence. Here, where the noise of the world fell away, they could speak of dreams yet to be realized, of challenges yet to be faced, and of the enduring love that had become their sanctuary. The grove was their witness, a keeper of secrets and silent vows renewed with each visit.

The legacy of Alex and Elena, while anchored in the past, continued to weave through the lives of those they led, a tapestry rich with hues of courage, wisdom, and love. Their story, now intertwined with the very identity of their pack, served as a compass for those who looked to the future, wondering what paths to tread, what destinies to embrace.

Under their guidance, the pack had become a beacon of hope, not only for their kind but for all who sought harmony within the natural world. The sanctuary of learning, proved by the Alpha couple, flourished, becoming a crossroads of cultures, ideas, and beliefs—a place where the future was shaped by understanding and respect.

The vision Alex and Elena held for a world of coexistence began to ripple outward, touching even the most distant of communities. Meetings under the cover of twilight, where once grievances and territorial disputes were settled, now became gatherings of collaboration, shared knowledge, and mutual support.

This era of peace and constructive engagement marked a new chapter in the history of their kind, one where the wisdom of the old melded with the promise of the new, forging a future undefined by past conflicts but inspired by the possibilities of unity and peace. As the wheel of the year turned once again, marking the passage of time with the beauty of nature's endless cycle, the pack gathered to celebrate the changing seasons, each festival a reflection of the life and vitality that flowed through their veins.

Alex and Elena, standing together as they had through countless seasons, looked upon the faces of their pack—old and young, weathered, and wide-eyed—and saw the reflection of their love and leadership. Their hearts swelled with pride, not for the battles won or the challenges overcome, but for the family they had built, the community they had nurtured, and the love that had blossomed and grown through the years.

Their story, etched in the stars and whispered by the wind, would endure through the ages, a beacon for those who walk the path of darkness seeking the light. And as long as their tale was told, the legacy of Alex and Elena—their unbreakable bond, their unwavering love, and their enduring commitment to their pack—would live on, a timeless reminder of the power of love to unite, to inspire, and to transform the world around them.

With each passing year, Alex and Elena instilled in their pack the importance of guardianship—not only of their own kind but of the natural world that sustained them They led expeditions to rejuvenate the forests, streams, and meadows that had given them shelter and sustenance, teaching their kin the sacredness of the balance between nature and werewolf.

Their efforts extended beyond the physical realm into the spiritual, fostering a deep connection with the earth that went beyond mere respect—it was a symbiotic relationship, one that ensured the vitality of their land and, by extension, their people for generations to come. Recognizing the wisdom of collective governance, Alex and Elena proved a council of elders, a gathering of the most respected and experienced members of their pack. This council served not just as advisors to the Alpha pair but as custodians of the pack's laws, traditions, and history.

This initiative ensured that leadership was not combined but a shared responsibility, reflecting the diversity of their pack and allowing for a multitude of voices to be heard. It was a testament to their belief in democratic principles, in the importance of everyone's contribution to the whole.

Throughout their lives, Alex and Elena saw the ebb and flow of life within their pack. They celebrated new births with joy, recognizing each new life as a continuation of their legacy, a new thread in the intricate tapestry of their kin. And when it was time to mourn those who were missing, they did so with the entire pack, each loss a reminder of the preciousness of life and the bonds that held them together.

Their leadership was marked not only by their strength in the face of external threats but by their compassion and empathy in moments of pain and loss. They understood that true leadership meant standing with their pack in times of joy and sorrow, in victory and defeat.

As the years turned into decades, the story of Alex and Elena echoed across the lands, crossing the boundaries of their own kind, and reaching others. Their tale of love, unity, and leadership underpinning a community that thrived on cooperation and mutual respect became a beacon across the supernatural world.

The legacy they were building was one of hope, a vision of a future where all beings, regardless of their nature, could find common ground and live in peace. It was a dream that had begun under the moon's tender watch, nurtured through trials and triumphs, and continued to grow, radiating outward like the light from a beacon fire.

In the quiet moments when the world seemed to pause, Alex and Elena found themselves in the sacred grove, where their journey had begun. Here, amidst the ancient trees, where the whisper of the wind carried the voices of their ancestors, they danced. It was not a dance of ceremony or ritual but one of two souls, eternally intertwined, moving through time and space as one.

This dance was their promise, renewed with each step, each turn—a pledge to continue to lead, to love, and to protect, if the moon guided their paths, and the stars watched over them. In the endless cycle of life, their love stayed a constant, as enduring, and powerful as the turning of the earth itself.

Their story, woven into the fabric of their world, became a legend that transcended time, a narrative emboldened by its truth and the profound impact it wrought upon the world. As the moon waxed and waned above them, marking the passage of time with its celestial grace, Alex and Elena saw the natural cycles of their world with a reverence born of years of guardianship. They found beauty in the constancy of change, in the way the moon's phases mirrored their own journey—times of brightness and shadow, of visibility and concealment.

In this celestial dance, they saw a reflection of their own lives, an endless cycle of renewal and transformation. They celebrated each full moon with their pack, each ceremony a reminder of the night they had pledged their hearts to each other and the enduring power of their bond.

Their story, continued the wind, whispered through the leaves, and reflected in the waters, became a source of wisdom for generations to come. Young werewolves grew up on tales of Alex and Elena's bravery, their love, and their unyielding commitment to their people and their principles.

These stories, enriched with each retelling, served not just entertainment but as moral guides, lessons in leadership, love, and the strength of community. They were a testament to the fact that legends were not born of myth but of actions—of made in moments of crisis and compassion shown in times of need. In the fullness of time, Alex and Elena saw their children, and their children's children, grow to maturity, each bearing the legacy their lineage with pride. They watched as new leaders appeared, inspired by the examples they had set, ready to guide the pack into the future with wisdom gleaned from the past.

This continuation of their legacy was their greatest achievement, more than any battle won or alliance forged. It was the enduring proof of their love and leadership—a circle of life unbroken, spinning ever onward. And though the day would come when Alex and Elena would no longer walk among them in the flesh, their spirits remained an integral part of the pack's soul. The grove where they danced, where they had shared their hopes and dreams, became hallowed ground, a place of pilgrimage for those seeking guidance or solace.

Their story, now immortal, continued to inspire, a beacon of light in a world often shrouded in darkness. It was a song of hope, of enduring love and unity, which would never cease to be chanted about the realm. As they stood together under the twilight sky, watching the first stars appear, Alex and Elena knew that their time as leaders was ending. rather than sorrow, they felt a profound sense of peace and fulfillment. They had built something that would endure, a legacy of love and leadership that would continue to thrive long after they were gone.

Hand in hand, they turned to face their pack one last time, their hearts full of love and gratitude. They had led with courage, ruled with compassion, and loved all their being. Now, they entrusted their legacy to the next generation, confident in the knowledge that, under the eternal dance of the moon and stars, their story would live on, a timeless testament to the power of unity and the enduring strength of love.

Chapter 12: *A New Alpha*

The moon hung low in the sky, casting a silvery glow over the clearing where the Blue Twilight pack had gathered for the ball. The air was jam-packed with the scent of pine and wildflowers, mingling with the musky scent of werewolves in their human forms. Rowan, the next alpha of the South Paw pack, stood at the edge of the clearing, his eyes scanning the crowd for any signs of trouble.

As the son of Miles and Lily, the current alpha and Luna of the South Paw pack, Rowan was trained to be a strong and capable leader. He was tall and broad-shouldered, with dark hair that fell in unruly waves around his face. His eyes were a piercing shade of blue, like the clear summer sky, and they missed nothing as he watched over his pack.

But tonight, Rowan's attention was dragged to a figure across the clearing. She moved with a grace and beauty that took his breath away, her long hair shimmering like spun gold in the moonlight. Calogera, half fae, and half wolf, was a rare and exotic beauty, with eyes the color of emeralds and a smile that could light up the darkest night.

As their eyes met across the clearing, Rowan felt a jolt of electricity shoot through him. He knew in that moment that she was his mate, the other half of his soul. Without a word, he crossed the clearing to stand before her, his heart pounding in his chest.

"Calogera," he said, his voice rough with emotion. "I am Rowan, son of Miles and Lily. Will you dance with me?"

Calogera's eyes widened in surprise, but she nodded, a smile playing at the corners of her lips. As they moved onto the dance floor, the music of the pack's musicians filling the air, Rowan felt a sense of peace settle over him. In Calogera's arms, he felt whole, complete.

As they danced, the other members of the pack watched in awe. It was rare for a werewolf to find their mate, and even rarer for it to happen at a ball hosted by another pack. But as Rowan and Calogera moved together, their bond was undeniable.

When the music finally stopped, Rowan led Calogera to a quiet corner of the clearing, away from the prying eyes of the other pack members. Under the light of the moon, he took her hands in his, his eyes searching hers.

"Calogera," he said, his voice low and intense. "I know we have just met, but I feel a connection to you that I cannot explain. Will you be my mate, my Luna, and stand by my side as we lead the South Paw pack together?"

Tears welled in Calogera's eyes as she nodded, her heart overflowing with love for this strong and gentle werewolf before her. In that moment, she knew that she had found her true home, her place by Rowan's side.

And as they embraced under the light of the moon, the other members of the pack gathered around them, their howls of joy echoing through the night. Rowan and Calogera, the next alpha and Luna of the South Paw pack, had found each other at last, bound together by fate and love.

As the days turned into weeks, Rowan and Calogera's bond only grew stronger. They spent their time exploring the vast forests that surrounded the South Paw pack territory, their laughter ringing out like music in the crisp morning air. Calogera's fae heritage brought a sense of magic and wonder to their days, as she showed Rowan the hidden beauty of the natural world.

But it was not all sunshine and roses for the new alpha and Luna. The responsibilities of leading a pack weighed heavily on Rowan's shoulders, and Calogera struggled to find her place among the pack members who still viewed her with suspicion because of her mixed heritage. Despite these challenges, they faced them together, their love and determination unwavering.

One evening, as they sat by the fire in their shared den, Rowan turned to Calogera with a serious expression on his face. "My love," he began, taking her hands in his. "I know that it hasn't been easy for you, being the only half-fae in a pack of werewolves. But I want you to know that I will always stand by your side, no matter what challenges may come our way."

Calogera's eyes filled with tears at Rowan's words, touched by his unwavering support and love. She squeezed his hands tightly, her heart overflowing with gratitude for the strong and compassionate alpha who had captured her heart.

"I love you, Rowan," she whispered, her voice barely above a breath. "And I will always stand by your side, through thick and thin. Together, we can overcome anything that comes our way."

And with those words, their bond deepened even further, a connection that transcended time and space. They were more than just alpha and Luna – they were soulmates, destined to walk the path of life together, hand in hand.

As the moon rose high in the sky, casting its silvery light over the pack territory, Rowan and Calogera sat together in peaceful silence, their hearts beating as one. In that moment, they knew that no matter what challenges lay ahead, if they had each other, they could conquer anything.

And so, under the watchful gaze of the moon, Rowan and Calogera's love story continued to unfold, a tale of passion, loyalty, and unwavering devotion that would stand the test of time.

As the seasons changed and the South Paw pack faced new challenges, Rowan and Calogera stood united, their bond growing stronger with each passing day. Together, they navigated the intricacies of pack politics, earning the respect and loyalty of their pack members through their unwavering dedication and leadership.

But their love story was not without its trials. As tensions rose between neighboring packs and threats of conflict loomed on the horizon, Rowan and Calogera found themselves evaluated in ways they had never imagined. The fate of their pack and their love hung in the balance, and they knew that they would have to fight with everything they had to protect what was most precious to them.

One fateful night, as the full moon rose high in the sky, a rival pack launched a surprise attack on the South Paw territory. Rowan and Calogera stood side by side, their eyes blazing with determination as they led their pack members into battle. The air was filled with the sounds of snarls and howls, the clash of teeth and claws echoing through the night.

During the chaos, Rowan caught sight of Calogera, her silver fur gleaming in the moonlight as she fought with a fierce determination that took his breath away. He knew then, more than ever, that she was his equal in every way – a warrior, a leader, and his true partner in life.

As the battle raged on, Rowan and Calogera fought back-to-back, their movements fluid and coordinated as they defended their pack with everything they had. In that moment, they were not just alpha and

Luna – they were a formidable team, united in purpose and resolve.

And when the dust settled and the rival pack retreated, defeated, Rowan and Calogera stood victorious, their pack members rallying around them in a show of unity and strength. In that moment of triumph, they knew that their love and their bond were unbreakable, forged in the fires of adversity and evaluated by the trials of life.

As they stood together under the light of the full moon, Rowan and Calogera shared a silent moment of gratitude and love, their hearts beating as one. In that moment, they knew that no matter what challenges lay ahead, if they had each other, they could overcome anything – for they were not just Alpha and Luna, but soulmates bound by destiny and love.

With the threat from the rival pack vanquished and a newfound sense of unity among the South Paw pack, Rowan and Calogera found themselves at a turning point in their journey as alpha and Luna. The trials they had faced had only served to strengthen their bond, and they appeared from the conflict more determined than ever to lead their pack with wisdom and compassion.

As the days turned into weeks and the weeks into months, Rowan and Calogera worked tirelessly to rebuild and fortify the South Paw territory, ensuring the safety and prosperity of their pack members. Together, they implemented new strategies for defense and diplomacy, earning the respect and admiration of neighboring packs and solidifying their position as leaders in the werewolf community.

But amidst the responsibilities of leadership, Rowan and Calogera made sure to carve out moments of peace and joy for themselves. They would often steal away into the forest, hand in hand, to bask in the beauty of nature and revel in the simple pleasures of each other's company. In those stolen moments, they found solace and strength, drawing comfort from the unbreakable bond that connected their hearts.

One evening, as they sat by the edge of a tranquil lake, the moon casting a shimmering reflection on the water, Rowan turned to Calogera with a soft smile on his face. "My love," he began, his voice gentle and warm. "I am grateful every day for the gift of your love and companionship. You are the light of my life, the anchor of my soul."

Calogera's eyes sparkled with emotion as she gazed into Rowan's eyes, her heart overflowing with love for the strong and compassionate alpha who had captured her heart. "And you, my dear Rowan," she replied, her voice filled with tenderness. "You are my rock, my protector, my everything. With you by my side, I am whole."

In that moment, as the moon hung low in the sky, Rowan and Calogera sealed their love with a tender kiss, a promise of forever etched in the depths of their souls. And as they embraced under the watchful gaze of the moon, they knew that their love story was far from over – it was only just beginning, a tale of passion, courage, and enduring love that would stand the test of time.

As the seasons changed and the South Paw pack thrived under the leadership of Rowan and Calogera, a new chapter in their love story began to unfold. The bond between the two packs, once strained by rivalry and conflict, grew stronger as the Blue Twilight pack, led by Alpha Onyx and Luna Amber, extended an olive branch of peace and cooperation.

A grand ceremony was planned to celebrate the union of the two packs, a symbol of unity and solidarity in the face of adversity. Rowan and Calogera stood at the forefront of the festivities, their hearts filled with hope and joy as they welcomed their newfound allies with open arms.

Under the light of the full moon, the packs gathered in the clearing where it all began – the place where Rowan and Calogera had first met and forged their bond. The air was filled with the scent of pine and wildflowers, mingling with the musky scent of werewolves in their human forms. The sound of laughter and music filled the night, a celebration of love and unity that echoed through the forest.

As Alpha Onyx and Luna Amber stood before the gathered packs, their voices strong and clear, they spoke of peace, cooperation, and the power of love to overcome all obstacles. Rowan and Calogera watched with pride and gratitude, knowing that their love had played a pivotal role in bringing the two packs together.

And as the ceremony ended, Rowan and Calogera stepped forward, their hands clasped together, a symbol of unity and strength. "We stand before you today as alpha and Luna of the South Paw pack," Rowan began, his voice ringing out with conviction. "And we pledge to honor this union, to protect and cherish each member of our extended pack family, and to lead with wisdom and compassion."

Calogera's eyes shone with emotion as she spoke, her voice filled with warmth and sincerity. "Together, we are stronger," she said. "Together, we will face whatever challenges come our way, united in purpose and bound by love."

And as the two packs howled in unison, their voices rising to the heavens in a chorus of unity and joy, Rowan and Calogera knew that their love story had transcended the boundaries of pack and species, becoming a beacon of hope and inspiration for all who saw it. In that moment, they knew that their love was not just a bond between two souls – it was a force of nature, a testament to the power of love to conquer all.

Chapter 13: *The Arrival of Multiples*

Amber checked her appearance in the mirror one last time before heading out to the local werewolf pack meeting. She could not help but feel nervous as she thought about what would happen when she saw her mate, Onyx, again. It had been years since they had been separated from their last set of triplets, and now they were starting a new chapter in their lives with another set of children.

As she arrived at the meeting, Amber scanned the room for Onyx. She finally spotted him standing with a group of werewolves, deep in conversation. She could not help but notice how handsome he looked, his dark hair falling in waves around his strong jawline. She took a deep breath and walked over to him, feeling her heart race with anticipation.

Onyx turned to face her as she approached, a warm smile spreading across his face. "Amber," he said softly, his voice sending shivers down her spine. "It's been too long." Amber felt a surge of emotion as she looked into his mesmerizing green eyes. "Yes, it has," she replied, trying to keep her voice steady. "I've missed you, Onyx.

"Before they could say another word, a new voice interrupted their reunion. "Amber! Onyx!" Clara called out, rushing over to join them. She was a beautiful werewolf with long blonde hair and piercing blue eyes, and she was accompanied by her mate, Archer, a tall and rugged werewolf with a mischievous smile. Clara and Archer had also been separated from their last set of triplets, and now they were starting fresh with a new set of children as well. The two couples had bonded over their shared experiences and had become close friends over the years.

"It's so good to see you both," Clara said, hugging Amber and Onyx tightly. "I can't wait to catch up and hear all about your new little ones." Onyx smiled warmly at Clara. "We can't wait to hear about your new triplets as well," he replied. "It's been too long since we've seen each other." As they settled into comfortable conversation, a sense of peace settled over the group. They talked about their lives since they had last seen each other, sharing stories of their children and the challenges they had faced. The bond between the two couples only grew stronger as they laughed and reminisced about old times.

As the night wore on, Amber felt a sense of contentment wash over her. She knew that no matter what challenges lay ahead, she had Onyx by her side, and her love for him only deepened with each passing moment. She looked over at Clara and saw the same love and devotion in her eyes as she gazed at Archer. Amber knew that the road ahead would not be easy, but she also knew that with her mate by her side, she could face anything. And as she looked into Onyx's eyes, she knew that their love would guide them through whatever trials they may face.

With a renewed sense of hope and determination, the two couples embraced the future, knowing that together they were stronger than they had ever been apart. And so, as the night drew to a close, they walked hand in hand, ready to face whatever challenges lay ahead, united in love and bound by a bond that could never be broken."

The moon hung high in the night sky, casting its ethereal glow upon the ancient forest. Amongst the towering trees, a pack of werewolves roamed, their silhouettes blending seamlessly with the shadows. In the heart of the pack, four individuals stood out, their lives intertwined in a dance of love and destiny.

Amber, with her fiery red hair and emerald eyes, exuded a vibrant energy that captivated all who laid eyes upon her. She was a force to be reckoned with, fiercely protective of her family. Her mate, Onyx, had a calm and steady demeanor, his midnight black fur shimmering under the moon's tender touch. Together, they were an unstoppable duo, bound by love and a shared purpose.

Clara, Amber's best friend, was a beacon of kindness and compassion. Her golden locks cascaded down her back, framing her gentle hazel eyes. Clara had found her soulmate in Archer, a strong and devoted werewolf with a rugged charm. His russet fur matched Clara's warmth, and his piercing blue eyes held a depth that whispered of secrets untold.

Amber and Clara had both been blessed with the gift of motherhood, their lives forever changed by the arrival of their precious little ones. Amber had given birth to a boy and two girls, their tiny forms a testament to the love between her and Onyx. Clara, on the other hand, had been blessed with a trio of boys, each one a reflection of the bond she shared with Archer.

As the moon's soft glow enveloped the clearing, the four werewolves gathered, their pups playing joyfully at their feet. Amber watched her son, a strong and curious little wolf, as he fearlessly explored his surroundings. Her daughters, with their mischievous eyes and playful natures, tumbled and tussled with their cousins, the bond of family growing stronger with each passing day.

Clara, her heart bursting with love, watched proudly as her boys romped and chased each other. They were a spirited bunch, full of energy and laughter. Archer stood by her side, his steady presence a reminder of the strength they had as a family. The love they shared was a beacon of light that guided them through the darkest of nights.

In this magical moonlit moment, the bonds between these two families were forged even deeper. The love between Amber and Onyx, Clara, and Archer, radiated like a beacon, illuminating the path ahead. They knew that their journey would not always be easy, but together, they were invincible.

As the night wore on, the werewolves retreated to their den, their pups nestled close, safe, and warm. The moon continued to watch over them, a silent witness to the love and devotion that filled their lives. In the embrace of their mates and the laughter of their children, Amber, Onyx, Clara, and Archer found solace and strength.

Their story was one of love and adventure, of overcoming obstacles and embracing the beauty of their unique family. And as the moon slowly descended in the sky, it whispered a promise of tomorrow, filled with endless possibilities and the unwavering love that bound them all.

In the depths of the forest, the werewolves slept soundly, their dreams filled with visions of a future where love conquered all. For in their hearts, they knew that their bond, forged under the watchful gaze of the moon, was unbreakable. And so, they embraced the night, knowing that with each new dawn, their love would only grow stronger.

Amber had long, flowing hair that shimmered like flames in the sunlight. Her fiery red hair cascaded down her back, adding to her vibrant and captivating presence. It was a unique and striking color that perfectly matched her bold personality.

Her eyes were like two sparkling emeralds, mesmerizing anyone who investigated them. They were a stunning shade of green, reminiscent of lush forests and deep, hidden treasures. Amber's eyes were full of depth and intensity, reflecting her inner strength and passion.

Overall, the combination of her fiery red hair and emerald eyes made Amber stand out in the crowd, radiating a sense of confidence and allure. Amber had long, flowing locks of golden hair that cascaded down her back in loose waves. Her hair was lustrous and shiny, reflecting light like a halo around her face. She took great care of her hair, nourishing it with natural oils and using gentle products to keep its health and vitality.

Her eyes were a mesmerizing shade of deep blue, like the calmest ocean on a sunny day. They sparkled with warmth and intelligence, always expressing her emotions with authenticity. When she looked at someone, it felt as though she could see into their soul, making them feel seen and understood.

Amber had a captivating sense of style that reflected her vibrant personality. She had a keen eye for fashion, effortlessly combining trendy pieces with timeless classics. Her wardrobe was a mix of bold colors, playful patterns, and elegant designs that always made a statement. Amber had the ability to turn heads wherever she went, leaving an impression with her impeccable fashion choices.

In addition to her physical beauty, Amber had a sharp intellect and a thirst for knowledge. She was a lifelong learner, constantly seeking new experiences and expanding her horizons. Her curiosity and intelligence made her conversations engaging and thought-provoking, as she was able to discuss a wide range of topics with depth and insight.

Amber had a warm and infectious laughter that could fill a room with joy. She had a deep sense of humor and could find humor in even the most mundane situations. Her laughter was contagious, bringing smiles to the faces of those around her and creating a positive and uplifting atmosphere.

Amber was a natural leader, inspiring others with her confidence and determination. She had a powerful sense of purpose and was not afraid to pursue her dreams and stand up for what she believed in. Her resilience and perseverance were qualities that made her an inspiration to others, encouraging them to believe in themselves and their own abilities.

Overall, Amber was a true embodiment of beauty, both inside and out. Her physical features and personal qualities combined to create a captivating presence that left an impression on everyone she encountered. She was a shining example of how beauty can go beyond appearances, encompassing kindness, intelligence, and a zest for life.

Amber had a passion for adventure and exploring the world. She loved to travel to recent places, immersing herself in diverse cultures and experiencing the beauty of diverse landscapes. From hiking through lush rainforests to diving into clear waters, Amber embraced every opportunity to connect with nature and create lasting memories.

She had a deep appreciation for the arts and was a talented Witch-wolf Hybrid herself. Whether it was painting, sculpting, or photography, Amber had a natural ability to capture the essence of a moment and express her creativity through various mediums. Her artwork was often inspired by her travels and the people she met along the way, displaying her unique perspective and Witch-wolf Hydridic vision.

Amber had a genuine love for animals and was an enthusiastic advocate for their well-being. She volunteered at local animal shelters, dedicating her time and energy to caring for abandoned and neglected animals. Her compassion and empathy were clear in the way she interacted with animals, providing them with love, comfort, and a second chance at life.

She was also a resolute philanthropist, actively involved in various charitable organizations. Amber believed in using her resources and influence to make a positive impact in the world. Whether it was supporting education initiatives, providing access to clean water, or fighting against social injustices, she was committed to making a difference and creating a more fair and compassionate society.

Amber had a close-knit circle of friends who cherished her for her loyalty, kindness, and unwavering support. She was a faithful friend, always there to lend an ear, offer advice, or simply share a laugh. Her genuine care for others created a sense of belonging and warmth within her friendships, making her a trusted confidante and a pillar of strength.

In her free time, Amber enjoyed immersing herself in books and literature. She had a voracious appetite for knowledge and found solace in the pages of a delightful book. Whether it was a classic novel, a thought-provoking non-fiction piece, or a collection of poetry, she found inspiration and enlightenment in the written word.

Amber's positive energy and zest for life were contagious. She approached each day with gratitude and a determination to make the most of every moment. Her presence was a ray of sunshine, brightening the lives of those around her and reminding them of the beauty and joy that can be found in the simplest of things.

Overall, Amber was a remarkable individual who embodied the qualities of compassion, creativity, and resilience. Her adventurous spirit, dedication to making a positive impact, and genuine connections with others made her a truly extraordinary person. She left an impression on everyone she encountered, and her legacy continues to inspire others to live a life filled with purpose, kindness, and passion.

Amber had a deep love for nature and the environment. She believed in the importance of preserving the planet for future generations and was actively involved in environmental conservation efforts. She took part in tree planting initiatives, beach clean-ups, and educational campaigns to raise awareness about sustainable living and the impact of werewolf activities on the Earth.

Her love for adventure extended to extreme sports and outdoor activities. She was an avid rock climber and enjoyed the thrill of scaling challenging cliffs and mountains. She also took part in exciting activities like skydiving, bungee jumping, and whitewater rafting, always seeking new adrenaline-pumping experiences that pushed her limits.

Amber had a curious mind and a thirst for knowledge. She constantly looked to expand her horizons and learn about diverse cultures, traditions, and languages. She would often immerse herself in the local communities during her travels, engaging with locals, trying new foods, and learning their customs and traditions. This curiosity and open-mindedness allowed her to form deep connections with people from all social classes.

As a Witch-wolf Hybrid, Amber experimented with various Witch-wolf Hydridic styles and mediums. She was not afraid to step out of her comfort zone and explore new techniques. From abstract paintings to intricate sculptures, her artwork reflected her versatility and willingness to embrace new challenges. She often held art exhibitions to display her work and used her talent to raise funds for charitable causes.

Amber was a strong advocate for mental health and believed in the importance of self-care and emotional well-being. She openly shared her own struggles with anxiety and depression, aiming to break the stigma surrounding mental health issues. She encouraged others to seek help, practice self-care, and prioritize their mental well-being.

In addition to her Witch-wolf Hydridic pursuits, Amber had a talent for storytelling. She would captivate her audience with vivid descriptions of her travel experiences, bringing to life the sights, sounds, and emotions she met along the way. Her stories transported listeners to different corners of the world, inspiring them to dream big and embrace their own sense of adventure.

Amber had a deep appreciation for music and its ability to evoke emotions and bring people together. She enjoyed attending live concerts and music festivals, immersing herself in the energy and rhythm of the performances. She also played the guitar and would often strum melodies to go with her artwork or to simply unwind and find solace in the power of music.

Overall, Amber was a multifaceted individual whose passion for adventure, creativity, and making a positive impact on the world touched the lives of many. Her zest for life, coupled with her compassion and determination, made her a truly remarkable individual. She continues to inspire others to embrace their passions, explore the world, and have influence in their own unique way.

Chapter 14: *The Beta's Son and The Rogue*

Casimir had never been one for grand gestures. He was a beta's son, raised to be steady, dependable, calm amidst the storm. Yet, as he stared at the half-finished birdhouse in his hands, he felt a surge of something reckless course through him. He was building this for Bronwen, the enigmatic, fierce she-wolf who had somehow captured his steady heart.

She was unlike anyone he had ever met. A whirlwind of contradictions: strong yet vulnerable, aloof yet fiercely loyal. Her lineage was a mystery, even to her. She was a foundling, raised on the fringes of different packs, never truly belonging. The only clue to her heritage was the faint scent of dragon fire that clung to her, a whisper of an ancient, powerful bloodline.

He knew his parents would not approve. Bronwen was a rogue, untethered to any pack, her loyalties uncertain. But Casimir saw something in her that transcended pack laws and traditions. He saw a kindred spirit, a soul yearning for a place to belong.

He met her on the edge of the Blue Twilight territory, where the ancient forest met the rugged cliffs. She was a blur of motion, fighting off three rogue wolves with a ferocity that belied her slender frame. He had intervened, drawn by a need to protect, a need he could not explain.

Their first meeting was a clash of fangs and claws, a whirlwind of growls and snapping jaws. But beneath the primal aggression, Casimir saw a spark of recognition in her golden eyes, a glimmer of gratitude that bloomed into a hesitant trust.

Since then, they had met in secret, stealing moments under the silver glow of the moon. He had learned about her life, her struggles, her fierce independence that was both a shield and a burden. He had glimpsed the loneliness she hid beneath her sharp wit and sardonic humor.

Building a birdhouse might seem like a mundane gesture for a werewolf, but Casimir knew it held a deeper meaning for Bronwen. It stood for a home, a haven, something she had never truly had.

He envisioned her delight, the way her lips would curve into a rare, genuine smile, the way her eyes would soften, losing some of their guarded wariness. He was lost in this pleasant daydream when a gruff voice shattered the silence.

"What in the name of the Moon Goddess are you doing, Casimir?"

His father, Archer, stood behind him, his face etched with disapproval.

"It's a birdhouse, Father," Casimir replied, his voice calm despite the nervous flutter in his chest.

"Don't play coy with me," Archer growled, his eyes narrowed. "We both know this isn't for some feathered creature. This is for that rogue, isn't it?"

Casimir met his father's gaze, his own chin lifting in a show of defiance he had not known he had. "Her name is Bronwen," he corrected, the words firm and clear. "And yes, it's for her."

The air crackled with tension, the age-old conflict between duty and desire playing out between father and son. Casimir, the dutiful son, was now walking a path he had not chosen, a path carved by the mysterious, captivating she-wolf who had awakened a longing he had never known he had.

Archer's eyes blazed with fury. "She's a danger to this pack, Casimir. A rogue with dragon blood, no less. Her loyalties are unclear, her motives unknown. You cannot trust her."

"You haven't even met her," Casimir retorted, the calmness he had always prided himself on dissolving under the heat of his father's anger. "She's not what you think. She is just—"

"Just what?" Archer interrupted, his voice like a whipcrack. "Just a lost soul? A vulnerable creature needing your protection. Do not be naive, son. Dragon blood runs hot and wild, unpredictable. You're playing with fire, Casimir, and you'll get burned."

Casimir's jaw clenched, his wolf rising within him, yearning for a confrontation that went against every fiber of his being. He was the mediator, the peacemaker, yet Bronwen had ignited a fire in his soul that threatened to consume the very foundations of his life.

"She saved my life, Father," he said, his voice low but steady. "I was cornered by those rogues, the ones who've been raiding our territory. She saved me. Does that sound like someone who is a danger to our pack?"

Archer's expression flickered, a brief glimpse of uncertainty in his eyes. He knew about the rogue incursions, knew that his son had been lucky to escape. But the prejudice against rogues, especially ones with dragon blood, ran deep.

"That doesn't change anything," Archer said, his voice regaining its firmness. "Gratitude is a fleeting emotion, Casimir. It does not erase the danger she stands for. She's a wild card, and wild cards can destroy everything we've built."

Casimir, however, had reached his limit. The years of obedience, of following the pack's rules, of being the dependable beta's son had molded him into a man of reason and control. But Bronwen had unleashed a primal force within him, a fierce protectiveness that refused to be silenced.

"I won't apologize for caring about her," he said, meeting his father's gaze with unwavering determination. "She's more than just a rogue, Father. She is... she is someone I—"

The words caught in his throat; the declaration of love too raw, too vulnerable to utter aloud. He could not bring himself to say it, not yet, not with the weight of his father's disapproval bearing down on him.

"She's someone you what?" Archer pressed; his voice laced with suspicion.

Casimir swallowed hard, his gaze dropping to the birdhouse in his hands. "She's someone who deserves a chance," he finally said, his voice softer now, the fire banked but not extinguished. "A chance to prove that she's not the monster you believe her to be."

Archer stared at his son, a mixture of anger and bewilderment swirling in his eyes. He saw the resolute set of Casimir's jaw, the unwavering conviction in his eyes, and he knew that something fundamental had shifted within his son. The beta's son, the dependable, steady presence in the pack, was gone. In his place stood a wolf driven by a force beyond duty, beyond reason, a force that was as wild and unpredictable as the dragon blood that flowed in the veins of the she-wolf who had captured his heart.

A tense silence stretched between them; the only sound was the rustling leaves of the ancient forest surrounding their home. Archer knew this was a battle he could not win. He could forbid Casimir from seeing Bronwen, could enforce pack laws and banish the rogue from their territory, but he could not control his son's heart.

The wolf within him, the alpha who demanded obedience, wrestled with the father who yearned for his son's happiness. He saw the depth of Casimir's feelings for this rogue, saw the unwavering loyalty in his eyes, and a grudging respect began to bloom within him.

"Bring her to the next full moon gathering," Archer finally said, his voice weary but resolute. "Let her stand before the pack, let her tell her story. We'll decide her fate then."

Casimir's heart leaped. It was not acceptance, not yet, but it was a chance, an opportunity for Bronwen to prove herself. He knew it would be an uphill battle, that prejudice ran deep within the pack, but he clung to the hope that they would see in her what he saw: a strong, resilient she-wolf worthy of their respect, even their acceptance.

"Thank you, Father," he said, the words laced with gratitude that transcended the conflict that had erupted between them. He knew this was not the end, but a beginning, a tentative step on a path fraught with uncertainty.

He found Bronwen by the river, her lithe form silhouetted against the shimmering moonlight. She was staring at the rushing water, her face lost in thought, her expression unreadable. He approached her cautiously, his heart pounding against his ribs.

"Bronwen," he said softly, his voice a bomb in the stillness of the night.

She turned, her golden eyes meeting his, a flicker of surprise crossing her face. He saw the question in her gaze, the unspoken query about his father's reaction.

He took her hand; her fingers cool and strong in his grasp. "My father wants to meet you," he said, his voice calm despite the turmoil swirling within him. "At the full moon gathering."

Bronwen's eyes widened, a mixture of apprehension and hope flaring in their depths. She had lived on the fringes, always on the outside looking in, never truly belonging. The thought of standing before the Blue Twilight pack, of revealing her lineage, of exposing her vulnerabilities, filled her with both trepidation and a yearning she could not ignore.

"Why?" she asked, her voice barely a whisper.

Casimir lifted her hand to his lips, pressing a gentle kiss against her knuckles. "Because I believe in you," he said, his voice filled with conviction. "And I want them to believe in you too."

He saw the flicker of uncertainty in her eyes, the ingrained wariness of a soul who had learned to expect rejection. He could not promise her acceptance, could not guarantee a smooth path, but he could offer her his unwavering support, his love that defied pack laws and challenged centuries-old prejudices.

As the moon bathed the forest in its silvery light, Casimir and Bronwen stood together, their hands clasped, their fates intertwined. They were a study in contrasts: the steady beta's son and the fiery rogue, the embodiment of order and chaos, yet somehow their differences harmonized, creating a melody that was both discordant and beautiful. The future stretched before them, uncertain yet full of possibilities, a testament to the power of love that dared to defy the boundaries of pack and blood.

The days leading up to the full moon gathering were a blur of nervous anticipation. Casimir found himself torn between reassuring his packmates and preparing Bronwen for the scrutiny she would face. The Blue Twilight pack was known for its strict adherence to tradition, its suspicion of outsiders, and the whispers about Bronwen's dragon heritage only fueled their apprehension.

Casimir, however, remained steadfast in his belief. He saw Bronwen's inherent goodness, her loyalty, and her fierce determination to protect those she cared for. He knew the dragon blood that ran in her veins was not a curse, but a source of strength, a testament to her resilience.

He spent hours talking to Bronwen, preparing her for the questions, the doubts, and the potential hostility she might meet. He saw her struggle, the conflict between her yearning for acceptance and the deep-seated fear of rejection that haunted her. Yet, he also saw her determination solidify, a fire ignited in her golden eyes, a resolve to face her past and fight for her future.

The night of the full moon arrived. The air thick with anticipation. The clearing in the heart of the forest, usually a place of celebration and unity, was now charged with an undercurrent of tension. The pack members gathered, their eyes fixed on the two figures standing at the edge of the clearing: Casimir, their beta's son, the embodiment of pack loyalty, and Bronwen, the rogue, the outsider, the unknown.

Archer, as beta, stood at the forefront, his gaze stern yet laced with a hint of curiosity. He had given Casimir his word, a chance for Bronwen to plead her case, but the decision rested with the pack.

Casimir felt Bronwen tense beside him, her hand gripping his tightly. He squeezed back, offering a reassuring smile, a silent promise of his unwavering support.

"Bronwen," Archer's voice boomed, echoing through the clearing. "You stand before the Blue Twilight pack, a rogue who has trespassed on our territory, who has captured the heart of one of our own. We demand to know your purpose, your lineage, your intentions."

A hush fell over the crowd as Bronwen stepped forward. She stood tall, her chin lifted, her golden eyes meeting the scrutinizing gazes of the pack. The scent of dragon fire, faint yet undeniable, wafted through the air, a whisper of ancient power that sent a ripple of unease through the assembled wolves.

"I am Bronwen," she began, her voice clear and steady despite the tremor that ran through her. "I have no pack, no lineage I can claim. I was a foundling, raised on the fringes, surviving by my wits and my strength. I have no memory of my parents, no knowledge of my heritage, save for the fire that burnt in my blood, a legacy I am only beginning to understand."

She paused, her gaze sweeping over the faces that surrounded her, their expressions ranging from curiosity to outright hostility. "I came to this territory seeking refuge," she continued, her voice gaining strength. "I was pursued, hunted by those who would exploit my power for their own gain. Casimir found me, offered me kindness when I expected only aggression. He saw beyond the label of rogue, beyond the whispers of my heritage, and offered me a chance at something I had never dared to dream of: acceptance."

Her words hung in the air, a challenge, a plea for understanding. The pack remained silent, their judgment held in check, but their gazes remained wary, their trust yet to be earned.

Bronwen took a step closer, her eyes meeting Archer's, her gaze unwavering. "I may not be one of you, not by blood or tradition," she said, her voice resonating with a conviction that surprised even her. "But I have come to care for this pack, for the bonds of loyalty and kinship that bind you. I am willing to fight for this pack, to stand beside you against any threat, to prove myself worthy of the acceptance that Casimir has offered."

Her declaration hung in the air, a bold statement that challenged the very foundation of the pack's traditions. The silence stretched, taut with anticipation, the fate of Bronwen, and even the future of the Blue Twilight pack, hanging in the balance.

Chapter 15: *The Moonlit Union*

In the realm where the shadows danced beneath the moon's silver glow, two worlds intertwined in a love that defied all boundaries. Henry, the noble Lycan prince, adorned in fur as dark as the night, and Piper, the enchanting princess of the Fairy world, who was half fae, half wolf, and half dragon, found solace in each other's arms.

Their love was forbidden, an ancient tale whispered among the trees and howled among the winds. But as fate would have it, the hearts of the prince and the princess beat as one, united by a bond stronger than any magic or decree.

Months turned into seasons, and whispers of a miracle appeared from the depths of the forest. Piper, with eyes that held the mysteries of the universe, felt the stirrings of life within her. The couple had yearned for a child, a symbol of their love that transcended realms, and now their prayers had been answered in a way they never expected.

As the moon waxed and waned, Piper's belly swelled not with one, but with six tiny hearts that beat in harmony with hers. The news of this extraordinary pregnancy spread like wildfire through the enchanted lands, igniting both awe and concern among the denizens of the night and the fae.

Henry, with his amber eyes filled with a mix of joy and trepidation, vowed to protect his mate and their unborn pups with his life. Piper, with her gentle smile and a strength that belied her delicate appearance, embraced the challenges that lay ahead with unwavering resolve.

Together, they navigated the trials of carrying a litter of pups, each day a testament to their love and the bond that bound them together. Henry's pack stood by their prince, offering their support and loyalty, while Piper's kin in the Fairy world showered her with blessings and protection.

As the moon reached its zenith, casting a silvery sheen over the expectant couple, Henry and Piper found solace in the knowledge that their love would conquer all obstacles. For they were not just prince and princess, Lycan and Fae—they were soulmates destined to rewrite the stars with the legacy of their extraordinary offspring.

And so, under the watchful gaze of the moon and the twinkling stars, Henry and Piper prepared for the arrival of their pups, a testament to the enduring power of love that transcended boundaries and united two worlds in a tale ancient itself.

As the days turned into nights and the nights into days, the time for the birth of Henry and Piper's pups drew near. The air crackled with anticipation, a palpable energy that hummed through the enchanted lands, heralding the arrival of a new era.

On a moonlit night when the stars aligned in a celestial dance, Piper's labor began. Henry, his fur bristling with a mix of nerves and excitement, stood by her side, his eyes never straying from his mate's face, where determination and pain mingled in a potent brew.

In a secluded glade deep within the heart of the forest, surrounded by the ancient trees that bore witness to the unfolding drama, Piper's cries pierced the stillness of the night. The Fairy midwives, their wings shimmering in the moonlight, fluttered around her, their hands glowing with healing magic as they aided in the miraculous birth.

One by one, the pups appeared into the world, their tiny forms a testament to the love that had created them. Each pup bore a unique blend of their parents' traits—some with fur as black as midnight, others with wings that glistened like dew-kissed petals—each a precious gift from the heavens above.

As the last pup made its entrance, a hush fell over the glade, broken only by the soft cries of the newborns and the gasps of awe that escaped the lips of those present. Henry, his heart overflowing with a love so profound it threatened to consume him, gathered his mate and their pups in his arms, a picture of pure bliss and contentment.

In that moment, as the moon hung low in the sky, casting a silvery glow over the scene of new life and boundless love, Henry and Piper knew that their union had created something truly extraordinary—a family that defied conventions and united two worlds in a tapestry of love and magic.

And so, under the benevolent gaze of the moon and the twinkling stars, Henry and Piper embraced their pups, their hearts brimming with a joy that transcended words. For in the midst of chaos and uncertainty, they had found a love that was unbreakable, a bond that would endure for all eternity—a love that had given birth to a new era, where werewolves and fairies stood united in a legacy of hope, acceptance, and undying love.

As the days turned into weeks and the weeks into months, the glade where Henry and Piper's pups were born buzzed with activity. The air was filled with the sounds of tiny yips and chirps, as the newborns grew stronger under the watchful eyes of their parents and the enchanted beings that surrounded them.

Henry, with his regal bearing and fierce protectiveness, stood guard over his family, his pack by his side, ready to defend their prince and the future of their kind. Piper, with her gentle touch and nurturing spirit, tended to their pups with a tenderness that belied her royal status, her wings fluttering in a protective embrace.

The pups thrived under their parents' care, their unique traits and abilities beginning to manifest as they grew. Some showed a talent for shifting between forms with ease, while others displayed a knack for harnessing the ancient magic that flowed through their veins—a legacy of their mixed heritage.

As the pups grew stronger and more independent, Henry and Piper knew that it was time to instill in them the values that would guide them in their journey through life. They taught them the importance of unity and acceptance, of embracing their differences and finding strength in their shared bond.

The glade became a haven of learning and laughter, a place where the pups frolicked and played under the watchful eyes of their parents and the wise elders of both worlds. They learned the ways of the forest and the secrets of the stars; their minds and hearts opened to the wonders that surrounded them.

And as the moon waxed and waned, casting its silvery light over the growing family, Henry and Piper knew that their legacy was secure. Their pups, with their diverse talents and boundless potential, would carry their love and their teachings into the world, a beacon of hope and harmony in a realm torn by ancient feuds and prejudices.

And so, under the watchful gaze of the moon and the twinkling stars, Henry and Piper stood united, their hearts entwined with the future of their kind. For they knew that no matter what challenges lay ahead, they would face them together, with love as their shield and family as their strength—a love that had defied all odds and birthed a new era of peace and unity in a world where werewolves and fairies stood side by side, bound by a love that knew no bounds.

As the seasons changed, and the pups grew into adolescence, Henry and Piper faced new challenges that evaluated the strength of their family and the bonds they had forged. The glade that had once been a sanctuary of peace and harmony now echoed with the whispers of change, as the pups embarked on their own journeys of self-discovery and growth.

Each pup faced their own trials and tribulations, navigating the complexities of their dual heritage and the expectations that weighed upon them. Some struggled to control their shifting abilities, while others grappled with the weight of their destinies as heirs to two powerful realms.

Henry and Piper, with hearts heavy with worry and love, stood by their pups through every hardship and triumph, their guidance and support a steady beacon in the tumultuous sea of adolescence. They watched with pride as their offspring embraced their unique gifts and forged their own paths, each step bringing them closer to their true selves.

Amidst the chaos and uncertainty, a dark shadow loomed on the horizon—a threat that neither werewolf nor fairy had faced before. A malevolent force, borne of ancient grudges and festering hatred, looked to divide the realms and plunge them into chaos and despair.

Henry and Piper knew that the time had come to unite their people in the face of this looming danger, to set aside old grievances and stand together as one against a common foe. With their pups by their side, each wielding their own strengths and powers, they embarked on a quest to rally the denizens of the forest and the fae in a battle for the very soul of their world.

The days grew darker as the forces of darkness gathered, their eyes gleaming with malice and their hearts consumed by a thirst for power. But in the heart of the glade, where the moon shone bright and the stars burned with a fierce light, Henry and Piper stood united, their love a shield against the encroaching shadows.

And as the battle lines were drawn and the fate of their world hung in the balance, Henry and Piper knew that no matter what trials lay ahead, they would face them together, with their pups by their side and a love that transcended all boundaries—a love that had given birth to a new era of hope and unity in a world torn apart by ancient feuds and darkness.

The air crackled with tension as the forces of darkness descended upon the glade, their malevolent presence casting a pall over the once serene landscape. Henry, with his fur bristling and his eyes ablaze with determination, stood at the forefront of his pack, his gaze unwavering as he prepared to face the oncoming threat.

Piper, her wings shimmering with an ethereal light, stood by his side, her heart filled with a mix of fear and resolve. Their pups, each bearing the mark of their unique heritage, lined up behind them, their faces set in expressions of fierce determination and unwavering courage.

As the first wave of darkness crashed upon them, a cacophony of battle cries and magic filled the air. Werewolves clashed with shadowy creatures, their fangs, and claws meeting in a dance of primal fury, while fairies weaved intricate spells that lit up the night like fireworks.

Henry and Piper fought side by side, their powers blending in a symphony of light and shadow that drove back the encroaching darkness. Their pups, each embracing their gifts and strengths, fought with a bravery that belied their youth, their hearts united in a common cause—to protect their home and their family at all costs.

The battle raged on, the glade bathed in the light of a thousand stars as werewolves and fairies fought as one against a foe that sought to tear them apart. With each strike and each spell cast, the forces of darkness faltered, their ranks thinning under the relentless assault of unity and love.

And as the moon reached its zenith, casting a silvery glow over the battlefield, a triumphant cry rang out through the night. The forces of darkness, their malevolent presence dissipating like mist in the morning sun, retreated into the shadows from whence they came, defeated by the power of unity and love that stood as a beacon of hope in a world plagued by darkness.

In the aftermath of the battle, as the glade lay quiet and still once more, Henry and Piper gathered their pups in a tight embrace, their hearts filled with pride and gratitude. They knew that their love had triumphed over adversity, that their family had appeared stronger and more united than ever before—a testament to the enduring power of love that transcended all boundaries and defied all odds.

And as the stars twinkled overhead, casting their gentle light upon the scene of victory and unity, Henry and Piper knew that their legacy would endure for generations to come—a legacy of love, unity, and hope that would shine bright in the hearts of werewolves and fairies alike, a reminder that in the face of darkness, love would always prevail.

Chapter 16: *Unexpected Adventures*

The forest of Eldergrove was alive with the whispers of the night, the leaves rustling softly as if sharing ancient secrets with the wind. The moon hung heavy and full, a silver sentinel watching over the world below. It was a night of power, a night of magic, and for Falcon and Ciara, a night of profound transformation.

Falcon and Ciara are preparing for the coming birth of their pups. They had been trying for years to conceive a pup. The Moon Goddess must have heard their prayers because on the trip back to the Blue Twilight pack she became pregnant but did not know she was expecting until Amber said something to her about it.

Ciara was sick halfway through the trip which took at least a week to complete. After the ball, Ciara went to the hospital to get checked out and to confirm her pregnancy. Thomas, the head doctor, who was also a werewolf, did a thorough exam on Ciara. He did blood and urine tests to confirm Ciara's pregnancy. However, she wanted video confirmation. Thomas ordered an ultrasound of the pup.

The ultrasound showed that she was carrying not one but five pups. She was over the moon with joy and could not wait to get home to tell her mate. When Ciara told Falcon the news that she was carrying five pups at once, he just dropped to the floor in a dead faint. Ciara was so shocked that she hollered for help! She thought that her news had killed her mate. But the fact remained that he just passed out from sheer shock of the news.

Ciara lay in the heart of their pack house, a sanctuary of warmth and earthy scents, her breaths coming in slow, rhythmic waves. Her belly was swollen with new life, five precious pups that stirred within her, each a tiny spark of the future they would soon share. Falcon, her mate, and guardian, sat by her side, his amber eyes reflecting the moonlight that filtered through the canopy above.

"You're so beautiful," Falcon murmured, his voice a low growl that vibrated with love and awe. His large, calloused hands rested gently on the curve of her abdomen, feeling the movement of their unborn children. "Our pups will be the strongest the pack has ever seen."

Ciara smiled, her emerald eyes shining with a mixture of excitement and trepidation. "And the most loved," she added, her voice a melodic whisper that seemed to dance with the leaves outside. "But Falcon, I'm scared. Five at once... it is unheard of. What if I am not strong enough?"

Falcon's gaze hardened with determination, the protective instinct of the alpha wolf rising within him. "You are Ciara, the moon's chosen, my chosen. Your strength is beyond measure. Our pups will be born under the blessing of the moon, and they will thrive because they are ours."

As the night deepened, Ciara's contractions began, each one a rolling wave that brought them closer to the moment their lives would change forever. Falcon was a constant presence, his strength her anchor, his voice a soothing balm that guided her through the pain and the fear.

Hours passed, each marked by the steady beat of two hearts becoming seven. And when the first cries of their newborns filled the pack house, the world held its breath. Falcon watched in wonder as Ciara tenderly cleaned each pup, nuzzling them close to her warmth. They were perfect, each a unique blend of their parents, with fur as soft as the night and eyes that sparkled like the stars.

As dawn approached, painting the sky with hues of pink and gold, Falcon stepped outside the den, his chest swelling with pride. The pack had gathered, sensing the arrival of the new members, their eyes bright with curiosity and joy.

"We have been blessed," Falcon announced, his voice carrying through the trees. "Ciara has given birth to five healthy pups, heirs to the Dark Moon pack."

A chorus of howls rose in celebration, a symphony of life and unity that echoed through the forest. Falcon's heart swelled with love for Ciara and their children, for the pack that stood by them, and for the life they had built together.

As he returned to the den, the first rays of sunlight spilled over the threshold, bathing his family in a golden glow. Ciara was resting, her body curled protectively around their slumbering pups. Falcon lay down beside her, his body a shield against the world, his spirit entwined with hers.

In the quiet of the morning, with the promise of a new day on the horizon, Falcon and Ciara shared a look of profound understanding. They were more than mates, more than parents. They were the embodiment of the pack's heart, the keepers of its future.

And as the pups stirred, their tiny whimpers a testament to the life force that coursed through their veins, Falcon and Ciara knew that they would face any challenge, overcome any obstacle, for they were bound by love, by destiny, and by the unbreakable bond of family.

Under a full moon's ethereal glow, in the heart of the enchanted forest, lived a pack of extraordinary werewolves. They were no ordinary wolves, for their spirits danced through moonlit nights, their primal instincts guided by love. Falcon and Ciara, the alpha pair, ruled with compassion and strength. Blessed with five beautiful pups, their love story unfolded like a fairytale, forever etched in the tapestry of their pack.

The firstborn, a handsome and courageous boy named Asher, inherited his father's piercing blue eyes and rugged charm. Possessing an unmatched love for adventure, Asher was always the first to lead his siblings into the heart of the wilderness. His playful spirit brought joy to the pack, and his bravery made him a natural leader.

Next came Willow, a spirited and compassionate girl, her caramel curls cascading like a waterfall. She had her mother's gentle touch, healing both body and soul. With a heart full of empathy, Willow embraced the wounded and offered solace to anyone in need. Her soothing presence brought harmony to their pack, and her wise counsel earned her siblings' admiration.

The middle child, Orion, exuded an aura of mystery and wisdom beyond his tender years. With sleek black fur and piercing green eyes, he embodied the elegance of his ancestors. Often found deep in thoughts, Orion swiftly understood the complexities of the world. His untamed curiosity made him an avid seeker of knowledge, unraveling the ancient secrets that lay hidden within the forest.

Between Willow and Orion was Luna, the epitome of grace and beauty. Her silver coat shimmered under the moon's tender caress, captivating all who beheld her. Luna had an enchanting voice, her melodious howls resonating through the night, harmonizing with the spirits of the forest. Her charming presence, both ethereal and mesmerizing, left all those in her wake spellbound.

Finally, was Aurora, the youngest and most mischievous of the pack. Her snow-white fur sparkled under the moonlight, reflecting her playful and free-spirited nature. Aurora's infectious laughter echoed through the trees, bringing joy to everyone around her. Her boundless energy and mischievous pranks reminded the pack of the joy that could always be found, even in the darkest of times.

Together, the five pups of Falcon and Ciara embodied the unity and strength of their pack. Each had unique qualities that complemented one another, forming an unbreakable bond that surpassed the realms of sisterhood and brotherhood. Their destinies intertwined, and their hearts beat in harmony, ready to face life's challenges and embark on a remarkable journey of self-discovery and love.

Little did they know that their lives were about to take an unexpected turn, for the enchanted forest held secrets yet to unfold. Ancient prophecies whispered through the rustling leaves, and an unforeseen danger lurked in the shadows. But amidst the uncertainties, a love that transcended werewolf comprehension stood as their guiding light.

As night turned into day, and the moon began its descent, the pups of Falcon and Ciara embarked on an extraordinary adventure. Their hearts, entwined by an unbreakable bond, were about to face unimaginable trials and pleasures. Within the depths of their souls, the flames of love burned brightly, igniting a mesmerizing tale of romance, destiny, and the power of a pack united.

As the cool morning sun stretched its golden rays through the forest, the pups of Falcon and Ciara began their day like any other, filled with boundless energy and playful antics. Little did they know their lives would soon be forever changed by the arrival of a mysterious stranger.

It was during their usual exploration of the distant borders that they stumbled upon a young wolf, wounded, and lost. His jet-black fur was matted with dirt, and his amber eyes flickered with a mix of fear and longing. Without hesitation, the compassionate Willow approached him, sensing his fragility.

"Are you lost?" she gently inquired, her voice carrying the tender melody of care.

The stranger's gaze met Willow's, and in that moment, a connection sparked between them. He introduced himself as Kieran, a lone wolf seeking refuge from his own troubled past. Kieran's presence ignited a curiosity within Luna, her silver eyes glimmering with intrigue.

Orion, with his wise demeanor, sensed something peculiar about Kieran. He believed this encounter had a deeper significance; an act of fate woven into the very fabric of their lives. With his keen intuition, Orion encouraged his siblings to embrace this newfound alliance, for he sensed that their paths were meant to intertwine.

As days turned into weeks, the bond between the five pups and Kieran grew stronger. In their shared adventures, laughter rang through the forest, and each pup discovered new depths within themselves. Asher found solace in Kieran's unwavering loyalty, bridging the gap between strength and vulnerability.

Aurora, ever the mischievous spirit, found a kindred soul in Kieran's playful nature. Their laughter echoed harmoniously, creating music that filled the forest and rose up to the heavens. Together, they unlocked a joy within themselves that knew no bounds.

But it was in the moonlit nights that Willow and Kieran's connection deepened further. The soft glow of the moon cast a spell upon them, and Willow realized that her healing touch could mend not only flesh but also the broken pieces of a wounded heart. With Kieran, she discovered a love so profound it transcended the physical realm, intertwining their souls in a mesmerizing dance of trust and affection.

Luna, with her ethereal presence, could not deny the growing stir within her. In Kieran's company, she felt her inner voice harmonize with his, their thoughts becoming a symphony of shared desires and dreams. Their connection was one rooted in a bond that went beyond what words could express, and it ignited a warmth within Luna's luminous heart.

In the heart of the enchanted forest, a love story unfolded, encapsulating the essence of romance, passion, and the undying bonds of a pack. Together, the five pups of Falcon and Ciara, alongside Kieran, embarked on a journey filled with trials and tribulations. Their love would be evaluated, and secrets of the past would appear, but their devotion to each other would remain unyielding.

Little did they know that their fates were intricately entwined, woven by the ancient magic that coursed through their veins. As the moon rose higher with each passing night, it whispered prophecies of their destinies, unveiling a future where love would conquer darkness and unity would triumph over despair.

In the mystical realm of werewolves, a romance blossomed, captivating their hearts, and captivating the very essence of their existence. Will their bonds withstand the tests that await them? Only time, the true orchestrator of destiny, would reveal the answers as their tale continued to unfold under the watchful gaze of the moon.

In the mystical lands of Silverwood Forest, under the glowing moon and twinkling stars, the legacy of the werewolf pack continued with the five pups of Falcon and Ciara. Born under an auspicious full moon, two boys and three girls appeared, each bearing traits of their mighty parents.

The eldest of the litter, Asher, had a powerful sense of leadership and an unwavering spirit. His piercing amber eyes held the wisdom of the ages, a trait inherited from his father, Falcon, the revered Alpha of the pack. Eager to prove himself, Asher took his role as the future leader of the pack seriously, always looking out for his siblings and ensuring their safety.

Next in line was Orion, with his charming personality and mischievous grin that never failed to capture the attention of others. Unlike his brother, Orion preferred diplomacy over dominance, often mediating disputes within the pack with his silver tongue. His deep blue eyes shimmered with an air of mystery, hinting at the secrets he held close to his heart.

Among the three sisters, the firstborn was Willow, named after the moon, itself. With her silvery fur and gentle nature, she was adored by all who knew her. Willow had a special gift for healing, inherited from her mother, Ciara, who had been known for her nurturing spirit. Her presence brought comfort to those in need, her gentle howls echoing throughout the forest as a beacon of hope.

Following Willow was Luna, known for her fiery temper and determination. Her vibrant green eyes mirrored the lush foliage of the forest, while her untamed spirit was a force to be reckoned with. Ivy held a deep connection to the earth and its secrets, often disappearing into the depths of the forest to commune with nature and draw strength the ancient trees.

Last but certainly not least was Aurora, the youngest of the litter, whose golden fur shimmered like the sun's breaking through the canopy above. Aurora had a gift for prophecy, her eyes reflecting visions of the future that she could not yet fully grasp Despite her youth, her insights were valued by the pack, for they held a promise of what was yet to come.

As the five siblings navigated the trials and tribulations of growing up in the pack, they discovered that the bond between them was unbreakable, a bond forged not only by blood but by shared experiences and a deep love for one another. Together, they would face challenges and adversaries, theories intertwined like the roots of the ancient trees that watched over them, their hearts beating as one in the rhythm of the forest. And amid the shadows and moonlit nights of Silverwood Forest, the tale of the five pups of Falcon and Ciara would be etched into the history of the werewolf pack, a story of love, loyalty, and the enduring power of family.

As the seasons changed and the pups grew stronger, they embarked on a journey of self-discovery, each embracing their unique gifts and learning to harness the untapped potential within them. Asher honed his leadership skills, earning the respect of the pack with his unwavering dedication and unwavering sense of justice. Orion, with his gift of diplomacy, forged alliances with neighboring packs and navigated the delicate balance of power in the forest.

Willow's healing abilities flourished, her gentle touch bringing solace to those in pain and suffering. Luna's connection to the earth deepened, allowing her to tap into the ancient energies of the forest and channel them into strength and resilience. Meanwhile, Aurora's visions grew clearer, offering glimpses of both promise and peril, guiding the pack through times of uncertainty.

Together, the five siblings stood as a formidable force, their unity a testament to the strength of family ties. Their bond was unbreakable, a shield against the dangers that lurked in the shadows of the forest. But as whispers of an ancient prophecy began to surface, foretelling a time of profound change and upheaval, the pups knew that their true test was yet to come.

Under the watchful gaze of the moon, the pack faced challenges that evaluated their resolve and unity. Dark forces threatened to divide them, and new alliances were forged to combat a common enemy. Through it all, the siblings stood side by side, their loyalty unwavering, their love for each other a beacon of hope in the darkness.

As the ultimate battle loomed on the horizon, the five pups of Falcon and Ciara knew that their destinies were entwined with the fate of the pack. Together, they would fight not just for survival, but for the future of their kind. And as the moon rose high in the sky, casting its silver glow over the forest, the legacy of the five siblings would be written in the stars, a tale of courage, sacrifice, and the enduring power of love.

Deep within the heart of Silverwood Forest, a sense of foreboding lingered in the air as the pack braced themselves for the impending storm. The ancient prophecy whispered of a great test that would find the fate of their kind, a test that would challenge the very fabric of their existence.

As the siblings rallied their packmates, Asher's voice rang out with authority, his eyes blazing with determination. Orion stood by his side, calm and collected, his words soothing the frayed nerves of the younger wolves. Willow tended to the wounded with gentle care, her healing touch a source of solace during chaos. Luna prowled the perimeter, alert and ready to defend their territory with fierce loyalty. And Aurora, her golden eyes ablaze with the fire of prophecy, offered guidance and foresight to guide their actions.

The night of the confrontation arrived, shrouded in darkness and uncertainty. The enemy lurked in the shadows, their howls echoing ominously through the trees. As the pack stood poised for battle, the five siblings shared a silent moment of solidarity, their bond unspoken but unbreakable.

The clash was fierce and unforgiving, the sound of snarls and claws clashing filling the night air. The pack fought with valor and determination. Their spirits united in a common cause. Asher led the charge, his strength and courage inspiring those around him. Orion negotiated alliances and strategies with tactical precision, turning the tide of battle in their favor. Luna's healing powers kept the pack in fighting shape, her presence a beacon of hope in the chaos.

Luna's connection to the earth bolstered their defenses, the roots and vines responding to her command to entangle their enemies and hold them at bay. And Aurora, with her prophetic visions, guided their movements and expected the enemy's next move, giving the pack a crucial edge in the heat of battle.

As the moon reached its zenith, casting a silvery glow over the battlefield, the tide turned in favor of the pack. Their unity and determination proved stronger than any force of darkness, their bond forged in blood and love unyielding in the face of adversity.

And when the dust settled and the victorious howls of the pack filled the night, the five pups of Falcon and Ciara stood together, their hearts full of pride and gratitude for the strength they found in each other. Their story, of courage, sacrifice, and unwavering love, would be told for generations to come, a testament to the enduring legacy of the werewolf pack of Silverwood Forest.

Chapter 17: *Moonlit Encounter*

In the mysterious realm of Silvermoon Forest, where the moon cast a soft glow over the towering trees, Luna, a young and spirited werewolf, roamed freely beneath the starlit sky. With her sleek silver fur and piercing amber eyes, she moved with a grace that was unmatched, her howls echoing through the night.

Among the pack, Luna stood out not only for her beauty but also for her fierce independence. She had always been drawn to the edges of the forest, yearning for something more than the confines of her pack's territory. It was on one night, as she followed a trail of moonlight deeper into the woods, that she stumbled upon Maximus.

Maximus was a formidable werewolf, his dark fur gleaming in the moonlight as he moved with a confidence that matched Luna's own. His piercing green eyes bore into hers, and for a moment, time seemed to stand still. There was a spark between them, a connection that went beyond words.

As they circled each other, a mixture of curiosity and desire swirling in the air, Luna could not help but be drawn to Maximus. He was unlike any wolf she had ever seen, his strength matched only by his tenderness. In his presence, she felt a sense of belonging she had never experienced before.

As they continued to dance beneath the moon, their movements fluid and dual, Luna felt her heart opening to Maximus in a way she had never thought possible. He saw her for who she truly was, fierce and wild, yet longing for a love that was as deep as the ocean.

Their connection deepened as they roamed the forest together, their bond growing stronger with each passing day. Luna and Maximus became inseparable, their love blossoming like the flowers that the forest floor. But as the moon waxed and waned, a shadow loomed over their newfound happiness.

A rival pack, envious of the connection Luna and Maximus shared, looked to tear them apart. Led by a cunning alpha determined to claim Luna as his own, they launched an attack on Maximus, hoping to drive a wedge between the two lovers.

But Luna, fiercely protective of her mate, stood by Maximus's side, her claws bared and her fangs gleaming. Together, they fought off their attackers, their love serving as a shield against the darkness that threatened to consume them.

In the aftermath of the battle, as the moon shone down upon, Luna and Maximus stood united, their love stronger than ever before. With their hearts intertwined and their souls entwined, they that nothing could ever come between them.

And as they howled at the moon in unison, their voices blending in a symphony of love and longing, Luna and Maximus knew that they were destined to be together, forever bound by the enduring power of their love.

As the seasons changed and the moon cycled through its phases, Luna and Maximus's love only deepened, growing with each passing day. They explored every hidden corner of the forest together, their paw-prints marking a path of shared memories and cherished moments.

Their bond transcended the boundaries of their werewolf existence. Luna found solace in Maximus's strength, his unwavering support grounding her in moments of doubt. In turn, Maximus reveled in Luna's fierce independence, her spirit inspiring him to reach greater heights.

One night, under the silvery glow of the full moon, Maximus led Luna to a tranquil clearing bathed in moonlight. With a glint in his emerald eyes, he lowered himself onto one knee, his gaze never leaving Luna's mesmerizing amber eyes.

"Luna," Maximus began, his voice a low rumble that resonated deep within her soul. "From the moment I laid eyes on you, I knew you were destined to be my mate. Will you do me the honor of becoming my Luna, the queen of my heart and the light of my life?"

Tears of joy glistened in Luna's eyes as she nodded vigorously, unable to form words through the overwhelming emotion coursing through her. Maximus stepped forward, a wolfish grin spreading across his face as he gently slid a delicate silver band onto Luna's outstretched paw.

In that moment, surrounded by the gentle symphony of the forest and the watchful gaze of the moon above, Luna and Maximus pledged their love to each other in a vow as ancient and eternal as time itself.

From that day forward, Luna and Maximus ruled the Silvermoon Forest with grace and strength, their love a beacon of hope and unity for all the werewolves who called the forest home. Together, they faced every challenge, every triumph, hand in paw, knowing that if they had each other, they could conquer anything.

And as they gazed up at the moon, their hearts intertwined and their souls ablaze with a love that defied all odds, Luna knew that she had found not only her mate in Maximus but also her truest companion, her fiercest protector, and her greatest love.

As time passed and their love continued to flourish, Luna and Maximus found themselves facing a new challenge that evaluated the very core of their bond. A darkness encroached upon the Silvermoon Forest, a malevolent force that threatened to tear apart everything they held dear.

Whispers of an ancient curse spread through the forest, causing unrest among the werewolf packs. Luna and Maximus knew they had to act swiftly to protect their home and their love from the impending danger.

With unwavering determination, Luna and Maximus embarked on a quest to unravel the mystery of the curse. They traversed through hidden caverns and treacherous terrain, their bond growing stronger with each obstacle they overcame together.

Their journey led them to the heart of the forest, where they discovered a long-forgotten relic that held the key to breaking the curse. With a mixture of courage and love guiding their every step, Luna and Maximus set out to undo the darkness that threatened to consume their world.

In a climactic battle against the malevolent force, Luna and Maximus fought side by side, their unity and love radiating like a beacon of hope in the face of adversity. With a final, powerful surge of energy, they shattered the curse, releasing the forest from its grip and restoring peace once more.

Embraced by the forest's renewed tranquility, Luna and Maximus stood together at the edge of the clearing, their eyes locked in a silent exchange that spoke volumes of the trials they had overcome and the love that had sustained them through it all.

The moon hung high in the night sky, casting a silvery glow over the dense forest that surrounded the territories of the Dark Moon pack and the Blue Twilight pack. Luna, a young werewolf from the Dark Moon pack, moved silently through the underbrush, her keen senses alert to any danger that might lurk nearby. She was the daughter of Falcon and Ciara, the Alpha, and Luna of the Dark Moon pack, and she carried herself with the grace and strength befitting her lineage.

As Luna patrolled the borders of her pack's territory, her thoughts drifted to the Blue Twilight pack, their long-standing rivals. She had heard stories of their Alpha's son, Maximus, a powerful and enigmatic werewolf whose reputation preceded him. Maximus was the son of Amber and Onyx, the Alpha, and Luna of the Blue Twilight pack, and he was said to be a formidable warrior with a heart as fierce as his loyalty to his pack.

Despite their packs' long history of conflict, Luna could not help but feel a curious pull towards Maximus. She had never met him in person, but his name whispered through the trees like a tantalizing promise, stirring something deep within her soul. She wondered what he was like, whether he shared her desire for peace between their packs, or if he was as fierce and unyielding as the stories claimed.

As Luna rounded a bend in the forest trail, her sharp ears caught the sound of footsteps approaching. She tensed, ready to defend her territory against any intruders, but her muscles relaxed when she saw Maximus appear from the shadows, his dark eyes meeting hers with a mixture of surprise and curiosity.

"Maximus," Luna greeted him, her voice soft but steady. "What brings you to the borders of the Dark Moon pack's territory?"

Maximus studied Luna with a gaze that seemed to strip away the layers of her defenses, baring her soul to his scrutiny. His voice was deep and resonant as he replied, "I come in peace, Luna. I wish to speak with you and your Alpha about forging a truce between our packs. The bloodshed has gone on for too long, and I believe it is time for us to find a way to coexist in harmony."

Luna's heart quickened at Maximus's words, her pulse thrumming with a mixture of hope and trepidation. Would it be possible, she wondered, that their packs could set aside their differences and embrace a new era of cooperation and understanding? The idea filled her with a sense of longing she could not name, a yearning for something she had never dared to dream of before.

"We will need to discuss this with my parents," Luna said, her voice steady despite the tumult of emotions swirling within her. "But I believe that peace is possible, Maximus. Let us meet with Alpha Falcon and Luna Ciara and see if we can find a way forward together."

Maximus's eyes softened with a glimmer of warmth and respect as he nodded in agreement. "Thank you, Luna. I look forward to speaking with your parents and beginning the process of healing the rift between our packs. Perhaps, in time, we can even find a way to bridge the gap between our hearts."

As Luna and Maximus turned to make their way back to the Dark Moon pack's territory, the moonlight bathed them in its ethereal glow, casting their shadows together in a dance of light and darkness. In that moment, as their paths converged under the watchful eye of the moon, Luna felt a spark of connection ignite between them, a bond that transcended the boundaries of their packs and unite them in a destiny neither could have foreseen.

Little did they know that their meeting was only the beginning of a love story that would defy the odds and evaluate the limits of their courage and loyalty. For Luna and Maximus were fated to embark on a journey that would challenge their beliefs, their passions, and their very identities as werewolves bound by tradition and duty.

In the days that followed their first meeting at the border between their packs, Luna and Maximus found themselves drawn to each other with an irresistible force that neither could deny. They met in secret, stealing moments away from their duties and responsibilities to explore the burgeoning connection that simmered between them like a hidden flame waiting to be ignited.

As they walked through the forest, their voices mingling with the rustle of leaves and the whisper of the wind, Luna and Maximus spoke of their hopes and dreams, their fears and doubts laid bare in the quiet intimacy of their shared conversations. They discovered that they had more in common than they had ever imagined, their hearts beating in unison with a rhythm that echoed the ancient bond between their packs.

Maximus revealed the depths of his longing for a world where werewolves could live in peace and harmony, free from the shackles of centuries-old animosities and rivalries. Luna, in turn, shared her vision of a future where love could conquer hatred, where unity could triumph over division, and where the moon's gentle light could illuminate a path towards reconciliation and understanding.

Their bond deepened with each passing day, growing stronger and more profound as they navigated the challenges and obstacles that threatened to tear them apart. They faced opposition from within their packs, where old wounds still festered and bitter memories lingered like shadows in the night. They confronted their own doubts and insecurities, grappling with the weight of expectations and the fear of the unknown that lay ahead.

But through it all, Luna and Maximus clung to each other with a fierce determination and unwavering faith in the power of their love to transcend the boundaries that looked to divide them. They found solace in each other's arms, strength in each other's words, and courage in each other's unwavering belief that together, they could overcome any obstacle and defy any fate that dared to stand in their way.

One night, as the moon rose high in the sky, casting its silvery light over the forest like a blanket of stars, Luna and Maximus stood at the edge of a cliff overlooking the vast expanse of their territories. The night air was cool and crisp, the scent of pine and earth mingling with the heady fragrance of their shared desire.

"I love you, Maximus," Luna whispered, her voice soft but sure. "I love you with all of my heart and soul, with every fiber of my being. I believe in us, in our love, in the future we can build together."

Maximus turned to face Luna, his eyes reflecting the moon's gentle glow with a luminous intensity that took her breath away. "And I love you, Luna," he replied, his voice a low and steady cadence that echoed through the night. "I love you more than words can say, more than the stars can count, more than the moon can witness. You are my heart, my soul, my everything."

In that moment, as their gazes locked and their hearts beat as one, Luna and Maximus knew that they were meant to be together, that their love was a force of nature that could not be denied or had. They embraced each other with a passion that burned like a wildfire, their bodies entwined in a dance of love and longing that transcended time and space.

And as they stood on the edge of the cliff, their souls intertwined in a bond that would never be broken, Luna and Maximus leaped into the unknown together, their love guiding them towards a future filled with hope, promise, and the eternal light of the moon that would forever illuminate their path.

As the night whispered its secrets to the wind and the forest echoed with the promise of a new dawn, Luna and Maximus walked side by side, their hearts beating in sync with the rhythm of a love that would forever change the course of their lives and the fate of their packs.

As they turned their gazes skyward to the moon, its soft light illuminating their intertwined forms, Luna and Maximus knew that their love was an unbreakable bond, forged in the fires of adversity and strengthened by their unwavering commitment to each other.

And as they howled in unison, their voices blending in a harmonious melody that echoed throughout the forest, Luna and Maximus understood that their love story was etched in the stars above, a timeless tale of two souls united in love, destined to roam the Silvermoon Forest together for all eternity.

Chapter 18: *Moonlit Desires*

The moon hung low in the velvety sky, casting a soft glow over the dense forest. Its ethereal light filtered through the towering trees, illuminating the hidden secrets that lay within. Amongst the shadows, a young woman named Willow found herself standing at the edge of clearing, her heart pounding with a mixture of fear and anticipation.

Willow was a woman of unparalleled beauty, with cascading chestnut locks that framed her delicate face and eyes as deep as the ocean. Her porcelain skin seemed to glow under the moon's gentle touch, and her slender figure was accentuated by the flowing white dress that clung to her every curve. But beneath her captivating appearance, she hid a secret that had plagued her since birth - a secret that would soon be revealed under the watchful gaze of the moon.

As the night grew darker, a haunting howl echoed through the forest, sending shivers down Willow's spine. She knew that the time had come for her to embrace her true nature, to shed the shackles that had held her back for far too long. For Willow was not just an ordinary woman; she was a werewolf, a creature of the night destined to roam the wilderness under the moon's enchantment.

With a deep breath, Willow closed her eyes and let the moon's energy flow through her veins. She felt a surge of power coursing through her body, awakening the dormant beast within. Slowly, her werewolf form began to change, her bones shifting and stretching as fur sprouted from her skin. Within moments, Willow stood before the world as a magnificent creature, a wolf with fur as black as the night itself.

As she embraced her newfound form, Willow's senses heightened, allowing her to perceive the world in a way she had never experienced before. The scent of the forest filled her nostrils, the rustling leaves whispered secrets in her ears, and the distant hoot of an owl became a symphony in her lupine heart. She was no longer bound by the limitations of her werewolf self; she was free to explore the wilderness, to run with the wind, and to follow her heart's desires.

But amidst the exhilaration of her transformation, Willow could not help but feel a pang of loneliness. She longed for a companion who would understand her dual nature, someone who would love her unconditionally, both as a woman and as a wolf. She yearned for a love that transcended the boundaries of the ordinary, a love that would ignite her soul and set her ablaze.

Little did Willow know that fate had a plan in store for her. As she ventured deeper into the forest, her heightened senses led her to a clearing bathed in moonlight. And there, standing before her, was a werewolf unlike any she had ever seen. His fur was a rich shade of silver, shimmering under the moon's gentle caress. His eyes, a mesmerizing shade of amber, held a depth that mirrored her own.

In that moment, Willow knew that she had found her kindred spirit, her soulmate. Their eyes locked, and an unspoken connection formed between them, transcending the boundaries of language. It was a connection that spoke of a love that had been written in the stars, a love that would defy the odds and conquer all obstacles.

As they circled each other in the moonlit clearing, their hearts beat in perfect synchrony. With every step, they drew closer, until finally, their bodies intertwined in an enthusiastic embrace. In that moment, the world around them faded away, leaving only their love and the moon as their witness.

Willow had finally found the missing piece of her soul, the one who would accept her for who she truly was. Together, they would embark on a journey of love and self-discovery, embracing their dual nature and defying the norms of society. For in the realm of werewolves, where the moon's magic reigns supreme, true love knows no boundaries.

And so, under the moon's watchful gaze, Willow and her soulmate embarked on a love story that would forever be etched in the annals of werewolf lore. Their love would be a beacon of hope for all those who dared to embrace their true selves, reminding them that in the face of adversity, love would always prevail.

As the moon continued its celestial dance, Willow and her soulmate reveled in the passion and freedom that their love brought. Together, they would navigate the challenges that lay ahead, their hearts forever intertwined in a love that would transcend time itself. For in the realm of werewolves, where love and destiny intertwine, anything is possible.

The moon hung low in the velvety night sky, casting a luminous glow over the dense forest. Willow could feel her heartbeat quicken as she ventured deeper into the mystical wilderness. Her hazel eyes darted around nervously, unsure of what awaited her. She had heard the rumors, the enchanting whispers of a pack of werewolves that roamed this very forest.

Marco, a ruggedly handsome man with piercing blue eyes and an air of mystery, appeared by her side. The allure of the unknown drew him here, his heart yearning for adventure. He had an unwavering determination to explore what lay beyond the boundaries of ordinary life. Willow and Marco had been inexplicably drawn together; their souls entwined in a web of fate.

Their path led them to a clearing bathed in moonlight, the sacred meeting place of the werewolf pack. The ancient magic saturated the air, enchanting their senses. Amongst the trees, the sound of rustling leaves echoed, captivating their attention. A chill ran down Willow's spine, while Marco stood firm, his curiosity unyielding.

Suddenly, a figure appeared from the shadows. Jackson, the leader of the pack, had an undeniable aura of power. His emerald-green eyes held a wisdom beyond his years, conveying a sense of responsibility that came with leading the pack. Willow's heart skipped a beat as their gazes met, a silent recognition passing between them. Marco watched intently, his heart stirring with a mixture of jealousy and intrigue.

As they drew closer, Willow felt a magnetic pull, an inexplicable connection that bound her to Jackson's very soul. His touch sent tingles dancing along her skin, awakening a dormant desire she had long buried. Marco's eyes darkened with a flicker of jealousy; his protective instincts stirred by this undeniable chemistry.

The moon reached its zenith, casting an ethereal glow upon them all. Willow's heart pounded in her chest as she voiced the question burning within her. "Are you truly werewolves?"

Jackson smiled knowingly, his voice carrying a comforting warmth. "Indeed, Willow. We are bound by the moon's whims, shifting between two forms. Our lives are intertwined with nature's embrace, and love binds us even stronger."

The realization washed over Willow like a tidal wave crashing upon the shore. She had stumbled upon a world filled with mythical creatures, where love knew no boundaries. Marco, though hesitant, could not ignore the intensity of their connection. He understood that sometimes the heart chose its own path, oblivious to logic and reason.

Willow found herself torn between two worlds. Her love and loyalty to Marco was undeniable, but the pull of the werewolf pack tugged at her very core. Jackson's eyes held the promise of a love she had never known, a love that would transcend time and shape-shifted forms.

As the moon began its descent, Willow made her decision. She took a step towards Jackson, her heart aching for both men who had captured her soul. With tears glistening in her eyes, she whispered, "I choose to embrace the magic that lies within the depths of your world. Together, we shall defy the odds and create a love story that will be whispered by generations to come."

In that moment, a bond formed, intertwining their destinies. Willow, Marco, and the werewolf pack would face trials and tribulations, but their love would persist, like an everlasting flame in the darkness.

Little did they know their embrace of the unknown would unleash a centuries-old prophecy, setting in motion a chain of events that would evaluate the strength of their love and the very fabric of their existence.

Willow's decision sent ripples of change throughout the forest, awakening ancient energies that had long remained dormant. The moon, witness to their love and the choices they made, cast a guiding light upon their path.

As Willow delved deeper into the werewolf pack, she discovered a hidden world of untold secrets. Timeless rituals and sacred traditions unfolded before her eyes, revealing a rich tapestry of history and heritage. Each member of the pack had their own unique story, their lives intertwined in a delicate balance.

Amidst this enchanting backdrop, Willow found herself navigating the complexities of her relationships with both Jackson and Marco. She treasured the love she shared with Marco, for it was pure and familiar, built upon a foundation of trust and shared experiences. But her connection with Jackson held an otherworldly allure, rooted in destiny and passion beyond mortal comprehension.

Marco, torn by his love for Willow, struggled to come to terms with his own emotions. Though he longed for her happiness more than anything else, the ache of losing her became an ever-present ache that plagued his heart. He watched in anguish as Willow and Jackson grew closer, their bond strengthening with each passing day.

As the moon waxed and waned, Willow sensed a darkness lurking in the shadows. Strange occurrences unfurled, threatening not only her newfound love but also the entire pack. Whispers of an ancient curse echoed through the forest, conjuring images of danger and peril. Willow, with her unwavering determination, vowed to uncover the truth and protect those she held dear.

She sought solace in the wisdom of the pack's elder, Abigail. With her sage guidance, Willow embarked on a journey of self-discovery. Through ancient texts and whispered prophecies, she unearthed a truth that sent shivers down her spine. The curse, woven through the ages, held the power to tear apart their love and plunge the pack into eternal darkness.

Determined to break the curse and save her loved ones, Willow marshaled her courage. She enlisted Marco's unwavering support, for his love for her knew no bounds. Together, they embarked on a quest, their hearts beating in unison, fueled by their undying love.

Across treacherous terrain and into the heart of forbidden territory, Willow and Marco forged ahead. In their darkest moments, their love proved to be a guiding light, warding off the encroaching shadows. They met mystical beings, faced daunting challenges, but their unwavering devotion remained unyielding.

Through their trials, Willow uncovered the key to breaking the curse—a sacrificial act of pure love that would rewrite their destinies. Love, the most potent of all magic, would be the catalyst for their salvation.

Armed with this newfound knowledge, Willow returned to the pack. She stood before them, her resolve unwavering. With conviction in her voice, she outlined the path forward, inspiring hope and unity. The pack rallied behind her, ready to battle the encroaching darkness and reclaim their future.

In the face of adversity, Willow, Marco, and the werewolf pack stood united, their love fortified by the knowledge that together they were stronger than any curse or darkness that dared to challenge them. And as the moon shone brightly above, illuminating their path forward, they embraced their intertwined fates, ready to face the unknown with hearts ablaze.

Little did they know that their love story would forever be etched in the annals of werewolf lore, a testament to the power of love, sacrifice, and the indomitable spirit within each one of them.

Chapter 19: *Moonlit Embrace*

The forest was alive with a symphony of night sounds as Athena, Amber and Onyx's daughter traversed through the dense undergrowth. Her heart pounded in her chest as she pushed through the brush, her senses heightened by the pull of the full moon hanging low in the sky. She could feel the change coming, the familiar ache that signaled the shift from her human form to that of her true self—a werewolf.

Athena, Amber, and Onyx's daughter had always known she was different from others. From an early age, she had felt a connection to the wild, a yearning for the freedom of the night and the call of the moon. Raised by a pack of werewolves deep in the heart of the forest, Athena, Amber, and Onyx's daughter had long ago accepted her dual nature and embraced the power that lay dormant within her.

As she ran through the forest, her fur bristling with the thrill of the hunt, Athena, Amber, and Onyx's daughter could sense a presence nearby. A scent on the wind caught her attention—a musky, earthy aroma that spoke of another of her kind. Instinctively, she slowed her pace and crept forward, her senses on high alert.

Through the dense foliage, Athena, Amber, and Onyx's daughter caught a glimpse of silver fur shimmering in the moonlight. A male werewolf stood before her, his gaze intense and unwavering. Athena, Amber, and Onyx's daughter felt a jolt of recognition as their eyes met, a spark of something ancient and primal that stirred deep within her.

The male werewolf stepped forward, his powerful muscles rippling beneath his fur as he closed the distance between them. Athena, Amber, and Onyx's daughter could feel the heat of his body, the raw energy of his presence sending a shiver down her spine. She knew instantly that he was different from any other werewolf she had met before.

"Who are you?" Athena, Amber, and Onyx's daughter's voice was hoarse with emotion, her eyes locked with his in an unspoken challenge.

"I am Fenris," the male werewolf replied, his voice deep and resonant. "And you, Athena, Amber and Onyx's daughter, are the most beautiful creature I have ever laid eyes on."

Athena, Amber, and Onyx's daughter felt her heart skip a beat at his words, a rush of warmth flooding through her as she gazed into Fenris's piercing gaze. In that moment, she knew that her life would never be the same—that this encounter in the moonlit forest was the beginning of a love that would transcend time and space.

Fenris reached out a hand, his touch gentle yet electrifying as he traced a finger along Athena, Amber, and Onyx's daughter's jawline. She felt a surge of desire coursing through her veins, a hunger that mirrored his own. Without a word, they learned closer, their lips brushing in a tentative kiss that ignited a firestorm of passion between them.

As the full moon cast its silvery light upon their entwined forms, Athena, Amber, and Onyx's daughter and Fenris surrendered to the primal urge that bound them together. In the heart of the forest, amidst the ancient trees and whispering winds, they found a love that defied all reason and logic—a love that would endure through the ages, unbreakable and eternal.

Their kiss deepened, unleashing a storm of emotions that had long been suppressed within both Athena, Amber, and Onyx's daughter and Fenris. The world around them faded away as they lost themselves in each other, their connection growing stronger with each passing moment. It was as though they had been drawn together by forces beyond their control, destined to find solace and passion in each other's arms.

As the moon continued its ascent in the sky, bathing the forest in a silvery glow, Athena, Amber, and Onyx's daughter and Fenris danced under its light, their movements fluid and graceful. Each touch, each caress ignited a spark between them, binding them closer together in a bond that transcended mere physical desire.

Athena, Amber, and Onyx's daughter felt a sense of completeness that she had never experienced before. With Fenris by her side, she felt whole, as though a missing piece of her soul had finally been found. The fierce intensity of their connection left her breathless, her heart pounding with a mixture of fear and exhilaration.

For Fenris, Athena, Amber and Onyx's daughter was like a vision from a dream—a wild and untamed beauty that captivated his heart and soul. Her strength and resilience drew him in, her fiery spirit a perfect match for his own. He knew deep down that she was the one destined to stand by his side, to share in the trials and triumphs that lay ahead.

As the night wore on, Athena, Amber, Onyx's daughter and Fenris roamed the forest together, reveling in the freedom and wildness of their shared existence. They hunted as one, their instincts honed and synchronized, a seamless dance of predator and prey. In each other's presence, they found a sense of belonging that had eluded them for so long.

As the first light of dawn began to break on the horizon, Athena, Amber, and Onyx's daughter and Fenris knew that their time together was ending. The harsh reality of their world beckoned, pulling them back to the responsibilities and duties they could not ignore.

But as they stood side by side, the bond between them unbreakable, they knew that their love would endure. No matter the challenges they faced, no matter the obstacles in their path, Athena, Amber, and Onyx's daughter and Fenris were united in a love that transcended the boundaries of time and space—a love that would endure for all eternity. And as they watched the sun rise together, their hearts entwined, they knew that their journey was just beginning.

As the sun rose over the horizon, casting a golden hue across the forest, Athena, Amber, and Onyx's daughter and Fenris found themselves standing at the edge of a clearing, their hearts intertwined in a love that defied logic and reason. The world around them seemed to hold its breath, as if in silent awe at the bond that had formed between the two werewolves.

With a heavy heart, Athena, Amber, and Onyx's daughter turned to Fenris, her eyes filled with a mixture of longing and determination. "We must return to our respective packs," she said, her voice filled with quiet resolve. "But know this, Fenris: no matter where we go or what challenges we face, my heart will always belong to you."

Fenris gazed deeply into Athena, Amber, and Onyx's daughter's eyes, his own filled with a fierce intensity that matched her own. "And my heart will always be yours, Athena, Amber and Onyx's daughter," he replied, his voice filled with unwavering conviction. "Together, we are stronger than anything the world can throw at us. Our love will endure, no matter the trials we face."

With a silent understanding that transcended words, Athena, Amber, and Onyx's daughter and Fenris shared one final embrace, their fur brushing against each other in a tender caress. In that moment, time seemed to stand still as they held onto each other, a silent promise passing between them—a promise of love, loyalty, and unwavering support.

And then, with a heavy heart, they turned away from each other, each taking a step back into the depths of the forest. As they disappeared into the shadows, the memory of their moonlit encounter lingered in the air, a bittersweet reminder of the love that had been kindled under the watchful gaze of the moon.

Days turned into weeks, weeks into months, and seasons changed in the forest as Athena, Amber, and Onyx's daughter and Fenris went about their separate lives. But no matter how far apart they were, their hearts remained connected, a bond that could not be broken by time or distance.

And as the moon rose once again in the dark night sky, casting its ethereal light over the forest, Athena, Amber, and Onyx's daughter and Fenris found themselves drawn back to the clearing where their love had first blossomed. Under the watchful gaze of the moon, they reunited, their hearts beating as one, knowing that their love was stronger than any obstacle that fate could throw their way.

In that enchanted forest, where werewolves roamed freely under the light of the moon, Athena, Amber, and Onyx's daughter and Fenris's love endured—a timeless, eternal flame that would burn bright for all eternity. And as they stood together in the moonlit clearing, their howls echoing through the night, they knew that their love was destined to last forevermore.

As the night enveloped them in its embrace, Athena, Amber, and Onyx's daughter and Fenris felt a sense of peace and contentment wash over them. The moon, their silent witness, illuminated the clearing with its gentle glow, casting a spell of magic over the pair of werewolves who stood together once more.

Athena, Amber, and Onyx's daughter reached out a hand to Fenris, her touch light and loving. "I never stopped thinking about you, Fenris," she whispered, her voice soft but filled with emotion. "Our love is a force that cannot be extinguished, no matter how far apart we may be."

Fenris took Athena, Amber, and Onyx's daughter's hand in his own, his eyes locked with hers in a silent promise. "I have carried you in my heart every moment since we parted, Athena, Amber and Onyx's daughter," he replied, his voice filled with a mix of longing and determination. "Together, we are bound by a love that transcends time and space."

In that moment, the world around them seemed to fade away, leaving only the two werewolves standing in the moonlit clearing, their hearts beating as one. It was as if the forest itself recognized the power of their connection, bowing to the strength of their love that defied all odds.

With a renewed sense of purpose and determination, Athena, Amber, and Onyx's daughter and Fenris pledged to stand by each other's side, to face whatever challenges may come their way with unwavering loyalty and steadfast devotion. Their love was a beacon of light in the darkness, guiding them through the trials and tribulations of their world.

As they howled at the moon, their voices rising in perfect harmony, a sense of unity washed over them. They were no longer two lone wolves wandering the forest, but a formidable pair united by a love that had withstood the test of time.

And as the night stretched on, filled with the sounds of the forest and the whispers of the wind, Athena, Amber, and Onyx's daughter and Fenris knew that their love was a rare and precious gift—a gift that they would cherish and protect with all their hearts, for as long as they walked the earth.

Under the watchful gaze of the moon, they danced together in the moonlit clearing, their silhouettes intertwined in a graceful and eternal embrace. And as the night gave way to dawn, they disappeared into the shadows of the forest, their love shining like a beacon in the darkness, forever burning bright in the depths of their werewolf hearts.

Chapter 20: *The Union of Hearts*

In the dense forest of Silverwood, where moonlight filtered through the ancient trees, Pandora roamed freely. Her feet pounded against the soft earth as she ran with effortless grace, her silver fur shining under the glow of the full moon. She was a werewolf, a creature of the night with a wild spirit that roamed the shadows.

Pandora was the Alpha of her pack, a position she had inherited from her father, who had passed it down to her before he vanished under mysterious circumstances. She ruled with strength and wisdom, earning the respect of her fellow werewolves with her fierce loyalty and unwavering courage.

One fateful night, as the moon hung low in the sky, Pandora caught the scent of a stranger in her territory. Intrigued and cautious, she followed the scent until she came upon a clearing where a lone wolf stood, his fur a mix of dark greys and deep blacks.

The stranger was Lucas, son of Clara and Archer, a rogue werewolf with a troubled past. He had wandered aimlessly for years, searching for a place to call home and a pack to belong to. His eyes met Pandora's, and something sparked between them—an unspoken connection that pulled them together like magnets drawn to each other.

The full moon hung low in the night sky, casting a silvery glow over the dense forest. The air was thick with the scent of pine and damp earth, and a sense of anticipation crackled in the air. In the heart of the forest, a lone figure moved gracefully through the shadows, her senses keen and alert.

Pandora Blackwood was a werewolf, a creature of the night with the power to shift between werewolf and wolf form at will. She moved with a fluid grace, her silver fur glinting in the moonlight as she prowled through the undergrowth. Her senses were sharp, picking up the faintest rustle of leaves and the distant hoot of an owl.

As she moved deeper into the forest, Pandora caught a whiff of an unfamiliar scent in the breeze. Intrigued, she followed the scent trail, her heart pounding in her chest. She appeared into a small clearing, where a figure stood waiting for her.

He was tall and lean, with dark hair that fell in unruly waves around his face. His eyes were a piercing shade of blue, and they seemed to see right through her. Pandora felt a shiver run down her spine as she met his gaze, a strange sense of recognition stirring deep within her.

"Who are you?" she asked, her voice low and husky.

The man smiled, a slow, lazy smile that sent a jolt of electricity through her veins. "My name is Lucas, son of Clara and Archer," he said, his voice deep and resonant. "I've been searching for you, Pandora." Pandora's heart skipped a beat at the sound of her name on his lips. She took a step closer to him, her senses reeling with the heady scent of his skin. "Why have you been searching for me?" she asked, her voice barely a whisper.

Lucas, son of Clara and Archer reached out a hand to touch her cheek, his touch gentle and warm. "Because I've been drawn to you, Pandora," he said. "There's something about you that calls to me, something I can't resist." Pandora felt a surge of desire wash over her, her body responding instinctively to his touch. She leaned into his hand, her eyes locked with his, and in that moment, she knew that her life would never be the same again.

In that moment, under the watchful gaze of the moon, Pandora and Lucas, son of Clara and Archer, felt a bond forming between them, a bond that neither could explain but could not ignore. It was as if fate had brought them together, weaving their destinies into an intricate tapestry of love and longing.

As they circled each other, their instincts warred within them. Lucas, son of Clara and Archer was a lone wolf, a drifter used to look out for himself, while Pandora was a fierce Alpha with a pack to protect. But despite their differences, they found themselves drawn to each other, unable to resist the pull of their shared desires.

With a flicker of understanding in her eyes, Pandora approached Lucas, son of Clara and Archer, her movements cautious yet inviting. She could sense the loneliness and pain that lay hidden beneath his rugged exterior, and something in her stirred with compassion and empathy.

Lucas, son of Clara and Archer, too, felt a stirring within him—a longing for connection and belonging that he had never experienced before. As Pandora drew closer, he found himself opening to her, revealing the scars of his past and the yearning in his heart for a place to call home.

In that moment, with the moon as their witness, Pandora and Lucas, son of Clara and Archer embraced, their fur intermingling as they shared a fleeting moment of connection and understanding. It was a moment that would change the course of their lives forever, setting them on a path filled with danger, passion, and untold mysteries waiting to be unraveled.

As the night wore on and the moon reached its zenith, Pandora and Lucas, son of Clara and Archer stood together in the clearing, their hearts beating as one. In the embrace of the night, they had found something rare and precious—a love that defied boundaries and a bond that transcended time and space.

And as the first light of dawn touched the horizon, painting the sky with hues of pink and gold, Pandora and Lucas, son of Clara and Archer knew that their destinies were forever intertwined, bound by a love that would endure through the trials and tribulations that lay ahead.

As the days turned into weeks, Pandora and Lucas, son of Clara and Archer forged a deep and unbreakable bond, their love blossoming like the wildflowers that carpeted the forest floor. They spent their nights exploring the vast expanse of Silverwood, wandering hand in hand through the moonlit groves and hidden glades, their hearts entwined in a dance of passion and mystery.

Pandora introduced Lucas, son of Clara and Archer, to her pack, a loyal and fierce group of werewolves who welcomed him with open arms. At first, Lucas, son of Clara and Archer hesitated, unsure of his place among them, but as he spent more time with the pack and saw their camaraderie and strength, he knew that he had finally found the family he had been searching for.

Under Pandora's guidance, Lucas, son of Clara and Archer embraced his true nature as a werewolf, honing his skills in hunting and tracking, and learning the ancient rituals and customs of their kind. He grew closer to Pandora with each passing day, his love for her deepening with every shared moment and whispered vow.

One night, as the Blood Moon rose high in the sky, casting an ethereal glow over the forest, Pandora and Lucas, son of Clara and Archer stood at the edge of a moonlit lake, its surface shimmering like liquid silver. They had come to this sacred place to make a pact, a solemn vow to each other and to the moon that bound them together in an unbreakable union.

With her eyes shining with determination, Pandora spoke the words of the ancient ritual, her voice carrying the weight of centuries of tradition and devotion. Lucas, son of Clara and Archer listened with reverence, his heart swelling with love and gratitude for the powerful she-wolf standing before him, her fur gleaming in the moon's radiant light.

"I, Pandora, Alpha of the Silverwood pack, vow to protect and cherish you, Lucas, son of Clara and Archer, with all that I am," she declared, her words echoing through the stillness of the night. "Together, under the watchful gaze of the moon, we shall walk this path as one, united in heart and spirit, bound by the threads of destiny that have brought us together."

Lucas, son of Clara and Archer, felt a surge of emotion welling up within him, his eyes locked with Pandora's as he spoke the words of his own vow. "I, Lucas, son of Clara and Archer, pledge my loyalty and love to you, Pandora, for all of eternity," he said, his voice steady and earnest. "With you by my side, I am whole, and together we shall face whatever challenges come our way, secure in the knowledge that our love will guide us through the darkest of nights."

As the last echoes of their vows faded into the night, the Blood Moon shone down upon them, its crimson light bathing them in a divine glow. In that moment, Pandora and Lucas, son of Clara and Archer sealed their pact with a kiss, their souls intertwining in a dance of passion and desire that transcended time and space.

And as they stood together on the shores of the moonlit lake, their hearts beating as one, they knew that their love was written in the stars, destined to burn bright and eternal like the flames that lit up the night sky, a beacon of hope and promise in a world filled with darkness and uncertainty.

Under the watchful gaze of the Blood Moon, Pandora and Lucas, son of Clara and Archer embraced, their love forging a bond that would withstand the trials and tribulations that lay ahead, a love that would endure through the ages, a love that would shine like a beacon in the darkness, guiding them through the shadows and into the light of a new dawn.

As the seasons changed and the moon waxed and waned in the sky, Pandora and Lucas, son of Clara and Archer faced new challenges that evaluated the strength of their bond and the depth of their love. The Silverwood pack thrived under their leadership, united in their loyalty and devotion to their Alpha pair, but danger loomed on the horizon, threatening to disrupt the fragile peace that had settled over the forest.

Rumors of a rival pack encroaching on Silverwood's territory spread like wildfire through the whispering trees, igniting fear and uncertainty among the werewolves. Pandora and Lucas, son of Clara and Archer, knew that they must stand united to protect their pack and defend their home from any who dared to challenge their authority.

Under the cover of darkness, Pandora and Lucas, son of Clara and Archer patrolled the boundaries of Silverwood, their senses alert for any signs of intruders. As they moved through the shadows, their steps silent and sure, they felt the weight of responsibility pressing down upon them, the burden of leadership heavy on their shoulders.

One fateful night, as the moon hung low in the sky, a pack of rogue werewolves appeared from the depths of the forest, their eyes gleaming with malice and hunger. They bore the mark of the Blood Moon, a symbol of their defiance and their thirst for power, and they demanded a challenge to find the rightful rulers of Silverwood.

Pandora and Lucas, son of Clara and Archer stood their ground, their fur bristling with tension as they faced off against the rogue pack. The air crackled with electricity, the tension thick and palpable as the two sides eyed each other warily, each waiting for the other to make the first move.

With a low growl, Pandora stepped forward, her eyes flashing with determination as she spoke with authority. "We will not be swayed by your threats," she declared, her voice firm and unwavering. "Silverwood belongs to us, and we will defend it with our lives if we must."

Lucas, son of Clara and Archer stood by her side, his gaze fixed on the leader of the rogue pack, a formidable werewolf with a scarred face and eyes filled with malice. "We challenge you to a duel," he proclaimed, his voice ringing out through the night. "Winner takes all but know this—we fight not for power or glory, but for the safety and prosperity of our pack."

The rogue leader snarled in response, his lip curling in a vicious sneer as he accepted the challenge. The moonlight cast a silvery sheen over the clearing, illuminating the combatants as they circled each other, ready to engage in a battle that would find the fate of Silverwood and its inhabitants.

As the clash of fangs and claws echoed through the night, Pandora and Lucas, son of Clara and Archer, fought with a fierce determination born of love and loyalty. They moved as one, their movements fluid and precise, their minds and hearts in perfect synchrony as they defended their pack and their home with a strength that could only come from the depths of their souls.

In the heat of battle, as the moon reached its zenith and the stars shimmered overhead, Pandora and Lucas, son of Clara and Archer appeared victorious, their foes vanquished, and their territory secured once more. The rogue pack retreated into the shadows, defeated but not destroyed, their defeat a testament to the unwavering bond that united Pandora and Lucas, son of Clara and Archer in a love that was as fierce as it was enduring.

As they stood together in the aftermath of the battle, their chests heaving with exertion and their fur matted with blood, Pandora and Lucas, son of Clara and Archer knew that they had faced the first of many trials that awaited them on their journey through the wilds of Silverwood. But with their love as their guiding light and their bond as their anchor, they were ready to face whatever challenges came their way, secure in the knowledge that together, they were unstoppable, their hearts beating as one in the dance of the moonlit night.

In the wake of the fierce battle that had evaluated their strength and unity, Pandora and Lucas, son of Clara and Archer, found themselves at a crossroads, their hearts heavy with the weight of the responsibilities that lay upon their shoulders. The threat of the rogue pack still lingered in the shadows, a constant reminder of the dangers that lurked beyond the safety of Silverwood.

As they surveyed the aftermath of the skirmish, Pandora and Lucas, son of Clara and Archer knew that they could not afford to let their guard down, for the whispers of dissent and treachery were already starting to spread among the pack. Rumors of betrayal and treachery gnawed at the edges of their consciousness, threatening to sow discord and division among their loyal followers.

Determined to root out the source of the unrest, Pandora and Lucas, son of Clara and Archer embarked on a quest to uncover the truth behind the whispers that echoed through the forest like a sinister melody. They ventured deep into the heart of Silverwood, their keen senses on high alert as they searched for any signs of deception or subterfuge.

Their journey led them to a secluded glen, hidden from prying eyes by a shimmering waterfall and a canopy of ancient trees. There, they discovered a lone werewolf, a member of their own pack, skulking in the shadows with a furtive gaze and a guilty demeanor.

With a sense of foreboding settling in their hearts, Pandora and Lucas, son of Clara and Archer confronted the rogue werewolf, his eyes widening in fear as they laid bare his betrayal. "Why have you turned against us?" Pandora demanded, her voice a mixture of anger and hurt. "What do you hope to gain by sowing seeds of discord among your own kind?"

The rogue werewolf hung his head in shame, his fur bristling with guilt as he confessed to his actions. "I was tempted by promises of power and influence," he admitted, his voice quivering with remorse. "I was weak, and I succumbed to the whispers of doubt and fear that clouded my judgment."

Pandora's heart ached with sorrow as she listened to his words, her eyes filled with disappointment and compassion. She knew that betrayal was a bitter pill to swallow, but she also knew that forgiveness and redemption were within reach for those who looked to make amends for their mistakes.

Lucas, son of Clara and Archer, stepped forward, his gaze piercing as he spoke with a voice that echoed with authority and conviction. "You have strayed from the path of honor and loyalty, but it is not too late to redeem yourself," he declared, his words a mixture of rebuke and encouragement. "Stand with us, and together we shall overcome the darkness that seeks to divide us."

The rogue werewolf nodded solemnly, his eyes filled with gratitude and resolve as he pledged his loyalty once more to Pandora and Lucas, son of Clara and Archer. With a heavy heart and a renewed sense of purpose, he joined them in their quest to restore peace and harmony to the pack, determined to atone for his past transgressions and earn back the trust of his brethren.

As they stood together in the dappled light of the glen, the water falling like liquid silver around them, Pandora, Lucas, son of Clara and Archer, and their newfound ally knew that the road ahead would be fraught with challenges and obstacles. But with their hearts united in a bond forged by love and loyalty, they were ready to face whatever trials awaited them, secure in the knowledge that together, they were stronger than any force that looked to tear them apart.

And as they made their way back to the heart of Silverwood, their steps light and their spirits lifted, a new sense of purpose filled their hearts, guiding them towards a future filled with hope, healing, and the promise of a brighter tomorrow. In the shadows of the forest, where secrets and whispers intertwined with the rustling leaves, Pandora and Lucas, son of Clara and Archer knew that their love would be their guiding light, shining bright like a beacon in the darkness, illuminating the path that lay ahead.

As the moon hung high in the sky, casting its silver light over the forest, Pandora and Lucas, son of Clara and Archer stood locked in an enthusiastic embrace, their hearts beating as one. In that moment, they knew that they had found in each other a love that would transcend time and space, a love that would endure for all eternity.

The bond between Pandora and Lucas, son of Clara and Archer deepened with each passing day. They spent their nights exploring the forest together, their wolf forms running side by side through the moonlit glades. Their connection was primal and intense, a merging of souls that transcended the boundaries of werewolf understanding.

As the weeks turned into months, Pandora and Lucas, son of Clara and Archer, found themselves drawn to each other in ways they had never imagined. Their love was a force of nature, wild and untamed, like the forest that surrounded them. They shared their hopes and dreams, their fears, and insecurities, laying bare their souls to each other in the quiet of the night.

But not everyone was happy about their burgeoning relationship. The leader of the werewolf pack, a formidable alpha named Fenrir, viewed their union with suspicion and mistrust. He saw Lucas, son of Clara and Archer, as a threat to the pack's hierarchy, a rival for power and dominance.

One fateful night, as the moon hung low in the sky, Fenrir confronted Pandora and Lucas, son of Clara and Archer in the heart of the forest. His eyes blazed with fury as he accused them of betraying their kind, of forsaking the ancient laws that governed their existence. "You have defied the pack, Pandora," Fenrir growled, his voice low and menacing. "You have chosen an outsider over your own kind, a werewolf who has no place among us."

Pandora stood tall and proud, her silver fur bristling with defiance. "Lucas, son of Clara and Archer is not just a werewolf," she said, her voice steady and strong. "He is my mate, my soulmate, and I will not abandon him, no matter the cost." Lucas, son of Clara and Archer stepped forward; his gaze unwavering as he faced Fenrir. "I love Pandora with all my heart," he said, his voice ringing with conviction. "I will stand by her side, no matter what challenges we may face."

Fenrir's eyes narrowed, his lips curling into a snarl. "Then so be it," he said, his voice dripping with malice. "If you choose to defy the pack, you will suffer the consequences. You will be cast out, exiled from our midst, forevermore."

With a flick of his tail, Fenrir turned and disappeared into the shadows, leaving Pandora and Lucas, son of Clara and Archer alone in the darkness. But despite the threat of exile looming over them, they knew that their love was worth any sacrifice, worth any hardship they might face.

And as they stood together under the watchful gaze of the moon, their hearts entwined in a bond that could never be broken, they knew that they were destined to be together, forever, and always.

As the days passed, the tension within the werewolf pack grew palpable. Whispers of rebellion and dissent spread like wildfire through the ranks, fueled by Fenrir's anger and resentment towards Pandora and Lucas, son of Clara and Archer. The pack was divided, torn between loyalty to their alpha and sympathy for the star-crossed lovers.

One night, under the light of the full moon, the pack gathered in a clearing deep in the heart of the forest. Fenrir stood at the head of the assembly, his gaze cold and unforgiving as he addressed the gathered wolves. "We stand here today to pass judgment on those who have defied our laws and traditions," Fenrir declared, his voice echoing through the night. "Pandora and Lucas, son of Clara and Archer have chosen to forsake their own kind in favor of their forbidden love. They have betrayed us, and they must face the consequences of their actions."

Pandora and Lucas, son of Clara and Archer stood side by side, their fur shimmering in the moonlight, their eyes locked in a silent exchange of love and determination. They knew that the trial ahead would evaluate their bond like never before, but they were prepared to face whatever challenges lay in their path.

The trial began with a series of tests designed to prove the strength of Pandora and Lucas, son of Clara and Archer's love. They were tasked with navigating a treacherous obstacle course, with traps and pitfalls designed to evaluate their agility and cunning. They were challenged to hunt and track together, their skills as a team put to the ultimate test.

Through it all, Pandora and Lucas, son of Clara and Archer stood strong, their bond unbreakable, their love unwavering. They faced each challenge with courage and determination, their hearts beating as one, their souls intertwined in a bond that transcended time and space.

And when the final test came, a battle against a fierce and powerful adversary, Pandora and Lucas, son of Clara and Archer fought side by side, their fangs and claws flashing in the moonlight, their love fueling their every move. Together, they appeared victorious, their victory a testament to the power of their love.

As the pack looked on in awe and admiration, Fenrir stepped forward, his eyes filled with grudging respect. "You have proven yourselves worthy," he said, his voice low and gruff. "You have shown that love knows no boundaries, that it can conquer even the greatest of challenges. You are welcome among us, as equals and as kin."

And as the pack howled their approval, Pandora and Lucas, son of Clara and Archer knew that they had passed the ultimate test, that their love had triumphed over adversity, and that they were destined to be together, forevermore.

With the trial behind them and the pack's acceptance secured, Pandora and Lucas, son of Clara and Archer, found themselves at a crossroads. They had proven their love to the werewolf pack, but now they faced a new challenge - how to build a future together in a world that was still filled with dangers and uncertainties.

As they roamed the forest together, their fur brushing against each other in a silent caress, Pandora and Lucas, son of Clara and Archer knew that they were stronger together than they could ever be apart. They shared their hopes and dreams, their fears, and doubts, laying bare their souls to each other in a bond that grew deeper with each passing day.

But even as they reveled in their newfound freedom, a shadow loomed on the horizon. Rumors of a dark force gathering in the depths of the forest reached their ears, whispers of a malevolent presence that threatened to tear their world apart.

Determined to protect their pack and their love, Pandora and Lucas, son of Clara and Archer set out to confront this new threat, their hearts filled with courage and their minds set on victory. They faced trials and tribulations, battles, and betrayals, but through it all, they stood together, their love a beacon of light in the darkness.

And when the final battle came, a showdown against the dark force that sought to destroy everything they held dear, Pandora and Lucas, son of Clara and Archer fought side by side, their fangs and claws flashing in the moonlight, their love a shield against the encroaching darkness.

As the days turned into nights and the moon cycled through its phases, Pandora and Lucas, son of Clara and Archer worked tirelessly to rebuild the trust and unity of the Silverwood pack. Their efforts bore fruit as the pack members rallied together, their loyalty to their Alpha pair reaffirmed and their resolve strengthened by the trials they had faced and overcome.

Yet, amidst the newfound harmony that permeated the forest, whispers of a shadowy figure began to surface, murmurs of a dark presence that haunted the edges of Silverwood, its intentions unknown and its motives shrouded in mystery. Pandora sensed a tremor of unease in the air, a feeling of foreboding that sent shivers down her spine and set her senses on edge.

One moonlit night, as Pandora and Lucas, son of Clara and Archer, patrolled the boundaries of their territory, a sudden chill swept through the forest, accompanied by an otherworldly howl that echoed through the trees like a mournful cry. The hairs on the back of Pandora's neck stood on end, her instincts alert as she scanned the shadows for any sign of the elusive figure that lurked in the darkness.

A sudden movement caught her eye, a flicker of movement in the underbrush that sent a wave of apprehension coursing through her veins. With a swift gesture, she signaled to Lucas, son of Clara and Archer, her eyes narrowed in concentration as they crept closer to investigate the source of the disturbance.

As they drew near, a figure appeared from the shadows, it forms a twisted mass of darkness and malevolence that seemed to pulse with an unholy energy. Pandora's heart skipped a beat as she recognized the intruder—a werewolf unlike any she had ever met, its eyes gleaming with a feral intensity that belied a deep well of ancient power and knowledge.

The figure spoke in a voice that sent chills down their spines, a voice tinged with malice and hidden agendas. "I am Lycaon, a creature of the night, bound by the shadows and the secrets that lie buried beneath the Earth," it declared, its words dripping with a venomous allure that filled the air with an oppressive weight.

Pandora and Lucas exchanged a wary glance, their instincts screaming a warning that reverberated through their actual bones. Lycaon's presence was a harbinger of danger, a threat that loomed large over their peaceful existence, its intentions veiled in darkness and deception.

With a voice filled with authority and resolve, Pandora addressed the enigmatic figure before them. "What brings you to Silverwood, Lycaon? What do you look for in our territory, and what dark designs do you harbor within your heart?" she demanded, her eyes fixed on the shadowy form that stood before them like a specter from a forgotten past.

Lycaon's lips curled into a sinister smile, its eyes flashing with a malevolent gleam as it spoke in a voice that sent shivers down their spines. "I have come to claim what is rightfully mine," it proclaimed, its words laced with a chilling certainty. "The power that flows through your veins, Alpha and Omega, is the key to unlocking the secrets of the past and reshaping the future in my image."

Pandora and Lucas tensed at the ominous declaration, their hearts pounding with a mixture of fear and defiance. They knew that Lycaon posed a grave threat to their pack and their way of life, a threat that could unravel everything they had worked so hard to build and protect.

With a steely gaze and a heart filled with determination, Pandora faced Lycaon head-on, her voice ringing out through the night with a fierce resolve. "You may be a creature of shadows and deceit, Lycaon, but we are werewolves of Silverwood, bound by honor and loyalty," she declared, her words a challenge and a warning. "We will not let you harm our pack or our home, for we are united in a bond that is stronger than any darkness that seeks to engulf us."

As the tension crackled in the air around them, the moon hung low in the sky, casting a silvery light over the forest as Pandora and Lucas, son of Clara and Archer, stood firm in the face of the looming threat that loomed before them. With their hearts intertwined in a dance of defiance and courage, they braced themselves for the battles that lay ahead, knowing that their love would be their guiding light in the shadows of uncertainty and fear.

The confrontation with Lycaon had set into motion a chain of events that would forever alter the course of Pandora and Lucas's lives. As the moon waned and waxed, casting its ethereal glow over the forest of Silverwood, tensions simmered beneath the surface, the specter of the dark figure looming over them like a shadow that refused to be dispelled.

Whispers of a prophecy began to circulate among the pack, stories of an ancient legend that foretold of a great conflict between the forces of light and darkness, a battle that would find the fate of the werewolf clans for generations to come. Pandora and Lucas, son of Clara and

Archer, found themselves at the center of the prophecy, their destinies entwined with the threads of fate that wove their lives together in a tapestry of love and sacrifice.

As they delved into the secrets of the past, seeking clues that would unravel the mystery of the prophecy, Pandora and Lucas, son of Clara and Archer discovered hidden truths and long-forgotten legends that shed light on the origins of their kind and the power that lay dormant within their bloodline.

They uncovered tales of a legendary werewolf pack, the Guardians of the Blood Moon, who had once stood as protectors of the forest and keepers of the ancient knowledge that bound their kind to the cycles of the moon. The Guardians had battled against the forces of darkness, led by a powerful adversary who looked to harness the power of the Blood Moon for his own malevolent purposes.

Through the whispers of the wind and the ancient trees, Pandora and Lucas, son of Clara and Archer uncovered the key to unlocking the mysteries of their past—a relic known as the Moonstone, a crystal of untold power that held the key to unlocking their true potential and fulfilling the prophecy that had been foretold centuries ago.

With Moonstone in their possession, Pandora and Lucas, son of Clara and Archer embarked on a quest to confront Lycaon and thwart his plans to plunge Silverwood into chaos and darkness. They ventured deep into the heart of the forest, guided by a sense of purpose and determination that burned bright within their hearts, their bond as Alpha and Omega strengthening with each step they took towards their inevitable destiny.

As they reached the ancient ruins where Lycaon awaited them, the air crackled with tension and anticipation, the shadows dancing with a malevolent energy that looked to ensnare them in their dark embrace. But Pandora and Lucas, son of Clara and Archer stood firm, their hearts united in a bond that was unbreakable, their souls intertwined in a dance of love and sacrifice that transcended the boundaries of time and space.

With a fierce battle cry that echoed through the forest, Pandora and Lucas, son of Clara and Archer confronted Lycaon, his form wreathed in shadow and malice as he unleashed his dark powers upon them. But they stood unyielding, their hearts beating as one as they called upon the power of the Moonstone to channel the ancient energy that coursed through their veins.

In a dazzling display of light and energy, Pandora and Lucas, son of Clara and Archer unleashed their full potential, their forms glowing with an ethereal radiance that illuminated the ruins with a divine light. The power of the Moonstone surged through them, filling them with a strength and vitality that transcended their wildest dreams, their eyes shining with a luminous glow that banished the shadows of doubt and fear that had clouded their minds.

With a final surge of energy, Pandora and Lucas, son of Clara and Archer channeled the power of the Moonstone into a beam of pure light that arced towards Lycaon, engulfing him in a blinding wave of energy that dispelled the darkness that had plagued their hearts. As the light faded and the ruins fell silent, Lycaon lay defeated at their feet, his shadowy form dissolving into the ether, his malevolent spirit vanquished by the purity of their love and the strength of their bond.

As the moon rose high in the sky, casting its silvery light over the forest of Silverwood, Pandora and Lucas, son of Clara and Archer stood victorious, their hearts filled with a sense of peace and fulfillment that had eluded them for so long. The prophecy had been fulfilled, the forces of light triumphing over the darkness that looked to extinguish their hope and their love.

In the aftermath of the battle, the werewolf clans of Silverwood gathered to celebrate the victory of their Alpha pair, their voices raised in a chorus of triumph and joy. Pandora and Lucas, son of Clara and Archer looked out over the assembled pack, their eyes alight with pride and gratitude, their souls at peace with the knowledge that they had fulfilled their destiny and embraced their true potential as guardians of the Blood Moon.

And as they stood together under the watchful gaze of the moon, their hands entwined and their hearts beating as one, Pandora and Lucas, son of Clara and Archer knew that their love was a beacon of hope and light that would guide them through the trials and tribulations that awaited them on their journey through the wilds of Silverwood, their destinies intertwined in a bond that was as unbreakable as it was eternal.

In the end, it was their love that saved them, that vanquished the darkness and restored peace to the forest. As the sun rose on a new day, Pandora and Lucas, son of Clara and Archer stood victorious, their hearts united in a bond that could never be broken.

And as they looked out at the world spread before them, filled with endless possibilities and new beginnings, they knew that their love would guide them through whatever challenges lay ahead, that together, they could overcome anything. And so, hand in paw, they set out on a new adventure, their hearts entwined in a love that would last for all eternity.

Chapter 21: *Moonlit Love*

The moon hung low and full in the midnight sky, casting a silvery glow over the dense forest where Ismay, a spirited young woman, found herself lost. She had heard the tales of the mysterious werewolves that roamed these woods, but she paid them no heed, confident in her ability to navigate the trees and find her way back home. As she walked, the only sound that filled the night was the soft crunch of leaves beneath her feet.

Ismay's heart pounded in her chest as she stumbled upon a clearing bathed in moonlight. Suddenly, a rustling in the bushes caught her attention, and before she could react, a tall figure appeared from the shadows. The man before her was handsome, with piercing blue eyes that seemed to glow in the darkness. Ismay's breath caught in her throat as she realized that he was no ordinary man — he was a werewolf.

"Who are you?" Ismay asked, her voice barely above a whisper.

The werewolf gave her a mysterious smile, his sharp canines gleaming in the moonlight. "I am Tristian, Fallon, and Alexa's son," he replied, his voice deep and melodic. "And you are trespassing in my territory, little werewolf."

Ismay's heart raced at the sight of the enigmatic werewolf standing before her. She had heard stories of the fierce and loyal werewolves that protected their lands with unwavering devotion. Despite the fear that coursed through her veins, she felt a strange pull towards Tristian, Fallon, and Alexa's son, as if some unseen forces were drawing them together.

As she gazed into his intense eyes, Ismay saw a hint of vulnerability hidden beneath his rugged exterior. She sensed a deep loneliness that mirrored her own, and a longing for connection that tugged at her heart. Without fully understanding why, she took a hesitant step towards him, her hand outstretched.

"I mean you no harm, Tristian, Fallon, and Alexa's son." she said softly. "I only seek to find my way back home."

Tristian, Fallon, and Alexa's son regarded her with a mixture of curiosity and wariness, his gaze flickering between her outstretched hand and her earnest eyes. Slowly, he extended his own hand towards hers, the tips of his claws grazing her skin ever so gently. A spark of electricity passed between them, igniting a fire that neither of them could deny.

In that moment, under the watchful gaze of the full moon, Ismay and Tristian, Fallon, and Alexa's son, forged a connection that transcended their differences. Bound by fate and drawn together by an irresistible attraction, they stood on the precipice of a love that would defy all odds and challenge the very fabric of their worlds.

As the night stretched on, they shared stories of love and loss, dreams and desires, fears, and hopes. With each passing moment, their bond grew stronger, weaving a tapestry of emotions that bound them together in ways they could never have imagined.

When the first light of dawn began to break over the horizon, Ismay knew that she had found not only her way back home but a love that would change the course of her life forever. And as she investigated Tristian, Fallon, and Alexa's son's eyes, she saw a reflection of her own soul, a kindred spirit who had found solace in the most unexpected of places.

Together, under the watchful eye of the moon, Ismay and Tristian, Fallon, and Alexa's son, embarked on a journey that would evaluate the limits of their love and the strength of their bond. And as they navigated the treacherous waters of a world divided by fear and prejudice, they clung to each other with fierce determination, knowing that their love was worth any sacrifice.

In the heart of the enchanted forest, where the spirits of the wild roamed free and the howls of the wolves echoed through the night, Ismay and Tristian, Fallon, and Alexa's son, discovered a love that was destined to endure for all eternity. And as they embraced beneath the silver light of the moon, they knew that no force in the world could ever tear them apart.

As days turned into weeks and weeks into months, Ismay and Tristian, Fallon and Alexa's son's love blossomed and grew, defying all expectations and standing strong against the trials that threatened to tear them apart. Every moment they spent together felt like a cherished gift, a fleeting reprieve from a world that looked to keep them apart.

Tristian, Fallon, and Alexa's son, with his strength and grace, showed Ismay a world she never knew existed—one where magic and wonder danced in the shadows, and where love could conquer even the darkest of fears. And Ismay, with her bravery and compassion, opened Tristian, Fallon, and Alexa's son's heart to a depth of emotion he had never dared to explore, revealing a vulnerability that he kept hidden from the world.

Together, they navigated the complexities of their intertwined lives, walking a fine line between their werewolf and wolf selves. Ismay embraced the wildness within her, reveling in the freedom it brought, while

Tristian, Fallon, and Alexa's son, found solace in her gentle touch, a balm to the wounds that had long plagued his soul.

But their happiness was not to last, for a shadow loomed on the horizon, threatening to shatter the fragile peace they had worked so hard to build. A pack of rival werewolves, led by the ruthless Alpha Magnus, descended upon the forest, looking to claim Tristian, Fallon, and Alexa's son's territory as their own.

Ismay and Tristian, Fallon, and Alexa's son, knew that they had to fight to protect their love, their home, and each other. With courage in their hearts and determination in their eyes, they stood side by side, united against the forces that looked like they were to tear them apart.

The battle was fierce and unforgiving, the clash of claw against claw, fang against fang, echoing through the trees. Ismay fought with a ferocity she never knew she had; her determination fueled by her love for Tristian, Fallon, and Alexa's son, his eyes ablaze with a fierce protectiveness, unleashed the full extent of his werewolf strength, his howls reverberating through the night.

In the heart of the chaos, Ismay caught sight of Magnus, his eyes burning with a deadly hunger. With a snarl, he lunged towards Tristian, Fallon, and Alexa's son, his claws slicing through the air. Without hesitation, Ismay threw herself in front of Tristian, Fallon, and Alexa's son, taking the brunt of the attack meant for him.

Pain seared through Ismay's body as Magnus's claws tore into her flesh, but she knew that she had to protect the one she loved, no matter the cost. Tristian, Fallon, and Alexa's son roared in fury, his fangs bared, as he launched himself at Magnus, his rage consuming him.

In a whirlwind of fur and blood, the battle raged on, the forest bearing witness to the clash of wills and the strength of love. And in the end, it was Ismay and Tristian, Fallon, and Alexa's son, who appeared victorious, their bond stronger than ever, their love unbreakable.

As the moon rose high in the sky, casting its ethereal light over the victorious couple, Ismay and Tristian, Fallon, and Alexa's son, stood hand in hand, their hearts beating as one. In that moment, they knew that their love was a force of nature, a beacon of hope in a world darkened by hatred and fear.

And as they gazed into each other's eyes, the promise of a future filled with love and happiness stretched out before them, a testament to the power of a love that transcended all boundaries. In the embrace of the moonlit night, Ismay and Tristian, Fallon, and Alexa's son, found the peace and fulfillment they had long looked for, knowing that together, they could overcome any obstacle that came their way.

For Ismay and Tristian, Fallon, and Alexa's son, their love was a legend in the making, a tale of two souls bound by destiny and united in a love that would withstand the tests of time. And as they walked hand in hand into the dawn of a new day, they knew that their love would endure, a beacon of light in a world shrouded in darkness.

In the aftermath of the battle, Ismay's wounds slowly healed, leaving behind faint scars that served as a reminder of the price she had paid to protect Tristian, Fallon, and Alexa's son. Despite the physical pain, her heart felt lighter knowing that they had appeared victorious, their love stronger than ever.

As they tended to each other's wounds in the quiet of the night, Ismay and Tristian, Fallon, and Alexa's son, found solace in the simple act of being together. Their bond had been evaluated, but it had only deepened, solidifying the connection between them in ways they never thought possible.

Tristian, Fallon, and Alexa's son watched over Ismay with a fierce protectiveness, his gaze tender and filled with unspoken emotion. He had never allowed himself to get close to anyone, fearing the vulnerability that came with opening his heart. But Ismay had touched him in a way that no one ever had, awakening feelings he had long buried deep within.

Ismay, too, felt a profound shift within her soul. Her love for Tristian, Fallon, and Alexa's son had only grown stronger in the face of adversity, her heart overflowing with a depth of emotion she had never experienced before. She knew that their love was rare and precious, a gift to be cherished and nurtured.

But as the days turned into weeks and the seasons changed, a new challenge loomed on the horizon, threatening to evaluate their love in ways they could never have imagined. A prophecy had been foretold, one that spoke of a powerful force that would seek to tear Ismay and Tristian, Fallon, and Alexa's son, apart, setting in motion a chain of events that would shape their destinies.

Ismay and Tristian, Fallon, and Alexa's son, knew that they had to face this new threat together, drawing strength from each other as they braced themselves for the trials that lay ahead. With determination in their hearts and a fierce determination to protect their love, they set out on a journey that would take them to the very edges of the mystical world they inhabited.

Guided by the whispers of the wind and the shadows of the moon, Ismay and Tristian, Fallon, and Alexa's son, ventured into the unknown, their path fraught with danger and uncertainty. Along the way, they met beings of incredible power and wisdom, each offering cryptic clues and enigmatic guidance that led them ever closer to the truth.

As they drew nearer to the heart of the prophecy, a sense of foreboding settled over them, their hearts heavy with the weight of what was to come. Ismay and Tristian, Fallon, and Alexa's son, knew that their love would be evaluated like never before, that the very fabric of their bond would be stretched to its limits.

And when the final confrontation came, when the forces of fate collided in a whirlwind of chaos and uncertainty, Ismay and Tristian, Fallon, and Alexa's son, stood together, their hands intertwined and their hearts united. In that moment, they knew that their love was a force to be reckoned with, a beacon of light in a world consumed by darkness.

As the prophecy unfolded and the truth was revealed, Ismay and Tristian, Fallon, and Alexa's son, faced their greatest challenge yet, their love serving as a powerful shield against the forces that looked like tearing them apart. And in the end, it was their unwavering devotion to each other that triumphed, their bond stronger than ever, their love eternal.

In the aftermath of the storm, as the dust settled and the world returned to peace, Ismay and Tristian, Fallon, and Alexa's son, stood together, their eyes filled with a deep sense of contentment. They had overcome every obstacle in their path, defied every expectation, and appeared victorious, their love standing as a testament to the power of the heart.

And as they embraced under the watchful gaze of the moon, their souls entwined and their hearts at peace, Ismay and Tristian, Fallon, and Alexa's son,, Fallon, and Alexa's son, knew that their love was a rare and precious gift, one that would endure for all time, a love that would transcend the bounds of mortality and shine brightly in the darkness, a beacon of hope and light in a world filled with shadows.

In the wake of their triumph over the forces that looked to tear them apart, Ismay and Tristian, Fallon, and Alexa's son, found themselves standing at a crossroads, their hearts filled with a newfound sense of purpose and renewal. The trials they had faced had only served to strengthen their bond, solidifying their love in ways that defied logic and reason.

As they stood side by side in the enchanted forest, surrounded by the gentle rustle of leaves and the soft whispers of the wind, Ismay and Tristian, Fallon, and Alexa's son, knew that a new chapter in their lives was unfolding. The prophecy had been fulfilled, the veil of uncertainty lifted, and they were left with a sense of freedom and possibility that filled them with hope.

Ismay looked at Tristian, Fallon, and Alexa's son, with a smile that reached the depths of her soul, her eyes shining with a light that reflected the love she felt for him. Tristian, Fallon, and Alexa's son returned her gaze with a tenderness that spoke volumes, his heart laid bare before her, his love an unspoken promise of forever.

"We have overcome so much, my love," Ismay whispered, her voice soft and filled with emotion. "And through it all, our love has remained strong and unwavering. I believe we are destined to be together, bound by a love that transcends time and space."

Tristian, Fallon, and Alexa's son enveloped Ismay in his strong embrace, his warmth a comforting presence against the chill of the night. "Ismay, you are my light in the darkness, my anchor in the storm," he murmured, his words a vow that echoed through the forest. "Together, we are unstoppable, our love a force of nature that will endure for all eternity."

As they stood together beneath the canopy of stars, Ismay and Tristian, Fallon, and Alexa's son, made a silent pact to cherish each moment, to hold onto the love that had brought them through the darkest of nights and into the light of a new day. They knew that their journey was far from over, that new challenges and adventures awaited them, but they faced the future with a newfound sense of courage and determination.

With the first light of dawn painting the horizon in shades of pink and gold, Ismay and Tristian, Fallon, and Alexa's son, set out on a new path, their hands clasped tightly together, their hearts beating as one. They knew that whatever lay ahead, they would face it together, their love a guiding star that would lead them through the uncertainties of life.

And as they walked hand in hand into the sunrise, their spirits light, and their hearts full of love, Ismay and Tristian, Fallon, and Alexa's son, felt a sense of joy and peace that transcended words. In that moment, they knew that they were truly blessed to have found each other, to have forged a love that was unbreakable and pure.

For Ismay and Tristian, Fallon, and Alexa's son, the future was a blank canvas waiting to be painted with the colors of their love, a tapestry of dreams and desires that they would create together, one brushstroke at a time. And as they journeyed forward into the unknown, their hearts filled with hope and their souls intertwined, they knew that their love story was only just beginning, a tale of two souls united in an unbreakable bond that would endure for all time.

Chapter 22: *A United Front*

Evelyn had always been drawn to the mysterious and untamed world of the supernatural. Ever since she was a young girl, she had been fascinated by the legends of werewolves that had been passed down through generations in her family. It was said that her ancestors had been werewolf hunters, and that a powerful werewolf curse ran through their bloodline.

As she grew older, Evelyn became increasingly obsessed with the idea of encountering a real werewolf. She spent hours reading books and researching online, trying to uncover any information she could about these mythical creatures. But despite her efforts, she had never been able to find any concrete evidence of their existence.

Evelyn paused at the edge of the dense forest, her heart racing with apprehension and excitement. The moon hovered high in the indigo sky, casting a silvery glow over the towering trees that whispered secrets in the night breeze. She took a deep breath, the crisp scent of pine filling her lungs as she stepped into the shadows of the ancient woodland.

As she ventured deeper into the heart of the forest, the silence enveloped her like a shroud, broken only by the soft rustle of leaves under her feet. Evelyn was on a mission—a quest to unravel the mystery that had plagued her dreams for so long. She had heard whispers of a pack of wolves that roamed these woods, their haunting howls echoing through the night.

Evelyn's steps quickened as she followed a narrow path that wound its way through the twisted maze of trees. The moonlight danced on the forest floor, illuminating the forest with an ethereal glow. Her heart pounded in her chest as she felt the weight of the ancient magic that permeated the air.

Suddenly, a low growl shattered the stillness, sending a shiver down Evelyn's spine. She froze in her tracks, her senses on high alert as she scanned the shadows for any sign of movement. And then she saw him—a magnificent creature appearing from the darkness.

He was a werewolf, towering and powerful, with eyes that blazed like twin orbs of liquid silver. His fur was sleek and black as midnight, rippling with the muscles beneath. He moved with an effortless grace, every step exuding a primal energy that stirred something deep within Evelyn's soul.

As their eyes met, a surge of recognition passed between them—a connection that transcended time and space. Evelyn felt a pull unlike anything she had ever experienced, drawing her towards the enigmatic werewolf with an irresistible force.

Without a word, he approached her, his gaze filled with a mixture of curiosity and caution. Evelyn held her ground, her heart thundering in her chest as she reached out a trembling hand towards him. And then, in a moment of pure instinct, she touched his fur, feeling the powerful thrum of his heartbeat beneath her fingertips.

The werewolf's eyes softened, a fleeting sense of vulnerability crossing his features before he turned and disappeared into the shadows once more. Evelyn stood there, her hand lingering in the air where he had been, a sense of loss and longing washing over her.

As the echoes of the werewolf's presence faded into the night, Evelyn knew that she had embarked on a journey that would change her life forever. The mysterious creature had ignited a fire in her heart, unlocking a passion and desire that she had never known existed.

And so, under the watchful gaze of the moon, Evelyn made a silent vow to seek out the enigmatic werewolf once more, to delve deeper into the secrets of the forest and the untamed magic that pulsed through her veins. Little did she know that this chance encounter would set into motion a chain of events that would evaluate the boundaries of love, destiny, and the enduring power of the heart.

One fateful evening, as Evelyn was driving home from work, she took a detour through the woods to clear her head. The sun had set, and the moon hung low in the sky, casting an eerie glow over the dark forest. Suddenly, Evelyn heard a rustling in the bushes. She stopped her car and stepped out to investigate, her heart pounding in her chest.

And then she saw him – a tall, muscular man with tawny fur and piercing amber eyes. He stood before her, his gaze intense and searching. Evelyn's breath caught in her throat as she realized what she was looking at – a werewolf, in the flesh.

For a moment, they stood there, locked in a silent gaze. Evelyn could feel the raw power emanating from the werewolf, and she knew that she should be afraid. But instead, a strange sense of familiarity washed over her, as if she had finally found something she had been searching for her entire life.

The werewolf took a step forward, his eyes never leaving Evelyn's. She could see the conflict in his expression, the struggle between his primal instincts and his human emotions. And then, to Evelyn's surprise, he spoke.

"My name is Carson, son of Archer and Clara," he said, his voice deep and gravelly. "I mean you no harm, Evelyn. I have been watching you for some time now, drawn to your scent."

Evelyn's heart raced at the sound of her name on his lips. She felt a deep connection to this mysterious creature, one that she could not explain. And as she looked into his eyes, she saw a vulnerability that made her want to reach out and touch him, to comfort him during his inner turmoil.

"I've always believed in your kindness," Evelyn said softly. "I've spent my whole life searching for you."

Carson, son of Archer and Clara's eyes softened, and a flicker of hope crossed his face. "You understand," he murmured. "You know what it's like to be different, to long for acceptance."

Without thinking, Evelyn reached out and touched 's fur-covered hand. It was warm and rough beneath her fingers, and she felt a jolt of electricity shoot through her at the contact. Carson, son of Archer and Clara's eyes widened in surprise, and then he smiled – a wolfish grin that sent shivers down Evelyn's spine.

In that moment, Evelyn knew that her life would never be the same. She had found the werewolf she had been searching for, and she knew that their meeting was no coincidence. It was fate, a twist of destiny that had brought them together in the darkness of the forest. And as the moon rose higher in the sky, casting its silvery light over the two of them, Evelyn knew that she had finally found her true mate – in the form of a werewolf named Carson, son of Archer and Clara.

Evelyn brushed her fingers through her long, crimson hair as she gazed up at the full moon hanging low in the night sky. It cast a silvery glow over the forest, illuminating the ancient trees and casting long shadows across the forest floor. The air was cool and crisp, carrying with it the musky scent of pine and earth.

As she walked along the winding path, Evelyn could not shake the feeling of being watched. Her heart pounded in her chest, a mix of fear and excitement coursing through her veins. Stories of the elusive werewolves that roamed these woods had always fascinated her, but she never honestly believed they could be real.

Suddenly, a rustling in the bushes ahead made her stop in her tracks. Her pulse quickened as she strained to see through the darkness. And then, appearing from the shadows, was Carson, son of Archer and Clara. Tall and ruggedly handsome, with piercing green eyes and a wildness in his gaze that sent a shiver down Evelyn's spine.

"Carson, son of Archer and Clara," she whispered, her voice barely above a breath. He stood before her, his presence commanding and powerful. She could sense the primal energy radiating off him, a force of nature that drew her in like a moth to a flame.

In that moment, under the watchful gaze of the moon, Evelyn and Carson, son of Archer and Clara, shared a connection that transcended the boundaries of the ordinary world. It was as if they had known each other for lifetimes, their souls intertwined in a dance ancient itself.

"Evelyn," Carson, son of Archer and Clara, spoke her name like a prayer, his voice deep and resonant. "I have been searching for you," he said, his gaze never leaving hers. A rush of emotions flooded through Evelyn—fear, desire, longing—all swirling together in a whirlwind of conflicting feelings. But deep down, she knew that this meeting was no mere coincidence. It was written in the stars, fated by the moon.

As they stood there, bathed in moonlight, Evelyn felt a primal urge stirring within her. It was as if a part of her had been awakened, a side of herself she never knew existed. And in Carson, son of Archer and Clara's eyes, she saw a reflection of that same wildness, that same un-tamed spirit yearning to be set free.

Their destinies had collided on this fateful night, two souls bound by a love that defied logic and reason. And as they stood there, on the edge of the forest, Evelyn knew that her life would never be the same again.

The howl of a wolf echoed through the night, a haunting melody that sealed their fate. And as Carson, son of Archer and Clara, took Eve-lyn's hand in his, leading her deeper into the heart of the forest, she knew that she was embarking on a journey unlike any other.

Their love was as timeless as the moon that watched over them, as powerful as the beasts that prowled the night. And as they disappeared into the darkness together, Evelyn knew that she had finally found where she truly belonged—in the arms of her werewolf soulmate, Carson, son of Archer and Clara.

The forest whispered secrets as Evelyn and Carson, son of Archer and Clara, ventured deeper into its ancient depths. The rustling of leaves, the call of nocturnal creatures, the distant howls of their kin—all added to the mystique of the night.

Carson, son of Archer and Clara's presence beside her brought a sense of comfort and exhilaration. His touch was electric, sending tingles down Evelyn's spine as they walked in silence, their steps synchronized as if they were two halves of a whole.

As they reached a clearing bathed in moonlight, Carson, son of Archer and Clara, turned to face Evelyn, his eyes ablaze with an intensity that made her heart race. Without a word, he cupped her face in his hands, his touch gentle yet possessive.

"Evelyn," he murmured, his breath warm against her skin. "I have waited countless lifetimes for you, my mate, my love." The word "mate" echoed in her mind, sending a surge of emotions coursing through her. It was a primal bond, a connection that transcended time and space. And as Carson, son of Archer and Clara, drew her into his arms, Evelyn felt a sense of completeness wash over her.

Their lips met in a searing kiss, igniting a fire that consumed them both. It was a kiss born of passion and longing, of destiny fulfilled in the embrace of the night. And as they melted into each other, the lines between human and beast blurred, their true natures laid bare under the watchful gaze of the moon.

The world faded away as Evelyn and Carson, son of Archer and Clara, surrendered to the pull of their shared destiny. Their bodies moved in perfect harmony, a dance of desire and need that spoke volumes without a single word. In each other's arms, they found solace, acceptance, and a love that defied all odds.

As the night wore on, their love blossomed like a flower in the darkness, its petals unfolding to reveal a beauty both fragile and eternal. And as they lay entwined beneath the stars, Evelyn knew that she had found her home in Carson, son of Archer and Clara's arms, in the heart of the wild and untamed forest.

Their love story was written in the stars, whispered in the wind, and written and sent with love and care that echoed through eternity. And as they drifted off to sleep, wrapped in each other's embrace, Evelyn and Carson, son of Archer and Clara knew that their love would endure, unbroken and everlasting, in the realm of the werewolves and beyond.

The days turned into weeks, and weeks into months, as Evelyn and Carson, son of Archer and Clara's love deepened and grew stronger. They faced challenges and obstacles, both from within and from the outside world, but their bond remained unbreakable.

As the full moon rose once again, marking the time for Carson, son of Archer and Clara's transformation, Evelyn stood by his side, unwavering in her loyalty and love. She watched as he shifted into his werewolf form, a sight that both terrified and fascinated her. But through it all, she never wavered, always seeing the man she loved beneath the beast.

Together, they navigated the complexities of a world that did not understand or accept their love. They faced prejudice and discrimination, hatred, and fear, but through it all, they stood strong, united in their love for each other.

But as the seasons changed and new challenges arose, Evelyn and Carson, son of Archer and Clara, found themselves evaluated in ways they never imagined. The arrival of a rival werewolf pack threatened to tear them apart, evaluating their loyalty and strength.

Days turned into weeks, and weeks into months as Evelyn found herself consumed by thoughts of the enigmatic werewolf she had met in the moonlit forest. Every night, she wandered the winding paths of the woodland, her heart aching with longing to see him once more. She knew that their meeting had been no mere chance encounter—it was fate weaving its intricate web around their intertwined destinies.

One crisp autumn evening, as the leaves turned fiery shades of red and gold, Evelyn's yearning led her deep into the heart of the forest once more. The air was heavy with the scent of fallen leaves and the distant murmur of a nearby stream. The rustling of the trees echoed her restless heart as she ventured further into the shadows, guided by an invisible thread that drew her closer to the werewolf she looked for.

And then, she saw him—standing at the edge of a moonlit clearing, his gaze fixed on her with a mixture of wariness and something else, something that stirred a tumult of emotions within Evelyn. She approached him slowly, her heart thudding in her chest as she met his intense silver gaze.

They stood there in silence; the only sound was the gentle rustle of leaves in the breeze. Finally, the werewolf spoke in a voice that resonated deep within Evelyn's soul.

"Evelyn," he murmured, the sound as soft as a breath of wind through the trees. "You have returned."

His words sent a thrill of recognition through her, echoing the unspoken connection that had bound them since their first meeting. Evelyn felt a surge of courage within her as she stepped closer to him, the distance between them shrinking with each heartbeat.

"I couldn't stay away," she confessed, her voice barely above a whisper. "There's something about you that calls to me, something...undeniable."

The werewolf regarded her with an intensity that made her heart race even faster. In that moment, Evelyn saw a flicker of something vulnerable in his silver eyes, a yearning that mirrored her own.

"I am not like other creatures, Evelyn," he said, his voice tinged with a hint of sadness. "I walk a path that is often dark and lonely, filled with shadows that I cannot escape."

Evelyn reached out a tentative hand towards him, her fingers brushing against his fur as she looked into his eyes with compassion and understanding.

"We all have shadows within us," she whispered, her gaze unwavering. "But I see something more in you—a light that shines even in the darkest of nights. Together, we can face whatever comes our way."

The werewolf's eyes softened at her words, a flicker of hope dancing in their depths as he took a step closer to Evelyn, closing the distance between them until they stood mere inches apart.

And in that moment, beneath the watchful gaze of the moon and the rustling canopy of leaves, Evelyn felt a bond form between them—a bond that transcended time and space, uniting two souls in a dance of fate and desire. Little did they know that their destinies were intertwined in ways they could never have imagined, leading them down a path fraught with danger, betrayal, and a love that would defy all odds.

As Evelyn stood face to face with the enigmatic werewolf in the moonlit clearing, a sense of destiny weaved its threads around them, binding their fates in an intricate tapestry of shadows and light. The forest whispered its secrets, the rustling leaves bearing witness to the fragile connection blossoming between them.

In the stillness of the night, the werewolf's silver eyes bore into Evelyn's with an intensity that sent shivers down her spine. His presence was both commanding and haunting, a reflection of the untamed wildness that lurked within him.

"I have roamed these woods for centuries, Evelyn," he spoke, his voice a low rumble that reverberated through the clearing. "A creature of shadows and solitude, haunted by a past I cannot escape."

Evelyn felt a surge of empathy welling within her as she listened to his words, her heart aching with a profound longing to ease the burden he carried. She reached out her hand, her fingers entwining with his fur as she held his gaze with unwavering determination.

"We all carry our burdens, but we do not have to bear them alone," she murmured, her voice threaded with compassion. "Together, we can face the darkness that threatens to consume us and find the light that shines within."

The werewolf's eyes softened at her words, a flicker of vulnerability shimmering in their depths. As the moon cast its ethereal glow over the clearing, he stepped closer to Evelyn, his powerful frame enveloping her in a protective embrace.

"You speak of a bond that transcends our natures," he said, his voice tinged with a hint of wonder. "A light that can illuminate even the deepest shadows of my soul. Will you walk this path with me, Evelyn, as equals in a world that does not understand us?"

Evelyn met his gaze with unwavering resolve, her heart beating in sync with his as she nodded in silent agreement. In that moment, they forged a pact—a promise to stand together against the forces that looked to tear them apart, to embrace the light and shadows that wove their destinies together.

Under the watchful gaze of the moon, Evelyn and the werewolf stood as one, their hearts entwined in a dance of shadows and light. Little did they know that their bond would be evaluated by challenges and adversaries that lurked in the depths of the forest, waiting to strike at the fragile threads that bound them together.

And so, with a silent vow etched in their hearts, Evelyn and the werewolf embarked on a journey that would unravel the mysteries of their shared destiny, leading them down a path fraught with peril and passion, where love and loyalty would be their guiding stars in a world shrouded in darkness and magic.

Amidst the turmoil and chaos, Evelyn and Carson, son of Archer and Clara, stood firm, their love a beacon of light in the darkness. They fought side by side, their bond growing stronger with each battle won and lost.

And as they emerged victorious, their love forged in the fires of adversity, Evelyn and Carson, son of Archer and Clara, knew that they were destined to be together, no matter the obstacles in their path.

Their love story was a timeless tale of passion and perseverance, of two souls bound by fate and united in love. And as they stood together, hand in hand, under the watchful gaze of the moon, Evelyn and Carson, son of Archer and Clara, knew that their love would endure, eternal and unwavering, in the world of the werewolves and beyond.

Chapter 23: *The Alpha's Heir*

In the heart of the enchanted forest, deep within the Blue Twilight pack territory, lived a family of extraordinary beings. Amber, the half-witch half-wolf, and her mate Onyx, the majestic Alpha, had three beautiful pups. The oldest three, Luna, Orion, and Nova, were now grown and ready to embark on their own journeys. But it was their eldest daughter, Aislin, who was destined to become the next Alpha of the pack.

Aislin had a rare gift, inherited from her mother's magical bloodline, which made her the strongest and most powerful of her siblings. She had a fierce determination and a kind heart, qualities that would serve her well in her future role as leader of the Blue Twilight pack.

As Aislin prepared to take on her new responsibilities, her younger siblings, Ember, Sage, and Rowan, barely ten years old, looked up to her with admiration and awe. They were eager to follow in their sister's pawprints and make their own mark on the pack.

One day, as Aislin was practicing her Alpha duties under the watchful eye of Onyx, a dark shadow fell over the forest. The air grew cold, and a sense of unease settled over the land. Amber sensed a familiar magic at work and knew that trouble was brewing.

Aislin's training was put to the test sooner than expected when a pack of rogue wolves, led by a ruthless Alpha named Shadowfang, descended upon the Blue Twilight territory. They looked to challenge Onyx for control of the pack and would stop at nothing to achieve their goal.

With Onyx leading the defense, Aislin stood by his side, ready to prove herself as the next Alpha. The battle was fierce and intense, but with Amber's magic weaving through the air, the Blue Twilight pack fought bravely and appeared victorious.

As the dust settled and the rogues retreated, Onyx turned to Aislin with pride in his eyes. "You have proven yourself worthy, my daughter," he said, placing his paw on her shoulder. "You are the Alpha's heir, and the future of our pack is in your paws."

Aislin felt a surge of power and determination coursing through her veins. She knew that her journey was just beginning, and that she would need all her strength and courage to lead her pack into a new era of peace and prosperity.

And so, with her family by her side and the spirits of the forest watching over them, Aislin took her place as the rightful Alpha of the Blue Twilight pack, ready to face whatever challenges lay ahead.

As the sun rose over the horizon, casting a warm golden glow over the Blue Twilight pack, Aislin felt a nervous flutter in her chest. Today marked the beginning of the trials that would find if she were truly ready to take on the responsibilities of being the next Alpha.

She stood before the pack, her parents Amber and Onyx flanking her on either side. The rest of the pack gathered around, their faces a mixture of excitement and apprehension. Aislin took a deep breath, trying to calm her nerves.

The first trial was a test of courage. Aislin had to face a fearsome creature that lurked in the depths of the forest. She squared her shoulders and set off, determination shining in her eyes.

The creature turned out to be a massive dragon, its scales gleaming in the sunlight. Its eyes glowed with a fierce intelligence as it snarled at Aislin, evaluating her resolve. Aislin stood her ground, her wolf instincts kicking in as she prepared to fight.

With a thunderous roar, the dragon lunged at her, fire spewing. from its jaws. Aislin dodged and weaved, her agility and quick reflexes helping her avoid the deadly flames. She leaped onto the dragon's back, her claws digging into its scales as she fought to bring it down.

After a grueling battle, Aislin appeared victorious, the dragon lying defeated at her feet. The pack erupted into cheers, their faith in their future Alpha bolstered by her bravery and strength. The next trial tested Aislin's wisdom and leadership skills. She had to navigate a series of challenges that required quick thinking and strategic planning. From solving intricate puzzles to mediating disputes among pack members, Aislin managed each task with grace and intelligence.

After hours of intense trials, Aislin finally stood before her parents, her chest heaving with exertion but her eyes shining with pride. Amber and Onyx looked at her with a mixture of love and respect, knowing that their daughter had proved herself worthy of the title of Alpha.

As the sun began to set, casting a soft pink hue over the clearing, Aislin was officially declared the next Alpha of the Blue Twilight pack. The pack howled in celebration, their voices echoing through the forest as they welcomed their new leader with open arms.

And as Aislin stood before her pack, her heart swelling with gratitude and determination, she knew that the challenges were only just beginning. But with the love and support of her family and pack behind her, she was ready to face whatever trials lay ahead.

As Aislin settled into her new role as Alpha, she quickly realized that being a leader was not just about bravery and intelligence. It also needed compassion and empathy, qualities that would be put to the test in the coming days.

One evening, a young pup named Luna came to Aislin, tears shining in her eyes. Luna was the runt of the litter, often overlooked by the rest of the pack. She had been bullied by some of the older pups, and her confidence was shattered.

Aislin knelt beside Luna, her heart aching for the young pup. She listened as Luna poured out her fears and insecurities, her voice trembling with emotion. Aislin gently wiped away Luna's tears, her eyes filled with understanding and kindness.

With a determined gleam in her eye, Aislin decided. She called a pack meeting, her voice strong and clear as she addressed the assembled wolves. She spoke of the importance of unity and acceptance, reminding them that every member of the pack had value and worth.

She then turned to Luna, her gaze soft and warm. She encouraged Luna to stand tall and proud, to embrace her uniqueness and strength. Luna's eyes widened in surprise, but a flicker of hope sparked in her gaze.

In the days that followed, Aislin worked tirelessly to foster a sense of community and inclusivity within the pack. She organized group activities and games, encouraging wolves of all ages to come together and bond as a family.

And as the weeks passed, Aislin watched with pride as Luna blossomed and grew in confidence. The other wolves began to see her in a new light, rallying around her and offering their support. But just as things seemed to be settling into a peaceful rhythm, a dark shadow crept over the forest. A pack of rogue wolves, led by a ruthless Alpha named Shadowfang, descended upon the Blue Twilight pack, their eyes glinting with malice.

Aislin knew that she had to act quickly to protect her pack. With a steely resolve, she rallied her wolves, organizing a defense strategy to repel the invaders. The air crackled with tension as the two packs clashed, fur and fangs flashing in the moonlight.

During the chaos, Aislin found herself face to face with Shadowfang, his eyes cold and calculating. But she stood her ground, her determination unwavering as she faced the enemy Alpha. In a fierce battle of wills, Aislin appeared victorious once again, her pack rallying behind her to drive off the rogue wolves. The forest echoed with the victorious howls of the Blue Twilight pack; their spirits undaunted by the challenge they had faced.

But as Aislin watched the retreating figures of the rogue wolves, a sense of foreboding settled in her heart. She knew that this was only the beginning of a much larger conflict, one that would evaluate her strength and courage to their limits. And as the dark moon rose high in the sky, casting a shadow over the forest, Aislin braced herself for the trials that lay ahead.

As Aislin settled into her new role as Alpha of the Blue Twilight pack, she felt a sense of pride and accomplishment wash over her. But amidst the celebrations and congratulations, a shadow of the past loomed over her. One night, as the moon hung high in the sky, a mysterious figure appeared at the edge of the pack territory. Aislin's senses tingled with unease as she caught sight of the stranger, a hooded figure cloaked in shadows.

The stranger approached, their presence sending a chill down Aislin's spine. Amber and Onyx stood by her side; their expressions wary as they faced the mysterious visitor. "I come seeking the Alpha of the Blue Twilight pack," the stranger spoke, their voice cold and devoid of emotion. "I bring a warning of a great danger that threatens your pack."

Aislin felt a knot form in her stomach as she listened to the stranger's words. What could pose a threat to their pack, she wondered, her mind racing with possibilities. The stranger revealed themselves to be a powerful sorcerer, one who had once been a member of the pack before turning to the dark arts. They spoke of a dark force that had been awakened in the depths of the forest, a force that looked to bring chaos and destruction to all who stood in its way.

Aislin knew that she had to act swiftly to protect her pack from this new threat. With the sorcerer's guidance, she set off into the heart of the forest, her parents by her side as they prepared to face the danger head-on.

As they journeyed deeper into the shadows of the forest, Aislin felt a sense of foreboding grow within her. The air grew thick with the scent of ancient magic, and the whispers of the trees seemed to echo with warnings of danger ahead.

Finally, they reached a clearing where a sinister figure awaited them. A creature of pure darkness, its eyes gleaming with malice as it prepared to unleash its power upon the world. With a fierce battle cry, Aislin charged forward, her claws extended as she prepared to face the darkness head-on. Amber and Onyx fought by her side, their strength and determination bolstering her own.

The battle raged on, the clash of magic and claws echoing through the forest. But in the end, it was Aislin's resolve and bravery that won the day. With a final burst of power, she banished the darkness back to where it came from, ensuring the safety of her pack once more.

As the sun rose over the horizon, casting a warm golden glow over the forest, Aislin stood victorious, her heart filled with determination and hope for the future. But she knew that the shadow of the past would always linger, a reminder of the challenges that she would face as the new Alpha of the Blue Twilight pack.

Aislin stood at the edge of the cliff, the cool breeze ruffling her fur as she gazed out at the expanse of the Blue Twilight territory. The responsibilities of being Alpha weighed heavily on her shoulders, but she was determined to lead her pack with strength and wisdom.

The pack had faced many challenges in the months since Aislin had become Alpha. Rival packs had tried to evaluate their boundaries, looking to take advantage of the perceived weakness of a new leader. But Aislin had proven herself repeatedly, leading her pack to victory with courage and determination.

As she surveyed the land before her, Aislin knew that her pack was stronger than ever. The bond between the wolves ran deep, forged through trials and triumphs that had only served to strengthen their unity.

But there was still one final challenge that lay ahead. A dark shadow loomed on the horizon, a threat that no one could have foreseen. A pack of rogue wolves, led by a ruthless Alpha looking to expand his territory, had set their sights on the Blue Twilight pack.

Aislin knew that the upcoming battle would be the most difficult they had ever faced. The rogue wolves were fierce and cunning, their numbers greater than any they had met before. But Aislin refused to back down, her determination unwavering as she prepared her pack for the inevitable confrontation.

The night before the battle, Aislin gathered her pack around her, the glow of the moon casting a silvery light over the clearing. She spoke to them with words of encouragement and strength, her voice steady and unwavering. "We stand together as one, united in purpose and spirit," Aislin declared, her eyes shining with determination. "We will not be broken; we will not be defeated. For we are the Blue Twilight pack, and together, we are unstoppable."

The pack howled in response, their voices rising to the heavens in a fierce declaration of solidarity. As they settled in for the night, Aislin felt a sense of peace settle over her. She knew that whatever the next day brought, they would face it together, as a family. And as the first light of dawn broke over the horizon, signaling the beginning of the battle, Aislin led her pack into the fray with courage and determination. The clash of fur and fangs echoed through the forest, the sound of battle ringing in their ears as they fought for their home and their pack.

In the end, the Blue Twilight pack appeared victorious, their enemies vanquished and their territory secure. Aislin stood at the edge of the cliff once more, the sun rising behind her as she gazed out at the land that was now safe and peaceful. And as she turned to her pack, her heart filled with pride and gratitude, Aislin knew that the Blue Twilight pack would thrive under her leadership, their future bright and full of promise.

Chapter 24: *The Guardians*

In the shadowed realm of their existence, where the line between myth and reality blurred under the moon's mystic gaze, Aiden and Luna, Amber and Onyx's Daughter, their love story took on an even deeper, more complex hue. Now not only bound by the intense emotions of the heart but also by the ancient, primal call of their true natures, their love became a beacon across both the human and the supernatural worlds.

Aiden, with his fierce spirit and unwavering loyalty, embodied the strength and courage of his lineage. From the moment he had laid eyes on Luna, Amber, and Onyx's daughter, within the ethereal moonlight, he saw not just the woman who would capture his heart but a fellow soul who shared his deep, intrinsic connection to the wild and untamed forces of nature. As a werewolf, Aiden was already a creature of incredible power and subtlety, but with Luna, Amber, and Onyx's daughter, by his side, he found a sense of completeness he had never dared dream possible.

Luna, Amber, and Onyx's daughter, for her part, brought light to the shadows that oftentimes envelop Aiden's world. Her transformation into a werewolf, though fraught with challenges, had unveiled a depth of character and resilience that impressed all who knew her. With Aiden, she embraced her new existence, learning to navigate the nuances of their shared identity with grace and determination. Together, they stood for a union of strength and harmony, a powerful testament to the potential for coexistence between the supernatural and the natural world.

Their love, now imbued with the visceral, undeniable truth of their werewolf heritage, took on new dimensions. experienced the world through senses heightened beyond human capabilities, reveling in the beauty of the night with eyes that could see its true splendor, hearts that beat in unison with the ancient rhythms of the earth.

Under the full moon, they ran together through the forests that bordered their home, their forms sleek and powerful, a perfect symphony of movement and intention. In these moments, with the wind in their fur and the moon lighting their path, Aiden and Luna, Amber, and Onyx's daughter, found a freedom and a joy that was entirely their own. Their connection deepened, transcending words, as they communicated through looks and touches, their bond unspoken but unmistakable.

The challenges they faced, both from within and without, were no less daunting in the light of their love and shared strength. The rogue factions that sought to disrupt the peace between their kind and humanity found in Aiden and Luna, Amber and Onyx's daughter's formidable opponents, a couple whose love for each other was matched only by their commitment to protect their world from those who would see it torn asunder.

Together, they stood as guardians of the balance, a role that took them from the deepest shadows to the brightest lights. Their love story, a blend of passion, loyalty, and unwavering determination, served as a beacon of hope to their kind, a reminder that even in the face of the unknown, love could flourish and thrive.

As Aiden and Luna, Amber, and Onyx's daughter, moved through the world, their love stayed constant, a force both powerful and gentle. It was a love that defied the traditional boundaries, which transcended the ordinary, and that spoke of a connection as ancient as the moon and as enduring as the stars. In each other, they had found not just a partner but a soulmate, a fellow traveler on a journey that would take them through the depths of night and into the light of dawn, together, always.

Amidst the ever-present challenges and the whispers of the night, Aiden and Luna, Amber and Onyx's Daughter's bond grew only stronger, a testament to the enduring power of love in a world that often seemed shrouded in shadow. Their every step was a dance of light and darkness, a harmony of contrasts that defined the essence of their existence.

The seasons turned, marking the passage of time in a world that was constant only in its change. With each full moon, they explored the depths of their connection, their love a beacon that guided them through the labyrinth of the night. They were each other's anchor in the tumultuous sea of their dual nature, a reminder of the tranquility that could be found even amidst the storm.

Aiden, as a leader within their community, took on the mantle of protector with a solemn grace, his actions guided by a deep-seated belief in justice and the inherent worth of all beings. Luna, Amber, and Onyx's daughter, with her intuitive understanding and compassionate heart, stood by his side, a voice of reason and a source of unwavering support. Together, they navigated the complexities of their responsibilities, mindful of the legacy they would one day leave behind.

As their story unfolded, Aiden and Luna, Amber, and Onyx's daughter, became legends, their lives a tapestry woven with the threads of courage, sacrifice, and undying love. They faced adversaries with a united front, their battles not just for their own survival but for the future of their kind and the preservation of the delicate balance between worlds.

The love between Aiden and Luna, Amber, and Onyx's daughter, was more than a personal bond; it was a symbol of hope for all who knew them. It spoke to the possibility of coexistence, of building bridges where walls had once stood. Theirs was a love that transcended the boundaries of the physical world, touching the very soul of those who saw it.

In quiet moments, away from the eyes of the world, they found solace in each other's embrace, a haven from the demands of their duties. These moments, though fleeting, were a balm to their spirits, a reminder of why they fought so hard for peace and harmony.

And when the world slept, bathed in the soft glow of the moon, Aiden and Luna, Amber, and Onyx's daughter, would steal away to the heart of the forest, where the magic of the night was strongest. Here, in the seclusion of the ancient woods, they could be their truest selves, free from the expectations and responsibilities that their roles imposed upon them. They would run wild and free, their laughter mingling with the rustling leaves and the distant howl of their kin, a melody of joy and freedom.

Their story, though rooted in the realm of the supernatural, was a mirror to the desires and struggles that exist in the heart of every being. Aiden and Luna, Amber and Onyx's daughter's love was a reminder that even in a world fraught with danger and uncertainty, there is always room for hope, for connection, and for love that defies all odds.

As the chapters of their lives continued to unfold, Aiden and Luna, Amber, and Onyx's daughter, steadfast, their love unyielding. They stood as guardians of the night and champions of the day, their legacy a beacon for generations to come. In their love, they found not just solace, but strength—a strength that came not from power, but from the unbreakable bond that held them together, through the moon's cycle and beyond, into the ever-unfolding tapestry of eternity.

Their legacy, while deeply personal, rippled through the fabric of their community, instilling a sense of unity and purpose that transcended individual desires. Aiden and Luna, Amber and Onyx's daughter's love became a cornerstone upon which the future could be built, a future where the harmony between the natural and supernatural was not just an ideal, but a reality.

As the years passed, stories of courage, wisdom, and, most importantly, their unyielding love, became the of legend. Young were-wolves looked up to them not just as leaders, but as exemplars of what it meant to live a life guided by love and respect for all beings. They proved that even in a life filled with the extraordinary, the most powerful magic of all was love—a force that could bridge worlds, heal wounds, and bring light to the darkest corners of existence.

Together, Aiden and Luna, Amber and Onyx's daughter, spearheaded initiatives that fostered understanding and cooperation between different factions, both within the supernatural community and with the human world. They worked tirelessly to ensure that the peace they cherished was not a fragile truce, but a robust foundation for the future. Their diplomacy and genuine desire for a better world brought about alliances that were once thought impossible, uniting diverse groups under shared goals and mutual respect.

Yet, amidst their achievements and the adulation of their peers, they remained grounded, always mindful of the simple truths that had guided them from the beginning: that every heartbeat with the same need for love, acceptance, and peace; that every soul, no matter how fierce or timid, held within its capacity for great good.

In the privacy of their home, amidst the laughter and love of their family, Aiden and Luna, Amber, and Onyx's daughter, cherished the quiet moments that were their sanctuary from the obligations of leadership. Here, where the moonlight filtered through the windows and the night sang its ancient lullaby, they found strength in each other's arms, solace in each other's eyes.

Their children, born of love and raised in a world where the impossible was every day, grew to embody the best of their parents. Courage and compassion, strength, and wisdom, were the gifts they carried into the world, the legacy of Aiden and Luna, Amber, and Onyx's daughter's love. Through them, the future held not just hope, but a promise—a promise of a world where harmony reigned, where differences were celebrated, and where love was the most powerful force of all.

As the moon continued its eternal dance across the heavens, marking the passage of time in a world ever-changing, Aiden and Luna,

Amber, and Onyx's daughter, stood together, their faces turned toward the night sky. They whispered promises into the darkness, vows of love and commitment that transcended the physical world, binding them together through whatever challenges and joys the future might.

Their story, etched in the stars and whispered by the wind, was more than a tale of love; it was a testament to the enduring power of the heart. In a universe vast and mysterious, amidst the myriad wonders and dangers, the love between Aiden and Luna, Amber, and Onyx's daughter, shone as a beacon, guiding those who followed them toward a future bright with possibility.

And so, beneath the watchful gaze of the moon, in a world where magic and reality intertwined, Aiden and Luna, Amber and Onyx's daughter's love endured a constant star in the ever-shifting skies, a symbol of hope, unity, and the transformative power of love.

Their enduring love story, woven into the fabric of their community, inspired not only their immediate kin but generations that followed. The legacy of Aiden and Luna, Amber, and Onyx's daughter, was not just their battles for peace or their leadership that bridged worlds; it was fundamentally about the profound impact of their love—a love that transcended the ordinary, transforming and uplifting all who came into its orbit.

In the twilight of their years, with their legacy firmly proven and the future of their community secure, Aiden and Luna, Amber, and Onyx's daughter, found themselves reflecting on the journey they had embarked upon together. They had seen the world change, seen the impossible become possible, and fought tirelessly for a vision of harmony that had seemed so fragile at the dawn of their union. Yet, through it all, their love had remained unbroken, a constant light in the shifting sands of time.

As they walked together through the ancient forest, now as guardians not just in title but in spirit, they felt the deep, unspoken understanding that had always been the true foundation of their bond. They had grown together, not just in strength but in wisdom and empathy, their love maturing and deepening with each passing moon.

The world around them had changed, but the forest remained a sanctuary, a place where the magic of the old ways still whispered among the trees. Here, where their love had first taken root, Aiden and Luna, Amber, and Onyx's daughter, felt a profound connection to the cycles of life and nature, a reminder that every ending was but a prelude to a new beginning.

They, now leaders, carried forward the ideals and values instilled in them by Aiden and Luna, Amber, and Onyx's daughter. They, too, believed in the power of unity, the importance of peace, and the strength to be found in love and compassion. The future, once a distant dream, was now a living testament to the enduring legacy of their parents' love.

As Aiden and Luna, Amber, and Onyx's daughter, stood beneath the full moon, hand in hand, they knew that their time as active guardians of their kind were ending. Yet, they felt no sadness, only a deep sense of peace and fulfillment. Their love had ignited a flame that would burn brightly through the ages, a beacon for all who looked to live in harmony with the world and each other.

Their story, a timeless tale of love, sacrifice, and hope, would continue to inspire long after they had returned to the earth. It would be told around campfires, whispered in the wind, and celebrated under the full moon, a reminder that love, in all its forms, was the most potent force in the universe.

And so, under the watchful gaze of the stars, Aiden and Luna, Amber, and Onyx's daughter, shared one last, lingering kiss, a silent vow that even in death, their spirits would find each other, their love enduring beyond the confines of time and space. They had lived a life filled with purpose and passion, unified in their vision, and bound by a love that had changed the world.

In the end, Aiden and Luna, Amber and Onyx's daughter's legacy was not just about the peace they had forged or the battles they had won; it was about the profound truth that in love, there is eternal strength. journey, marked by the phases of the moon and the passage of the seasons, was a testament to the enduring magic of love—a magic that, like the moon's gentle light, would guide the hearts of generations to come.

Chapter 25: *Moonlit Pleasures*

The night was alive with the sound of the forest, a symphony of rustling leaves and distant howls that echoed through the trees. Paxton prowled through the dense undergrowth; his senses heightened by the full moon that hung low in the sky. As the son of Clara and Archer, the Betas of the Blue Twilight pack, leaders of the werewolf pack, Paxton was no stranger to the wild and untamed world of the supernatural.

His keen eyes scanned the darkened forest, his wolf instincts on high alert as he sought out any sign of danger. Suddenly, a flicker of movement caught his attention, and he froze in his tracks, his ears pricking up in curiosity.

Appearing from the shadows was a figure, lithe and graceful, moving with an otherworldly elegance that captivated Paxton's gaze. As she stepped into the moonlight, Paxton caught his breath at the sight of her – Isolde, a witch-wolf hybrid like his childhood friend, Amber.

Isolde moved with a fluid grace that spoke of hidden power, her dark hair cascading in waves down her back as she moved through the forest with a sense of purpose. Her eyes, a mesmerizing shade of green, held a depth of mystery that drew Paxton in like a moth to a flame.

Unaware of his presence, Isolde moved closer, her every movement a dance of the supernatural. Paxton felt a strange pull towards her, a connection that he could not explain but could not ignore. As she moved past him, their eyes met, and in that moment, time seemed to stand still.

For Isolde, the encounter was a strange one. She had always felt different, an outsider in a world that she could not understand. Raised by her mother after her parents' separation, she had never known the truth of her heritage – that she was half-witch, half-wolf, a powerful combination that made her unique among her kind.

As she gazed into Paxton's eyes, something stirred within her, a feeling of recognition that she could not explain. His presence felt familiar, comforting in a way that she had never experienced before. And yet, she could not shake the feeling that there was more to this encounter than met the eye.

Paxton stepped forward, his movements slow and deliberate as he closed the distance between them. Isolde held her breath, her heart pounding in her chest as she felt the heat of his gaze upon her. In that moment, she knew that her life was about to change in ways she could never have imagined.

As the moon shone down upon them, casting a silvery glow over the forest, Paxton and Isolde stood face to face, two souls on the brink of a love that would defy all odds. In that moment, the world faded away, leaving only the two of them, bound together by fate and the ancient magic that pulsed through their veins.

As the full moon rose high in the sky, casting its ethereal glow across the forest, Paxton found himself wandering through the woods, his wolf senses heightened by the moon's magical pull. The son of Clara and Archer, the beta of the Blue Twilight pack, Paxton was a strong and noble werewolf, fiercely loyal to his pack and always ready to protect those he cared for.

On this night, as he roamed the forest with his pack members, his attention was attracted to a figure standing alone in a clearing. She was immersed in the silver light of the moon, her long hair cascading around her like a shimmering waterfall. Paxton's heart skipped a beat as he recognized her - Isolde, the mysterious and alluring newcomer to the pack.

Isolde was unlike any other werewolf Paxton had ever met. She owned an otherworldly beauty that captivated him from the moment they first laid eyes on each other. But there was something more to her, something that set her apart from the rest of the pack. Unbeknownst to Isolde, she was a witch-wolf hybrid, a rare and powerful combination of were-wolf and witch blood.

As Paxton approached her, he could sense the magic that flowed through her veins, a spark of something wild and untamed. But Isolde herself was unaware of her true nature, her parents having kept her heritage a closely guarded secret.

"Isolde," Paxton called out softly, his voice carrying through the still night air. She turned to face him, her eyes reflecting the moon's light like twin pools of silver.

"Paxton," she replied, a hint of surprise in her voice. "What are you doing here?" "I could ask you the same question," Paxton said with a smile. "But I'm glad I found you. There is something about you, Isolde. Something... magical."

Isolde blushed at his words; her cheeks flushed with a rosy hue. "I... I do not know what you mean," she stammered, unable to meet his gaze.

Paxton took a step closer to her, his hand reaching out to gently cup her cheek. "You're different, Isolde. Special. And I want to help you discover who you truly are."

As the moon shone down upon them, casting a spell of enchantment over the forest, Paxton and Isolde stood together, their hearts entwined in a dance of destiny. Little did they know that their fates were intricately entwined together, bound by a love that transcended both time and space.

And as they gazed into each other's eyes, lost in the magic of the moment, they knew that their love would endure, unshakeable and unbreakable, like the eternal bond between the moon and the stars.

As the night wore on, Paxton and Isolde found themselves drawn to each other in ways they could not explain. There was a magnetic pull between them, an unspoken connection that transcended words. With each passing moment, their bond grew stronger, weaving a tapestry of love and longing that neither could resist.

Together, they wandered deeper into the forest, their footsteps soft against the forest floor. The air was thick with the scent of pine and earth, the sounds of nocturnal creatures echoing through the trees. And yet, during it all, Paxton and Isolde only had eyes for each other.

"I've never felt like this before," Isolde whispered, her voice barely above a breath. "It's like... like I've known you my whole life."

Paxton smiled, his heart swelling with affection for the enchanting woman by his side. "I feel it too, Isolde. It's like we were meant to find each other, destined to be together."

As they walked, their hands brushed against each other, sending shivers of electricity racing through their bodies. The moon watched over them, a silent witness to their budding romance, its silvery light illuminating their path.

The full moon hung low in the night sky, casting a silvery glow over the dense forest that surrounded the Blue Twilight pack territory. Paxton, the son of Clara and Archer, the beta of the pack, prowled through the woods, his senses heightened by the moon's magic. As a young werewolf, he was eager to prove himself and make a name for himself within the pack.

As he moved through the trees, his keen ears picked up the sound of rustling leaves and snapping twigs. Paxton froze, his muscles tensing as he prepared for a threat. But instead of an enemy, he found himself face to face with a young woman standing in a clearing, her eyes wide with surprise.

The woman, Isolde, was a striking beauty with long, flowing hair the color of midnight and eyes that sparkled like stars. She was a witch-wolf hybrid, like the Luna of the Blue Twilight pack, Amber, but unlike Amber, Isolde was unaware of her magical heritage. Her parents had kept her true nature a secret, fearing the prejudice and fear that often went with being a witch-wolf hybrid.

Paxton felt a strange pull towards Isolde, a connection that he could not explain. He approached her cautiously, his wolf instincts telling him that she was not a threat. Isolde, too, seemed drawn to Paxton, her eyes softening as she took in his handsome features and strong, confident stance.

"Who are you?" Paxton asked, his voice low and rumbling with the power of his wolf.

"I'm Isolde," she replied, her voice as soft as a whisper. "I... I do not know how I ended up here. I was just walking in the woods and suddenly I was lost."

Paxton's heart went out to the beautiful stranger standing before him. He could sense her confusion and fear, and he felt a strong urge to protect her. Without hesitation, he offered her his hand, a gesture of trust and friendship.

"Come with me," he said gently. "I'll take you back to the pack territory. You'll be safe there."

Isolde hesitated for a moment, her eyes searching his face for any sign of deception. But she saw only sincerity and kindness in Paxton's gaze, and she nodded, placing her hand in his and allowing him to lead her through the forest.

As they walked, Paxton and Isolde talked, sharing stories and laughter as they made their way back to the pack territory. Paxton learned that Isolde was a talented artist, with a love for painting and drawing that matched his passion for music. Isolde, in turn, discovered that Paxton was a fierce warrior, skilled in combat and fiercely loyal to his pack.

By the time they reached the edge of the pack territory, Paxton and Isolde had formed a deep bond, a connection that went beyond mere friendship. As they stood under the light of the full moon, their eyes met, and in that moment, they both knew that their lives would never be the same.

Little did they know that their meeting was not a mere coincidence, but the hand of fate at work, weaving their destinies together in a tale of love, magic, and the power of the moon.

And so began the romance of Paxton and Isolde, a love that would defy all odds and conquer all obstacles, as they navigated the treacherous waters of pack politics, magical secrets, and the mysteries of their hearts.

As Paxton and Isolde's relationship blossomed, they found themselves drawn to each other in ways they could not explain. Their connection deepened with each passing day, and soon they were inseparable, spending every moment they could together, exploring the woods, sharing their hopes and dreams, and falling more deeply in love with each other.

But as their love grew, so did the shadows of the past that loomed over Isolde's life. Unbeknownst to her, her parents had kept a dark secret from her, one that would change everything she thought she knew about herself.

One fateful night, as the moon rose high in the sky, Isolde's mother, Elara, appeared at the edge of the pack territory, her eyes filled with sorrow and regret. She sought out Paxton and Isolde, her heart heavy with the burden of the truth she had kept hidden for so long.

"Isolde, my daughter," Elara began, her voice trembling with emotion. "There is something I must tell you, something that will change everything you thought you knew about yourself."

Isolde and Paxton exchanged worried glances, sensing the gravity of Elara's words. They listened in silence as Elara revealed the truth about Isolde's heritage, about her dual nature as a witch-wolf hybrid, a being of both magic and moonlight.

Isolde was astonished, her world spinning as she tried to come to terms with the revelation. She had always felt different, out of place among the other wolves in the pack, but she had never imagined that she was part witch, part magical being with powers beyond her wildest dreams.

Paxton also was shaken by the news, but his love for Isolde remained unwavering. He took her hand in his, offering her strength and support as she grappled with the truth of her identity.

Together, Isolde and Paxton faced the challenges that lay ahead, navigating the complexities of Isolde's newfound powers and the prejudices of those who feared what they did not understand. But through it all, their love remained a beacon of light in the darkness, guiding them through the stormy seas of uncertainty and fear.

As the moon shone down upon them, casting its silver light over the forest, Isolde and Paxton stood side by side, united in their love and their determination to overcome whatever obstacles stood in their way.

And as they gazed up at the moon, they knew that no matter what trials lay ahead, if they had each other, they could face anything together, their love strong enough to conquer even the darkest of shadows and the most powerful of magic.

And so, under the watchful eye of the moon, Paxton and Isolde embarked on a new chapter of their lives, one filled with magic, mystery, and the boundless power of love.

As Isolde embraced her newfound identity as a witch-wolf hybrid, she began to explore the depths of her magical abilities with a sense of wonder and curiosity. With Paxton by her side, she delved into the world of witchcraft, learning to harness the power of the elements and the moon to enhance her already formidable werewolf skills.

Together, Isolde and Paxton trained tirelessly, honing their abilities, and strengthening their bond as they faced the challenges that came with Isolde's unique heritage. They met resistance from some members of the pack who viewed Isolde's powers with suspicion and fear, but Paxton's unwavering support and Isolde's determination helped them weather the storm and appear stronger than ever.

As they navigated the complexities of pack politics and the ever-present threat of rival werewolf packs, Isolde and Paxton found solace in each other's arms, finding refuge and strength in the love that bound them together. Their connection deepened with each passing day, growing into a love that was as fierce and unbreakable as the bond between the moon and the night sky.

But their happiness was not to last, for a dark shadow loomed on the horizon, threatening to tear them apart and shatter the fragile peace they had fought so hard to build.

One night, as the moon hung low in the sky, a group of rogue werewolves descended upon the Blue Twilight pack territory, their eyes filled with malice and their fangs bared in a snarl of aggression. Led by a powerful alpha determined to claim the territory for his own, the rogues launched a brutal attack, catching the pack off guard and plunging them into chaos.

During the chaos, Isolde and Paxton fought side by side, their love fueling their determination to protect their pack and each other. With Isolde's newfound magical abilities and Paxton's fierce strength, they battled the rogues with a ferocity that struck fear into their enemies' hearts.

But just as victory seemed within their grasp, tragedy struck. In the heat of battle Isolde was fatally wounded, her body torn and bloodied by the rogue werewolves' savage attacks. Paxton's heart shattered as he watched his beloved fall, her life hanging in the balance as he fought to protect her from further harm.

As the moon cast its silver light over the battlefield, Paxton knelt beside Isolde, his hands trembling as he tried to stem the flow of blood from her wounds. Tears filled his eyes as he whispered words of love and desperation, praying to the moon and the stars for Isolde's survival.

And in that moment of darkness and despair, a miracle occurred. As the moon's light bathed Isolde's broken body, a shimmering glow surrounded her, weaving a tapestry of magic and healing that sealed her wounds and restored her to life.

With a gasp of wonder and awe, Isolde opened her eyes, her gaze meeting Paxton's with a love that burned brighter than the stars themselves. In that moment, they knew that their love was a force of nature, a power that could conquer even death itself.

And as they embraced under the light of the moon, their hearts beating as one, they knew that no matter what trials and tribulations lay ahead, as long as they had each other, they could overcome anything, their love shining like a beacon of hope in the darkness of the night.

As Isolde and Paxton appeared from the chaos of the battle, their love stronger than ever, they knew that they had faced their greatest challenge and appeared victorious. The rogue werewolves were forced off, their leader defeated, and the Blue Twilight pack stood united once more, stronger, and more resilient than before.

But the scars of the battle ran deep, both physical and emotional. Isolde bore the physical wounds of her ordeal, but it was the emotional toll that weighed heaviest on her heart. The fear of losing Paxton, being separated from him by forces beyond their control, haunted her dreams and cast a shadow over their happiness.

Determined to protect Isolde and ensure her safety, Paxton vowed to never leave her side, to always be there for her no matter what challenges they faced. Together, they sought solace in each other's arms, finding comfort and strength in the love that bound them together.

As the days passed and the wounds of the battle began to heal, a sense of peace settled over the pack territory. Isolde and Paxton spent their days exploring the woods, basking in the warmth of the sun and the beauty of the natural world around them. They reveled in the simple joys of life, cherishing each moment they shared.

But their happiness was once again threatened by a new danger, one that lurked in the shadows and whispered of betrayal and treachery. A rival pack, envious of the Blue Twilight pack's strength and unity, plotted to overthrow them and claim their territory for themselves.

As tensions rose and the threat of war loomed on the horizon, Isolde and Paxton knew that they would have to stand together, united in their love and their determination to protect their pack and each other. With Isolde's magical abilities and Paxton's fierce strength, they prepared for the battle that lay ahead, knowing that their love would be their greatest weapon against the forces of darkness.

And so, under the watchful eye of the moon, Isolde and Paxton faced their greatest challenge yet, their hearts beating like one, their souls intertwined in a bond that would never shatter. As they stood side by side, ready to face whatever trials and tribulations came their way, they knew that together, they could conquer anything, their love shining like a beacon of hope in the darkness of the night.

And as the first light of dawn broke over the horizon, casting its golden glow over the forest, Isolde and Paxton knew that a new day was dawning, a day filled with promise and possibility, a day when their love would triumph over all obstacles and shine brighter than the sun itself.

As the battle with the rival pack loomed closer, Isolde and Paxton stood united, their love a beacon of light in the darkness that threatened to engulf them. With the strength of their bond and the support of their pack behind them, they faced their enemies with courage and determination, ready to defend their home and their love at all costs.

The clash of claws and fangs echoed through the forest as the two packs met in a fierce and brutal confrontation. Isolde's magical powers blazed like a wildfire, her spells weaving a protective shield around her and Paxton as they fought side by side, their hearts beating as one.

In the heat of battle, as the moon shone down upon them, a sense of calm washed over Isolde and Paxton. They knew that no matter what the outcome, if they had each other, they could face anything together.

And then, in a moment of triumph and glory, the rival pack was beaten, their leader vanquished, and peace restored to the Blue Twilight pack territory. Isolde and Paxton appeared victorious, their love stronger than ever, their bond unbreakable.

As the dust settled and the sun rose high in the sky, Isolde and Paxton stood together, their hands clasped tightly, their eyes filled with love and gratitude. They knew that they had faced their greatest challenge and appeared victorious, their love shining like a beacon of hope in a world filled with darkness.

And so, under the golden light of the sun, Isolde and Paxton celebrated their victory, their hearts full of joy and their souls intertwined in a bond that would last for eternity. They knew that no matter what trials and tribulations lay ahead, if they had each other, they could overcome anything, their love a force of nature that could conquer even the darkest of shadows.

And as they embraced, their hearts beating as one, they knew that their love was a gift, a treasure beyond measure, a love that would endure for all time, a love that would light their way through the darkest of nights and the brightest of days.

And so, Isolde and Paxton walked hand in hand into the future, their love a beacon of light in a world filled with darkness, their hearts forever entwined in a bond that would never shatter. And as they gazed into each other's eyes, they knew that their love would last for all eternity, a love that would shine like the stars in the night sky, a love that would guide them through the trials and triumphs of life, a love that would be there forever and always.

Hello, my name is Carmalena but I go by CJ, I'm a single mother who has always pushed my children to be the best they could be and the same with my nieces and nephews. I live in a quiet town called Falling Waters in West Virginia, I have been writing since I was 16 but finally got the opportunity to publish my works and I hope a lot of people can relate to what I write. I have a 24 year old daughter and a 22 year old daughter as well as a 3 year old grandson.

She got news that changed her life forever.

A week before her 17th birthday she got news that changed her life forever. A week later her pack threw a party she did not want. At this party, she meets her mate. He is the notorious alpha of the Blue Twilight pack. He has a bad reputation for killing rogues. However, that changed when he met her. She does not know she is a hybrid. Her best friend goes with her when she moves to her new pack. The beta of the Blue Twilight pack knows that her friend is his mate.

Six months later,
there is an attack
on the Blue Twi-
light pack. She is
taken. Her friend is
wounded. The al-
pha and others go
to find her. When
they do find her,
she is held captive.
When they see the